VIRTUALLY LONDON
Neighborlee Book 3

Michelle L. Levigne

Two Olde Dragons Writing Wyrd Stories

Ye Olde Dragon Books

www.YeOldeDragonBooks.com

Previously released as *London Holiday*, 2014
Revised

Ye Olde Dragon Books
P.O. Box 30802
Middleburg Hts., OH 44130

www.YeOldeDragonBooks.com

2OldeDragons@gmail.com

Copyright © 2020 by Michelle L. Levigne
ISBN 13: 978-1-952345-04-3

Published in the United States of America
Publication Date: September 1, 2020

Cover Art Copyright by Ye Olde Dragon Books 2020

Welcome to Neighborlee, Ohio.

Where? Somewhere on the North Coast of Ohio, south of Cleveland, right off I-71, north of Medina, in the heart of Cuyahoga County.

What is it? That's a little harder to explain.

Neighborlee is a place you need to experience.

The most important thing you need to understand: Neighborlee is *magic*. Some people say the town is alive. It exists to protect the weird and wonderful (and sometimes a little bit scary) from the cold, practical, material world.

More important, Neighborlee protects the outside world from the weird and wonderful that come to visit ... and sometimes come to stay.

First stop: Divine's Emporium, a four-story Victorian house sitting on a hill overlooking the Metroparks. Whatever you really need, you can find at Divine's. Even if you don't know what you're looking for when you walk in the door. The shop is often bigger inside than it is outside. Angela is the proprietor. Please stay on the first floor. You don't want to find out what is hidden and locked safely away upstairs. Like Aslan, Angela is good, but that doesn't mean she's safe. And neither are the secrets and wonders and doorways to other worlds that she protects ... and keeps securely locked.

Come in and explore. Meet the people who help Angela guard Neighborlee. Share their adventures of magic and wonder, danger and sacrifice. You never know who or what you'll run into as you walk the streets and listen to the stories of their lives.

Chapter One

Before there was London Holiday, there was London *Halliday*.

The former...well, even after all this time, I still don't know what the right term is for her. Starting with the question of if she's real. What defines *real*? I don't know anymore.

As for the latter, she's real. Flesh and blood and down-to-earth. Call her Doni, for one thing. Even for those of us who knew all the details, sometimes the similarity in names got confusing.

Where do I get the right to tell the story? I was there when London Holiday was born. In a sense, I was the midwife. Using that analogy, Doni was as close to a mother as London Holiday would ever get. Doni and I were cousins -- our mothers were sisters. Her parents were killed in a mine explosion while researching a book, when she was nine. The Hallidays thought we, the Longfellows, were just plain weird. From their point of view, "weird" was lower in rank than "common," and if they had thought they could get any profit from Doni, we never would have known Aunt Lenore and Uncle Thaddeus were dead.

(Yes, my last name is Longfellow. And no, we're not related to the poet. Granddad was an orphan, one of the many orphans through the generations who arrived from nowhere on the edge of town and landed in the Neighborlee Children's Home. He loved poetry, so he chose Longfellow when someone gave him the chance to choose his own last name.)

The Hallidays didn't dump Doni on us when her parents were killed. That would imply some effort to make sure she ended up on our doorstep, which they most certainly did not.

Wednesday morning, the first week of June. I was on my way to Neighborlee High, where I was a sophomore. We only had three more days of classes before summer break, and I was running late, as usual. We had the Yearbook Staff thank-God-it's-over party to look forward to, and since Miss Lanie was our advisor, it was going to be good. I grabbed my backpack, jammed full of goodies for the party, and was looking over my shoulder as I headed for the door, yelling for Uncle Jinx to hurry up. He promised to drive me to school on his Harley on his way out of town. Jinx wanted to be as far away from Neighborlee as he could get when Senior Prank Night hit--the first Wednesday of June every year--so he wouldn't be blamed for whatever happened.

(Jinx got in major trouble with his Senior Prank, and the general consensus was that the idiots in the years that followed got in trouble trying to top what he did. What did he do? Something having to do with a pond in the Metroparks on Thursday where there *wasn't* a pond on Tuesday.)

I stepped out onto the front porch and almost tripped over Doni and her two pitiful little pieces of luggage. I stubbed my toe on her backpack full of books and jumped backwards, biting my tongue against a howl. I was barefoot, with my sneakers in my other hand. I planned on putting them on while I waited for Jinx to get his motorcycle.

"Does Mrs. Longfellow live here?" this skinny little kid with bottle bottom glasses half-whispered.

"Yeah. Why you looking for her?"

Hey, I was just a tenth-grader in a big hurry. So sue me for sloppy speaking.

"I'm London," she whispered, and raked one hand through white-blond hair that stuck out from her head like dandelion fuzz.

"Hi, London. Nice to meet you. I'm her granddaughter, Athena."

Yes, the penchant for weird names runs in my family. Doni was named London because she was born there. I was named Athena because my flaky mother, Portia--who went to a sperm bank when her biological clock went off instead of putting up with the mess of the dating scene--thought that would influence me to be wise.

She forgot Athena was a goddess of war and, according to some of the stories, a real smart-alec with an attitude problem and a penchant for nasty jokes. Not a good role model. Mom never figured that part out before she dumped me on Gram and joined the Peace Corps when I was a toddler. The last I heard from her, she was running an orphanage among the former cannibals in Papua New Guinea. Somewhere along the way, she figured it was easier to be a mother to twenty kids than to one.

I never said logic ran in my family.

It took about three seconds for what Doni said to sink through my gotta-hurry-for-the-last-day-of-school panic. I had an excuse. The fuzzy-headed, awkward kid in front of me was not the little girl in a Minnie Mouse costume in the frame on Gram's mantle. Aunt Lenore wasn't real big on photos. She wasn't real big on writing home, either.

"You're London? My cousin? Lenore and Thad's daughter?"

My first thought was to ask where her parents were, because obviously they weren't anywhere in sight. I liked Aunt Lenore and Uncle Thad, although I had never seen them face-to-face. They called whenever they were in the States, going from one investigative assignment to another, and sent pictures maybe once every twenty months or so. Usually those were pictures someone else took. They had an aversion to cameras that weren't used for their research. They sent cool presents from places no tourist ever visited, and books by the ton. All of us learned to read at least two languages besides English so we could make use of those books.

I had the sense not to ask Doni where her folks were, while my brain skidded through questions and possibilities and discarded most of them in the space of a few seconds. I'm not bragging when I say that. Gram claims I got electrocuted by a computer when I was a baby, crawling all over Granddad's desk and teething on the mouse cord. I've had an affinity for the frustrating, fascinating gizmos ever since. Part of that affinity meant my brain wanted to process a dozen different tracks at the same time, searching for information. Unlike computers, I had a tendency to get sidetracked by anything that caught my attention. Call it ADHD if you want, but I always preferred calling it the Neighborlee Effect.

(See how distracted I just got, telling you about me, when this is Doni's story?)

Jinx roared up the driveway from the shed in the back, where he stored his motorcycle, and skidded to a stop in the gravel. He gunned the engine a few times, twisting the handlebars and gave me his, "Weren't you in a hurry?" look. I signaled for him to cut and he did. Jinx was a lot more alert than people gave him credit for. He only pretended to be off in another dimension to irritate people.

"It's London." I pointed at her.

Jinx shrugged.

"Aunt Lenore's London."

Jinx jumped off his motorcycle so fast he almost knocked it

3

over. He was up on that front porch with such speed, the force of the wind from his movement made the screen door bang open and then shut again. He grabbed Doni by her shoulders and turned her around and out of the shadows of the porch.

"Hey, sugar," he said, in a thick molasses drawl. For some reason, he always talked like a good-old-boy to anyone under four feet tall. Don't ask why. "Where's your folks?"

That was *so* not the thing to say.

Doni's eyes welled up with tears and her lower lip trembled. She didn't burst into tears. Doni was never a crier and certainly never a wailer or a sniveler. I didn't know that then. All I knew was that my cousin had showed up on the porch without any warning, without any parents, and looked like she was going to burst into tears. I panicked.

"Gram!" I grabbed Doni's shoulder to drag her into the house.

I didn't get to school, and I ended up sharing my bag of treats with Doni, which helped. She liked those particular candy bars. Candy at eight in the morning helped her relax a little and open up and talk. My theory was, she figured someone who would unload a whole gob of candy bars on her had to be friendly.

Gram was happy to see her, even though Doni brought the news that Aunt Lenore and Uncle Thad had died. More than four months before. The Hallidays couldn't be bothered to notify our family. Aunt Lenore's maiden name wasn't known to the foreign media, and the death of a do-gooder scholar who never caused any scandals to report didn't create much of a blip to the media in the U.S., either.

If the Hallidays had found some profit from keeping Doni, we never would have known about her parents' deaths until Gram's birthday came with no phone call or card. Then Uncle Jinx and Granddad would have started making calls and harassing people for answers.

Time to back up and give some history:

The Hallidays have always been and always will be high society, wealthy-out-the-wazzoo greedy jerks. When Aunt Lenore and Uncle Thaddeus died, his family didn't know the right questions to ask. They also didn't have the sense to employ underlings who knew how to ask the right questions. The top page of the report from their lawyers' investigation said Doni had a meager (by Halliday standards) allowance to pay for school and living expenses, and no one could touch her trust fund until she was twenty-one.

The Hallidays thought they knew how much Uncle Thad was worth, and how much of the share of the Halliday conglomerate belonged to him and would belong to Doni someday: a miserable five percent of the Halliday "empire." Even if she did wear their name, they didn't care to try to get around her "bad genetics" to ensure she grew up a true Halliday: shallow, egocentric, living off of others, intimidating everyone into giving her everything she wanted, and fighting tooth and nail to live in the world's spotlight. Their mercenary little minds calculated it wasn't worth their while to spend twelve years indoctrinating Doni while they waited for her to grow up and turn her trust fund over to them.

They didn't read the rest of the report. While Uncle Thad owned a small percent of the Halliday conglomerate, Aunt Lenore was worth twenty times as much. He was a genius, writing social investigative tomes that took triple PhDs to understand. She had the Midas touch for investments. Longfellows have strange and useful talents. That was hers.

Thad and Lenore were that rare type of geniuses who actually had their feet on the ground. They put everything in Aunt Lenore's name. If his family had ever learned just how much they were worth, they would have put a guilt trip about family loyalty on Uncle Thad until he handed things over while Aunt Lenore's back was turned. They proved what geniuses they were when they realized his family wouldn't even think to check what was in her name.

The Hallidays considered Aunt Lenore a gold-digger with no fashion sense, and ignored her. Uncle Thad was something of a black sheep in the Halliday clan (would it be more accurate to call him the white sheep?) since he considered wealth a responsibility, to be used for the betterment of the world. That's what got him killed, so maybe his relatives' scorn wasn't entirely off base.

Their scorn for anything "tainted" with Longfellow blood meant Doni ended up on our doorstep. The Hallidays found no use for her. Since when does family have to be of "use"? Just the fact that Doni was of our blood was enough reason to welcome her with open arms.

Gram fussed over Doni. She called her Doni, which the fuzzy-headed, exhausted, brave little critter seemed to like. From the moment the family lawyer retrieved her from the authorities who had custody of her after the accident, she had been hearing "London," spoken with tones of disapproval and command. Later, when she had nightmares and talked in her sleep about those horrid months of hanging in limbo, I learned no one ever sent her out of the room before they talked about what a burden and bother she was.

The rest of the morning was spent in getting Doni settled in the room next to mine, digging through the attic and the cellar for some furniture, getting her a long soak in the old-fashioned claw-foot tub with orange-scented bath salts, and then filling her up with a huge breakfast feast. Gram was just like Mrs. Zephyr, and believed in healing through lots of good cooking.

Doni was pretty quiet the whole time we got her settled. Every once in a while, I looked over and saw her lip trembling a little, but she never cried, never whined, never said much of anything. She also never smiled, except when Gram hugged her and Uncle Jinx swore for three minutes straight after hearing how the Hallidays didn't even have the decency to deliver a nine-year-old when they relinquished custody of her. They sent her by plane, alone, and then she figured out how to take a bus from the airport. I think the fact that someone got really cussing hot furious on her behalf raised her self-esteem about fifty points.

After Doni's bath, Gram sent us to Divine's Emporium to do some shopping. She wanted Doni to decorate her new room to suit herself, and get more furniture than just a bed, a chest of drawers, and some shelves. Besides, wandering around Divine's would distract both of us while she and Uncle Jinx got to work on tying up all the legal details. Gram went to school with Mr. Carr of Carr, Cooper and Crenshaw, the big-wig law firm in town, so he was our family lawyer.

More important than getting Doni away from the house while Gram took care of serious business was introducing Doni to Angela, the owner of Divine's Emporium. If there was something "broken" inside her, Angela would sense it first and get to work, and give us some clues about what to do to help her.

Granddad always said Angela was the heart of the town. I was always ready for another excuse to go to Divine's and look for treasures. Introducing Doni to one of my favorite places in town was just one more thing I could do to help her settle in and feel welcome. We had a line of credit at Divine's. There was always something new and wonderful to find there, and Gram never got mad when I brought home something. Other girls liked shoes and clothes and makeup. I liked the odd treasures and books and just digging in the back rooms and dreaming. Mostly dreaming that one of these days, a sleek new computer like no one had ever seen outside an electronics show would mysteriously appear on one of the shelves, and I could bring it home for a song.

It also helped that I was best friends with Bethany Miller, Angela's goddaughter. Since Bethany almost grew up there, when she wasn't at her dad's diner, I nearly grew up there, too.

"You like books?" I said, about the hundredth question I had asked since we took off across town on Uncle Jinx's ancient mopeds. The motors were quiet enough we could talk, and there was hardly any traffic because everybody was either in school or at work.

About then, I realized I had missed the Yearbook party. Not good. But on the plus side, I had missed a lot of boring end-of-the-year activities in my other classes. Some of our teachers gave us quizzes that didn't affect our grades at all, and they thought we didn't know it.

"Love books." A little spark of interest lit Doni's eyes, and I nearly fell off my moped in shock.

"Great. Angela has a huge book room. You can take anything you want. But show me what you pick, because we might already have it at home. Most of the rooms on the third floor are library."

"Really?" Doni put both feet down and the moped stopped short, whirring a little before the engine shut off. Her eyes were wide and she had color in her cheeks for the first time since her hot bath faded.

"Yeah, really. Granddad lives in books. Gram was a librarian. That's how they met. He was stealing from the research section and she caught him. Wrestled him to the ground and... Let Gram tell you. She tells it a lot better. Or wait until Granddad gets home from his fishing trip, and he'll tell you and act it out."

"I love books." She pushed off with both feet and hit the control that got the moped's pitiful little motor humming again.

Right about then, pity for my long-misplaced cousin turned to active "like." We had a couple things in common, besides being dumped on Gram by relatives who couldn't find any use for us.

"I had lots of books. Mom and Dad got tons of books everywhere we went and sent them home. We added a new room on our house to hold all the books. *They* wouldn't let me keep any. *They* sold every last one." The growling break in her voice when she said *they* gave me a good idea how Doni felt about the Hallidays.

Okay, maybe it was immature of me, but I liked her a little more, knowing she really despised them. It meant Doni was with us all the way. She wouldn't be calling her Halliday relatives, begging them to take her out of this weird little town any time soon.

Don't get me wrong. I despised them, too. Anybody who would take a kid's books away was the lowest of the low. But the anger put Doni more squarely with us and against them. And since I had so little in the way of family, I was a greedy kind of kid who wanted to hold onto the ones I had as tightly as I could.

Then I thought of something.

"You know, Aunt Lenore used to send crates of books to Gram all the time. Chances are good a lot of them were duplicates of the books your folks sent home."

Doni stopped her moped again and stared at me, her face glowing, her eyes shining like crystals, full of tears. I liked that feeling, of knowing I had made her feel that good, given her that kind of hope. I decided right then, I was going to be Doni's protector, as well as the big sister Gram asked me to be.

At Divine's Emporium, Angela was waiting on the front step. She had a big bucket full of bubble solution and all sorts of wands and blower contraptions that looked like squirt guns with fans attached to them. She looked like she was just enjoying a quiet spell at the shop by goofing off, relaxing in the balmy weather.

I knew better. Angela had the pulse of the town, and there were times I was pretty sure she either could read minds or the Wishing Ball was actually a crystal ball that let her spy on everyone. She always seemed to know when people had problems and were coming to see her.

She waved to us and blew an enormous bubble, about four feet wide, that shimmered in all shades of purple and green and blue. It spun as the warm morning breezes lifted it higher, and I saw all sorts of images and figures chasing around in those swirls of colors. There were at least three Angelas in that bubble. One had the blue granny-style dress she always wore. The second wore an elegant gold and emerald Renaissance-style gown. The third was in crimson, a Regency-style high-waisted gown, like she usually wore for the Christmas decorating party she held every year.

Those multiple images of her vanished and other pictures appeared in the bubble. Par for the course. I didn't mention them to Doni, on the off chance I was the only one who could see them. The bubble rose up to the ornate gutters on the third floor, hooked onto a cornice, and popped. The most delicious smells of honeysuckle and newly mown grass and fresh bread showered down on us.

Doni stared for about five seconds, looking scared. Then she got that resolved look on her face I had seen her wear five or six times as she adjusted to her new situation. She pressed her lips flat, nodded once, her eyes half-closed, and I imagined her processing everything like a super-computer. Then she smiled at Angela.

"I'm guessing from those eyes and the shape of your chin and nose, you're Athena's cousin, London," Angela said, rising from her porch step. "I remember your mother. She loved this place, and I'm sure you will, too." Then she held out her arms and Doni stepped inside them and let Angela hug her.

That just proved how smart Doni was. And yes, how hurt she was, desperate and hungry for all the love anybody wanted to shower on her. Another good reason for taking her to Angela and Divine's ASAP.

Despite Neighborlee being such a great place to live, filled with magic and mystery, we had our share of creeps and general slimedogs trying to sneak into town and hurt people, steal, and profit from the innocent and defenseless. The nice thing about Neighborlee was that people watched out for each other, and we had some defenses a lot of towns didn't have.

The last thing Doni needed at this painful, scraped raw point in her life was to run into a jerk who would try to take advantage of her when she needed all the loving she could get--such as the Grandstone family. They considered themselves the elite of society and tried to convince everyone that they were not only wealthier than God, but they were the natural leaders and arbiters of what was good and worthwhile. Thank God, there were no Grandstone children in our generation.

We sat on the steps for a while, blowing bubbles and trying to connect them together to make weird creatures. It was a lot more fun than people might think. The typical high school sophomore would probably be disgusted by the baby game of blowing bubbles, but that was the thing about Divine's Emporium and the entire town of Neighborlee: nobody and nothing was "typical." We might have looked like an ordinary, small college town. Kind of sleepy. Maybe twenty years behind the times. But that was just a watercolor scrim that faded away when we least expected it, revealing lights and sounds and colors and...otherness.

When we went inside after about half an hour, it was only to be expected that the penny candy behind the counter in the main room included Doni's favorite, a mixed-up assortment of gummies in all flavors and colors and shapes. I would never expect anything less from Divine's. Sometimes the magic was incredible, and sometimes it could be a little frightening. I learned when I was a little kid not to look too closely when a room appeared where there had been a blank wall the week before.

Angela never said word one about me not being in school, though it wasn't even noon yet. She made Doni laugh by producing a plastic bag to fill from the penny candy jars, and then pulling out those mini bottles of blue cream soda that Granddad loved. It turned out Doni loved blue cream soda too.

Once she had her candy picked out, we explored the furniture room. After all, it was the official excuse for coming to Divine's. We found a couple pieces from a matching set. Pale blue, painted with misty pastel rainbows; nightstand, dressing table, and two tall, skinny bookshelves that would fit just perfectly between the outside corner of Doni's room and the windows on either wall.

"Don't worry," I told her, when I saw the longing in her eyes as she ran her fingertips along the rainbow streaking one of the shelves. She definitely had Granddad's love for books, and I understood it, even if the book bug hadn't bit me quite as strongly. "Granddad will be home from his fishing trip day after tomorrow, and then we can haul all this home and get your room set up. It'll take that long to go through the book rooms and pick out what you want on your shelves."

"I don't know." She gave me one of her rare smiles, and I

thought she might even laugh in another minute. "I'm really, really good at finding books fast."

"Angela?" Mr. Zephyr stuck his head into the furniture room. "What are you doing here, Athena? Isn't this thank-God-it's-over day for Yearbook?"

The Zephyr family (Charlie, Rainbow, and their three adopted children, Lanie, Harry and Pete) were always involved in what each other was doing. Miss Lanie had her parents come talk to our Yearbook and journalism classes each semester, so they knew us on sight. Heck, there were only twelve of us in Yearbook, so that wasn't too hard. Besides, our families went Neighborlee Gospel Church. Mr. and Mrs. Zephyr were writers, and traveled all over the world doing research on really cool, unusual books, finding out the truth behind things like St. Elmo's Fire and ghost ships and ancient legends of monsters.

"This is London, Athena's cousin. She's come to live with the Longfellows, and Athena is doing her duty as a big sister. And doing it quite well," Angela said.

Nothing like outright approval from Angela to make me feel like I had made up for a lot of stupid, selfish things I had done in the past couple of months.

"Well, hey, welcome to Neighborlee." Mr. Zephyr stuck out his hand and stepped all the way into the room to shake Doni's.

There wasn't anything scary about him, but I had seen grown men take a step back and look Mr. Zephyr over when they first met him. For one thing, he had a gray-white ponytail hanging almost to his waist. His tie-dyed T-shirt of red and black swirls formed a bull's-eye right over his belly button. Plus the tattoo of a Chinese firebird curled around his right forearm seemed to spread its wings for flight as the muscles flexed when he held out his hand.

Doni tipped her head to one side and hesitated only two seconds before holding out her hand to shake. She didn't look scared, just thoughtful.

I knew right then, even without the test of falling in love with Divine's Emporium, my little cousin was going to fit in just fine in Neighborlee. She was definitely a Longfellow.

Mr. Zephyr won her heart when he offered to take the furniture home for us. He had a couple things he wanted to drop off at our house, some books he had borrowed from Granddad, that he wanted to give back to him before he and his wife headed out of town in another week or two. He had actually stopped by to bring some books to Angela for safekeeping. They were trying to rent out their house while they were gone on this research trip, since Miss Lanie had her own place now, Pete would stay with her, and Harry was attending Cleveland State and living Downtown.

"Well, I think that's our cue to show you the library," Angela said, tucking a stack of books under one arm and gesturing with the other hand for Doni to follow her.

Doni hesitated in the archway of the room full of books next to the furniture room, while Angela headed for the stairs.

"That's the book room for tourists," I explained. "Those are the used books that people expect to find. We're going up to the really good books." That got another grin from Doni.

Divine's Emporium, for those who have never seen it before, was a big old Victorian-style house, sitting at the end of a dead-end street on a slope looking down on the Metroparks. The first floor was the main body of the shop, and sometimes there seemed to be more rooms or different rooms, from one visit to another. Other times, like at Christmas when more space was needed, they looked wider or taller, to suit the need. The second floor was mostly Angela's living area. I was in and out of there a lot with Bethany. Sometimes Angela had us both over for sleepovers or just to sit and drink tea on rainy days, and talk about books and what we wanted to do with our lives when we grew up.

At least, that was the routine when Bethany was around. She had been acting in commercials and community theater since middle school. She finally landed an agent after winning a talent contest that got her a bit part on a pilot for a new show on Nickelodeon. Every other month, she went out of town to film for a few days, more bit parts that put a nice chunk of change in her bank account and built up her resume. She wanted to be an actress, and her dad was the kind of great guy who let her pursue her dreams instead of demanding she follow in his footsteps and take over his diner when she grew up.

The third and fourth floors were storage, and only friends and special customers were brought up there to look around. Angela had two rooms full of books on the third floor. Old books. Rare. Unusual topics. I loved the library in Neighborlee, but I had learned early that if I couldn't find what I wanted there or through inter-library loan, I could always find the book I wanted at Divine's. When I thought the subject was unusual or specialized enough, I often went to Divine's first.

There were rumors that the fourth floor held more books, but they were kept locked up, with burglar alarms and whatever "magic" Angela used for extra protection. Rumors also said there was a room full of paintings that no one had ever seen. But tales like that always made me ask, "If no one has seen them, then how do you know they're up there?" Nobody ever had an answer for that kind of logical question.

We went into the third floor library rooms, and Doni fell in love. Angela and Mr. Zephyr wandered around, chatting about the research he and his wife were going to do on this trip, while she put the books away on a shelf marked, "Property of Charlie and Rainbow Zephyr." Doni walked up and down the narrow aisles of shelves. She just looked, hands clasped in front of her, eyes glistening like she would bust out crying any second, and grinning even wider than when Angela offered her the blue cream soda.

That was another cool thing about Angela. She let us carry our bottles around the shop and drink as we shopped, instead of insisting we not take any liquids out of the little soda fountain/coffee shop corner of the main room. Doni held that bottle in both hands, her fingers interlaced so tight they were white. I thought she might shatter the bottle at any minute.

Once I knew she wasn't going to do anything but look, I headed for the room across the hall, where I could sometimes find nifty, weird little gadgets. Maybe as a reward for taking care of Doni, that computer I wanted would be magically on a shelf?

No computer, but there was a manual on programming language I hadn't heard about yet. I snatched it up and tucked it under my arm and checked out some of the bits and pieces sitting in bins. Things like circuit boards and memory chips and little micro-miniaturized motors. I made a note of them, because Granddad liked to build things just for the fun of seeing what they would do. He sometimes had Kurt Hanson over and they would sit in his workshop in the cellar and talk electronics and robotics. Kurt had even more of a gift for gizmos than Granddad did, and sometimes he could fix or figure out what had escaped Granddad for months. Not that I was interested in Kurt, but I liked finding new bits and pieces for his mechanical experiments and telling him where to find them.

Once she finished drinking her soda, Doni got down to business, snatching up books she had spotted the first time around the book room. She had picked out a stack of books almost too tall for her arms, by the time Mr. Zephyr asked if we were ready to go home. Yeah, she and Granddad were going to get along just fine.

"What if we already have these at home?" Doni said, as Angela tallied up our purchases and wrote up a receipt and put them in the hand-written ledger book of our account for the store.

"You can bring them back, no problem." Angela winked at her. "But I can almost guarantee, you don't have these at home."

That almost-normal grin Doni gave her put this tight, hot feeling in my chest. Just what had those rotten Hallidays done and said to her over the last four months, that she would be so happy to know she didn't have to return some books?

Then it struck me a moment later: she said "home" without hesitating. Yeah, that made me feel good. Doni knew she belonged and she was wanted.

Mr. Zephyr loaded the furniture and our mopeds in the back of his VW bus and we were off. It wasn't that long of a drive to our house, but arms full of books would have made the trip kind of uncomfortable and tricky on the mopeds.

"Ford still hasn't come into the twentieth century and got a cell phone, has he?" Mr. Zephyr said, when I mentioned we would have had to wait until Granddad came back with his truck to haul Doni's new furniture home, if he hadn't helped us. He chuckled when I shook my head. Granddad claimed he was allergic to "that new-fangled techno-wizardry," which didn't make sense to me, because he was a wizard with gizmos. "How about I take a drive up to his old fishing hole and let him know the family's a little bigger?"

Chapter Two

"That'd be great, thanks. That is, if Uncle Jinx didn't think of it." I wished I had thought of it. Jinx and Gram had been talking fast and hushed for a long while before he took off. Maybe he had gone after Granddad and nobody had mentioned it to me.

A funny little hitch socked me in the chest, when I looked at Doni and realized something. Aunt Lenore was *dead*, but in all the fuss of Doni showing up and getting her settled and being so furious on her behalf, that little fact had slipped right past us. Who was going to tell my mother that her sister was dead? Had anybody thought of that yet?

I felt about twenty years older all of a sudden, and tired. Tragedy sure created a lot of work and a lot of things to think about. Even if--maybe especially if?--that tragedy was four months old.

What was wrong with those Hallidays, that they couldn't be bothered to call and say, "Oh, by the way, your daughter is dead. We don't want her daughter. She's on her way"?

Doni turned and looked at me with those big, sad eyes, and I shuddered at a new thought: Maybe it wasn't that they *didn't* care about her. Maybe they *hoped* something nasty would happen to her. Then there would no one to claim whatever inheritance she had coming to her, so they could take it over.

Of course, that begged the question of just what these people had done to Doni in the four months since her parents died. Why had they held onto her all that time, and only now cut her loose?

"Hey, Doni, how long after Aunt Lenore and Uncle Thad...well, after they had their accident--"

"There were a lot of government people and protective services people and lawyers." Her eyes got bigger and full of shadows, but there was no feeling in her voice. That was kind of scary.

Mr. Zephyr gave her that look I had seen him and Police Chief Tanner use when someone tried to snatch a little girl from the playground at the middle school back in March. The middle school was next to the high school, and I was trying out for the track team with Miss Lanie when it happened. Someone screamed. Miss Lanie vanished, like she flew from the running track to the playground. Then she was back, holding that little girl, who was so scared she didn't start crying until Miss Lanie told us what happened and sent someone to call school security. The kidnapper got away, though.

Suddenly there were people coming from every side of town. Police and teachers and Mr. Zephyr and Pastor Rocky. They got those sad, determined looks on their faces, just like he had now. Nobody ever said what happened, but there was a big time gap between when they caught up with the kidnapper on the edge of the Metroparks, and when he showed up at the police station.

That kind of look can be scary, but make you feel really safe, all at the same time.

"So they took care of you until your relatives showed up?" Mr. Zephyr said. His voice was so gentle, it made me want to cry. Doni nodded. She sniffled a little when I reached up to her in the front passenger seat and took hold of her hand. "How long was that?"

"About..." She frowned for a few seconds and the fingers on the hand I was holding twitched a little, so I guessed she was counting. "About seven weeks."

Mr. Zephyr growled something that sounded Chinese. It was a good guess he was cussing, like Granddad did sometimes. Doni's eyes got big. Then she giggled.

"Sorry about that." He shook his head and gave us both a crooked grin. Then he pulled into the driveway of our house, right behind the glossy black Lincoln that belonged to Mr. Carr.

The nice thing about Mr. Carr was that he wasn't afraid to do manual labor or get his hands or even his clothes dirty. Of course, there wasn't any dust on the furniture or books we hauled home from Divine's, but the possibility of it counted. Mr. Carr came outside in his light gray, three-piece summertime lawyer suit, and helped haul that furniture upstairs to Doni's room.

Before that, he bowed to Doni and shook her hand and said he was very pleased to meet her. Gram had told him the whole story already, so he didn't ask any questions. Instead, he talked about Mr. Zephyr's upcoming research trip, and offered to help find someone to rent the big old Zephyr farmhouse while they were away.

"Charlotte, did you send Jinx to get Ford, tell him the news? Or would you like me to run up to the old fishing hole and get him?" Mr. Zephyr said, when they came down after the final trip, hauling the last set of bookshelves.

"Oh, you'd better believe it," Gram said. "That boy wasn't in so much a hurry to get out of town that he'd overlook something like that." She chuckled and gestured with her tray of lemonade and fresh sugar cookies, out onto the porch. We all settled down. Doni curled up next to Gram on the three-seater swing with one of her new books.

"Get out of town?"

"Senior Prank Night." I took my usual spot on the steps with my back against the big support pillar Uncle Jinx had carved to look like dragons had wrapped around it. The other pillar had unicorns chasing each other around and around up to the top.

"Oh, joy." He shared grins with Mr. Carr. "Forgot about that."

"What's Senior Prank Night?" Doni asked, and sprayed a few crumbs from her mouthful of sugar cookie.

It was kind of nice to see she was a normal little kid in some aspects.

We explained about the long-standing tradition in Neighborlee for graduating seniors, on the first Wednesday of June, to play some extravagant prank. Sort of to leave their mark on the town before they headed off into adulthood. If they survived. Some members of the police and fire departments, and teachers spent Senior Prank Night on patrol. They tried to head off any pranks that got out of control, and prevent expensive or long-term damage to people, places, and things.

"Lanie swears some of these kids don't want to attend their own graduation ceremony," Mr. Zephyr said with a chuckle.

"We're still trying to figure out how she and her friends threaded those tires on the flagpoles in front of the schools, the board of education office and the police department," Mr. Carr said. "No ladder in this town tall enough to get to the top of those flagpoles. I tend to think that friend of hers, the one with the gift for gizmos--" He looked around, stumped for a moment.

"Kurt Hanson," I supplied.

"That's right." He nodded. "I think he rigged some elaborate pulley system to lift those tires up and over. At least Lanie's prank didn't get anyone hurt." He chuckled. "And they used ordinary, worn-out tires that could be cut off easily. As I recall, the year that idiot Grandstone and his friends tried to blow up Blackwater Pool, some other fool in their graduating class put steel-belted radials on the shorter flagpoles in front of the bank and the post office. Brand new ones. That's what got them caught, as I recall."

"How?" Doni sat up, eyes wide, her fourth cookie in her hand.

"They tracked the tires back to the store where they were stolen and the fools were caught on the security tape. Had to get a special saw to cut those tires off the flagpole." He nodded to Mr. Zephyr. "Nobody was hurt or upset, and didn't cost the town or the schools a penny to remove those tires, the year Lanie graduated."

"Yeah, Rainbow and I raised our kids right, I think," Mr. Zephyr said.

"I suppose Lanie is on patrol tonight," Gram said.

"You can bet on it."

After Mr. Zephyr left, Gram took Doni upstairs to show her some things she had dug out of storage for her room: rugs and curtains and pictures and things like that. I was alone with Mr. Carr for a little while. He settled down at the kitchen table, covered with all sorts of documents and lots of handwritten notes. I put away the lemonade and cookies and washed the dishes we had used.

"How's your cousin settling in?" he asked me, when I'd finished rinsing the last glass.

"She's a pretty tough little kid. There were a couple times I thought she'd start crying..." I shrugged and looked up at the ceiling. Gram and Granddad's room was over the kitchen, with the big cedar closet right next to it, and I could track Gram and Doni's movements by the faint creaking of the boards overhead. "They took all her books away."

"Eh?" He slid his glasses off the end of his nose and sat back, looking at me.

"Aunt Lenore was like Granddad--loved books. Doni's the same way. I'm pretty sure all those books Aunt Lenore and Uncle Thad sent to us, they had the same books for themselves. So that's like thousands, maybe. They had to build an extra room on their house for all the books, Doni said. Well, the Hallidays sold all her books. Except for that backpack full, that she stole when she figured what they were doing. Who'd be so mean to a little kid?"

"Indeed, I've been wondering what kind of people these Hallidays are. I met Thad, after he married Lenore. A good man. It amazes me that such a kind, generous man could come of such people. Then again, serial killers often pop up in loving, moral, strong families, so who can say?" He tapped the papers in front of him, written in a bold, square handwriting. "Charlotte and I have been planning what to say and do. The way this whole affair was handled is unforgivable. She isn't a woman to seek vengeance, but this is her granddaughter who has been irretrievably injured by the cold callousness of these people. It pained her to admit she suspects the way everything was handled indicates these people were maneuvering to profit from Thad and Lenore's deaths. The secrecy, and holding onto London, and then casting her off the way they did." He shook his head, his eyes dark with stern disapproval.

His eyes got darker when I told him what Doni had said, about being in the care of the authorities for seven weeks before the Hallidays showed up.

"I believe I shall take great joy in...hounding these people, causing them as much inconvenience and frustration as I can."

~~~~~

Doni and I were upstairs in the library rooms, looking for copies of her favorite books, when Mr. Carr finished talking and planning with Gram and left. She brought a late lunch up to us and we had a somewhat dusty picnic among all the books, slowly adding to the stack of Doni's finds. Every time we had a stack tall enough to wobble, we took the books downstairs and loaded them into the new bookshelves.

She was just like Granddad, filing her books on specific shelves for specific topics or types of books. The bookshelf on the right wall was for fiction, mostly fantasy and science fiction or old adventure stories, like Robin Hood and the Scarlet Pimpernel. The left wall had all the research books, a lot of history and botany. And a whole shelf of books just about horses. It was kind of funny that Doni didn't have any Black Stallion books. When I mentioned my collection and offered to let her read them, she made this funny little jerking motion, a combination of stepping toward me and opening her arms a little. Like she might hug me.

Well, that was a start, anyway. After all, she hadn't even been with us a whole day yet.

We were still upstairs digging through the books when Granddad came home. I heard the truck pull into the driveway, but it just didn't register, because we were debating whether we should run back to Divine's to see if there might be another set of shelves to match the first. It was already obvious that Doni was running out of shelf space and needed more.

Granddad stepped through the door and the torch lamps brightened for a few seconds, like they always did. We had to have lamps on, even though it was early afternoon, because all the windows in the libraries were covered up with floor-to-ceiling bookshelves. My theory was that he carried an electrical charge in his body that kind of boosted the circuitry in our old house. Gram, of course, maintained that the house was half-aware and was just saying "hello" whenever he stepped through the door. Maybe we were both right?

Anyway, Doni kind of flinched and half-rose up from the floor. She had been sitting, sorting through the piles in front of her, the books to go into her room now and the ones that had to wait for more shelf space.

"What happened?" she asked.

I got that funny hitching feeling in my chest at that flicker of fear in her eyes. I already wanted to blame every twitch and discomfort Doni had on the Hallidays. Just what had they done and said to her during the two months she was stuck living with them, before they tossed her?

"Oh, that's just the house welcoming your Granddad home." Gram hopped up from the little three-legged stool she kept in the library, for sitting and searching low shelves, and held out her hand. "Come on, let's go meet him before he tears the house apart looking for us." She said it with a giggle and sparkles in her eyes, so Doni actually looked like she might laugh with her. I followed a few steps behind, wiping my dusty hands on my jeans.

Granddad was on the second floor landing, trotting up with the speed of some of the guys on the baseball squad. I had to admit, he looked kind of fierce, with his shiny bald head and thundercloud gray, bushy eyebrows sticking out about two inches, and his snow-white beard hanging down to his shirt pockets. It wasn't a Santa Claus-type beard, either. More like ZZ Top. His big grin and the delight in his eyes when he saw Doni overrode any hesitation when he called her name and opened his arms wide.

She ran to him and he picked her up and spun her around, laughing. Granddad put her down and made a show of sniffing at

Doni before he stepped back. "Smells like somebody's been digging around in the library."

"You can smell that?" Her eyes got big with wonder.

"The best smell in the world. Paper and ink and book dust." He caught her chin in his big, gnarled hand. "It's good to see you, honey. I wish your folks were here, but they're in our hearts, and they know you're home now. That's all that matters. You're home where you belong. You got me?"

She nodded, eyes wide, bottom lip trembling for a few seconds. Then she let him take her hand and lead her downstairs.

Granddad got a lot more of her story out of Doni than Gram or I had. He had that talent. All it took was for him to sit and hold her hand. That same funny energy that made the lights react created a link between them. That was my theory. He never asked any questions that would make her freeze up, and when she got that hurting, wide-eyed look, he would stop and stroke her hand and ask the question a different way.

They settled in the kitchen to talk while Granddad had his late lunch. He had the most amazing ability to eat at any time and still be hungry when it was time for a meal. He never got that old man potbelly. He always claimed it was part of being one of the Lost Boys. That was what he and Principal Wellington and a few others called themselves; children who were found abandoned in the surrounding county and went to Neighborlee Children's Home. Granddad blamed a lot of weird things on being a Lost Boy.

I finally thought about skipping school. I decided to call Bethany to find out what I had missed. She called me as I was reaching for the phone. We did that a lot, calling when one of us had been thinking about the other. She was all excited about a phone call she just got from her agent, about a bigger-than-usual part she was going to audition for in a couple weeks. We talked for a little bit and I razzed her about how she was heading for Hollywood to stay, and she'd forget all about us small town folks.

When I got off the phone and went looking for the rest of the family, they were upstairs, hanging some rainbow curtains Gram dug out of the cedar closet that nearly matched the furniture from Divine's. Granddad agreed that Doni needed more bookshelves. We would go back to Divine's in the morning. For now, though, the rest of the day was for introducing Doni to Neighborlee.

We took the walking tour of town, as Gram called it. Our neighborhood, through the center of town, the shopping district that everyone referred to as the Mall. Then the Neighborlee Schools grounds: high school, middle school, elementary school and Board of Education building, all on one plot. Then we hit the highlights of the Willis-Brooks College buildings. Granddad was particularly proud of some of those old buildings covered with ivy and dark with age, built of the granite and sandstone quarried right here in Neighborlee a century-and-a-half ago.

The quarries had long since been abandoned, and either turned into fishing and swimming holes, made part of the Metroparks, or just nominally barricaded from general traffic. That didn't mean that suicidal idiots and risk-takers couldn't get in there and make a mess of their bodies and other people's lives.

We planned to have a picnic in the back yard that evening, but by the time we got home, Granddad took a look at the bright blue sky and announced a major storm was coming in. He chuckled when Doni tipped her head back and looked up at the few streaks of bright white clouds, her doubt clear on her face.

"Nope, you can't see it coming, but I can smell it. Rain's coming. Cold and hard. Mark my words."

"Not quite tornado season," Gram muttered as she climbed the steps to the back door into the kitchen.

"No self-respecting tornado would come within a mile of the borders of Neighborlee," he retorted, still chuckling.

I had my doubts about whether a storm or tornado could be aware enough to be "self-respecting," but I believed Granddad when he said we were safe from tornados. That was one of his Lost Boys gifts. It wasn't like he could predict the future, because I knew he couldn't. But when he said the weather was changing and his word contradicted the weatherman on TV or the weather site on the Internet, I always listened to him. Kids had started the day at school razzing me because I wore my slicker when it was sunny and hot, but by the end of the day they were all drenched and begging rides off the seniors, the only students allowed to drive to school, while I strolled home cozy and dry and smug.

So we had our picnic in the living room. Gram put green cloths on the lampshades to tint the light so we could pretend we were outdoors, and lit some pine candles, and I found some of my environment CDs and put them on the stereo. We ate to the sound of crickets and birds. Then we spent the evening playing board games, sitting on the floor. Doni laughed when the CD changed over to the one of wolves howling. Granddad just scowled at me, teasing, when the sleep soundtrack came on, consisting of different kinds of rainstorms.

"That's not part of it," I insisted, when a low rumbling of thunder slid through the steady drone of drumming rain.

"What'd I tell you?" Granddad got up from the blanket spread on the floor and pulled aside the curtains. I put the stereo on mute, and the drumming of rain continued, along with more thunder.

"Teach me how to do that, Granddad?" Doni said.

"Well, honey, I'll try, but it's gotta be something that's born inside you."

Lightning flashed, followed by a sharp clap of thunder only two seconds later. I got up and went to unplug my computer, just in case. When I came downstairs again, Gram remarked that she hoped the seniors had enough sense not to go out in this weather.

"Senior Prank Night, Gram," I said, sitting down next to Doni. She was eyeing the last two Ho-Hos beyond me, so I reached for them, ripped the package open and flipped one onto her plate. "Tradition."

"Tradition." She snorted delicately. "Seems to me pneumonia is a tradition, too, if you're fool enough to go out in this weather."

I had to agree, and hoped that when I was a senior the weather would be nice and warm and dry. I shivered a little, thinking of Miss Lanie and any other teachers who would be driving around in this weather, making sure the seniors weren't too nasty or stupid with their pranks.

Granddad distracted us by performing some of his magic tricks. He claimed they were sleight of hand, but since I could never seem to get the knack for it, I chose to believe it was magic. Doni, however, learned the few simple things he taught her right off. Flipping a quarter between the fingers of one hand and making it vanish, only to appear in the other hand. Knotting a handkerchief and then undoing the knots just by shaking it out a few times. Things like that. She sounded like an ordinary little girl, squealing with triumph when she picked up everything he taught her.

She also whined like an ordinary little girl when Gram put her foot down at about eleven and said it was time for her to go to bed. She didn't whine long, got up when Gram held out her hand, and followed her to bed easily enough. The poor little thing was probably exhausted from everything that happened today.

I could imagine how I would feel in her situation, after all the things she had endured. Unwilling to close my eyes and go to sleep, in fear of finding out in the morning that my incredible, fun day with my new family was just a dream--meaning I was stuck back with the horrid people who took me when my parents died.

"Think she'll be okay, Granddad?" I said, when the plumbing banged, meaning Doni was washing up for bed.

"It'll be a while, but yeah, as right as anyone can be after going through what she did. Neighborlee's our home. The air and soil, they feed us, heal us. Give her time to put down roots..." Granddad sighed and stretched his arms out along the seat of the couch he leaned against. "She'll make her place and be just fine."

"I want to pound them." My throat hurt when I said that, like a couple thousand hard words inside me wanted to come out, but I swallowed them down.

"Yeah, me too." That was the nice thing about Granddad. He always understood what I was saying. He knew I was thinking about the Hallidays and how they treated Doni. "You gotta understand something, Athena-gal. Justice is slow moving, because the Good Lord is merciful, too. If all we have is justice in this world, we'd get walloped the moment we even think of doing something mean-spirited and cruel. But mercy means we all get a chance to change our minds and make up for what we did."

"That just means the slimedogs get more chances to hurt people."

"True. And it means that the rest of us who know to do right, we have lots of chances to help other people. It's not enough to do right. You gotta get out there and persuade the other folks to stop doing wrong, too."

~~~~~

Just like Gram feared, some idiots were determined to have Senior Prank Night despite the weather. Toby Malone and his two buddies, Jay Parker and Steve Muldoon, stole two vehicles from the service fleet. Toby's dad worked for Neighborlee and had keys, which made it easy for Toby to do it. The original plan was to steal the bell from the Taco Bell out by the highway, but someone overheard their plotting and rumors got around, and they decided to just park those trucks in the quarries.

There were no lights in the quarries, because, duh, people weren't supposed to go in there. In the rain and mud, driving was pretty treacherous. Toby got lost and took the dump truck down a steep road that ended in a cliff. His coat got snagged on the truck when he lost control and tried to jump.

Miss Lanie got Toby loose before that truck went over a high drop-off. Good for Toby, but she broke her back.

The stories were confused for a long time after that. At first, people said she died a couple times and had to be resuscitated, she was that badly hurt. Then the word was that she was paralyzed from the shoulders down.

The funny thing was, by the end of the summer, Miss Lanie was out of the hospital and getting around town in a wheelchair-- and not a motorized one, either. She could even stand for short periods of time, and on a good day she could walk a little. When I got a chance to visit her, she said it was all from the prayers of the people in our church, and a good chunk of Neighborlee weirdness thrown in to help. I wasn't sure what to think, but I was glad she wasn't going to be doing the Christopher Reeve routine, needing help just to eat and sometimes even breathe.

She didn't go back to teaching, which angered me and a lot of other people. She was our basketball and track coach, as well as heading up the school newspaper and yearbook. A lot of people wanted Toby, Jay and Steve tossed directly into jail for a good long time. The judge gave them the option of going into the military, though, and they took it.

So when school started up in the fall for my junior year, I opted out of Yearbook and the school newspaper (dumb, because who was I punishing other than myself?) and took all the computer classes offered. Not that I needed those classes. Granddad said I figured things out better by simply doing and experimenting, than if I sat in a classroom.

I wonder sometimes how everything would have turned out if I hadn't taken those classes. If I hadn't decided to go into computer programming and design, to set up my own computer service and repair shop someday. If I had just left my computer as a hobby.

~~~~~

That summer, I spent a lot of time with Doni. Not just because I realized early what a smart, quietly fun kid she was. And not because I felt sorry for her. Bethany left town. It wasn't any fun working at Miller's Diner without her. We had always asked for the night shift because first, the tips were better with the evening menu and second, we liked to have our mornings free. We liked sleeping in. Exploring what new treasures had arrived at Divine's Emporium. Or just sitting somewhere quiet in the park and reading or daydreaming about our futures.

Well, Bethany's future not only arrived, it snatched her up and dragged her off to Hollywood. So I was pretty much alone. Yeah, I had friends, but nobody I really liked to hang with, day in and day out. I kept my night job at the diner, because I was still saving for my dream computer.

Mornings were for Doni and me. She was quite happy to spend her afternoons and evenings hanging with Gram and Granddad, talking about books, working in Gram's garden, making a place for herself. Roots.

She needed those roots when the Hallidays fought back.

They got pretty offensive because they had to get defensive. Mr. Carr went after them with everything he could think of, to protect Doni from them in the future. We would have preferred to let sleeping dogs lie, meaning doing everything possible to avoid reminding the Hallidays we existed and Doni was with us. However, the smart thing was to look for landmines now. We had been dealing with the Grandstones for generations, here in Neighborlee. So we knew to anticipate the Hallidays pulling the same kind of dirty tricks, and worse, once they learned just how rich Doni would be when she reached twenty-one.

For example, the Grandstones had bought up a bunch of old buildings, intending to get rich off urban renewal. Kurt Hanson worked for a garage they bought. He quit when that jerk-face Reggie Grandstone marched into the garage and boasted that he was now Kurt's boss. A year later, when Kurt sold a security alarm system he had been working on at the garage, the Grandstones claimed that anything invented by their employees was automatically their property. Even when they didn't sign any agreement regarding intellectual property and work-for-hire.

26

The Grandstones sued, and lost. Kurt had proof he had been inventing and tinkering with the system for years before that tiny window of time between them buying the garage and when he quit. So he didn't "invent" the system while he was still working for the garage. Mr. Carr got involved, and proved the single paycheck Kurt received after the Grandstones bought the garage came from the previous garage owner. Technically he never worked for them. They outsmarted themselves, making the former owner pay for any accounts payable generated before they took over.

The Grandstones regularly tried to claim property their family had never owned, and inventions they had never contributed to. Mr. Carr advised us to tie up Doni's legal status nice and tight to protect against similar tactics from the Hallidays. Eventually they would learn about Doni's trust fund, and then they would probably claim we had kidnapped Doni and brainwashed her. We had to prove from the start that they knew where she was living and wanted nothing to do with her ever again. If possible, we wanted it in writing that they renounced all claims to her.

Mr. Carr threw everything he had at them. He had been lawyering for nearly fifty years and stayed on top of the latest legal developments and cases. He had an awful lot of quasi-dirty legal tricks at his disposal.

The first battle Mr. Carr won was getting hold of Aunt Lenore and Uncle Thad's living trust. For about three weeks, the Halliday lawyers claimed it didn't exist. Other than some academic and alumni groups, Doni got everything. The trust specifically stated that no trustee got a penny, and Doni had the right to *choose* who would be her guardian and trustee of her estate.

When the Hallidays finally showed up overseas to take custody of Doni from the child welfare people, they took all her folks' paperwork without looking at it. All they cared about was getting into Doni's house and her parents' bank accounts. They still hadn't looked through those boxes of paperwork when Mr. Carr showed up with his clerks and enough court documents to choke several mules.

That tactic was totally necessary, to avoid counterclaims in the future. Unfortunately, it was a red flag, signaling the Hallidays that there was something worth fighting over. Doni was our priority, but the Hallidays zeroed in on financial profit and power and dove into the battle. They first claimed there wasn't any legal paperwork. Doni and her inheritance were in limbo. Translation: Uncle Thad and Aunt Lenore were irresponsible and unprepared. Mr. Carr anticipated that trick and proved them wrong before their lawyer finished his first lying speech. Plus, he had witnesses and copies of paperwork, proving the Hallidays had all those documents they claimed didn't exist. After all, they used all that paperwork to get custody of Doni, then get into her parents' house and bank accounts. The Hallidays arrived with a moving truck and started to fill it within hours of arriving in town. On the second day, they put a for sale sign on the front lawn.

When Mr. Carr showed up, the Hallidays were initiating a lawsuit to force a rezoning of the entire neighborhood, so they could sell the house for commercial development. They were still in the house, it hadn't been entirely emptied, and the moving truck was still there.

The neighbors hated them. Again, that worked for us. There were a lot of nasty clashes between them and people who had loved Uncle Thad and Aunt Lenore. All fodder for the legal mill. Mr. Carr had the paperwork and the support of two police officers accompanying him to get him into the house immediately.

The Hallidays couldn't get away with saying, "We'll look for the paperwork. Come back tomorrow." Chances were good that if he waited to come back the next day, all he would have found would be ashes.

When Mr. Carr tracked down the lawyers who handled Uncle Thad and Aunt Lenore's estate, he found out they didn't know Doni's folks were dead. In fact, they had received an email just a week before, talking about her folks' research project in England.

From that point on, there were twice as many legal minds gunning for the Hallidays. Even though they had the slipperiest lawyers rotten money could buy, they didn't stand a chance.

They had one weak spot: the Hallidays lived and died in the media. As soon as Mr. Carr figured that out, he put together a campaign that would destroy them in the public eye for generations to come. Then he showed them all the news releases, backed up with facts and statements from witnesses, ready to be released to the media. Interviews detailing how a grief-stricken nine-year-old had been left to cry herself to sleep in a cold, dark room in an abandoned wing of the Halliday mansion after they took custody of her. How her relatives had emptied her family home and wouldn't let her keep her floppy stuffed dog. How she had to break into the library in her own home at night to retrieve a few favorite books. How those relatives sold everything out from under Doni when they had no legal right to anything, and kept every penny. How they bought her a plane ticket that only got her halfway to Neighborlee, and didn't arrange for anyone at the airline to watch out for her. That backed up my theory that they wanted something bad to happen to Doni, but technically leave their hands clean.

The Hallidays claimed to be the injured parties. They tried to claim they adored Doni, that Aunt Lenore had alienated Uncle Thad from his loving family, and he had wanted them to be Doni's guardians. They insisted Doni was so distraught over the loss of her parents, she had run away.

Yeah, right, like any reputable ticketing agent at an airport would let a nine-year-old buy a ticket, without asking any questions? She couldn't even see over the counter.

I had spent the previous summer doing computer work for Carr, Cooper and Crenshaw. That was when Mr. Carr told me the best tactic was to anticipate every nasty trick, lie, and above-board legal trick the opposition might employ. And then turn those tricks against the people who might use them, before they used them.

Mr. Carr was the best of the spin doctors because he used the truth. No exaggerations, half-truths, or speculations. He laid out the facts and promised to let the infuriated media do what they wanted with it. The Hallidays caved within half an hour of the meeting where he gave them a list of all the reporters, newspapers, gossip sheets and bloggers he was about to contact with all the gory, salacious, entirely truthful details. It helped that all those people already loathed the Hallidays.

Just to pound a dozen extra nails into the coffin, Mr. Carr got the court to appoint a guardian *ad litem*. The court hired a child psychologist to examine Doni and get her side of the story. A guardian *ad litem* is appointed by the court to examine the child's circumstances and determine what is in the child's best interests, with no input from any disputing parties.

The guardian *ad litem* and psychologist examined us, examined Neighborlee, examined the Hallidays and their so-called friends, the environments Doni would grow up in, and interviewed a good dozen-odd friends of Aunt Lenore and Uncle Thad. Those friends hadn't learned they were dead yet, either. Another strike against the Hallidays and their secretive actions. All those people wanted to take Doni, too.

We won. We were judged the most healthy and supportive and healing environment. Of course, it helped that Aunt Lenore and Uncle Thad's friends met with us, saw she was happy with us, and threw their support on our side.

Then Mr. Carr dug the knife in and twisted it around a couple times for good measure.

Chapter Three

Mr. Carr waited until we had finished the last session of arbitration, left the meeting room in the Justice Center in Downtown Cleveland, and were waiting for the elevators to take us down. We made a pretty odd sight--the Longfellow party in our Sunday best clothes, facing the Hallidays dressed all in glossy black from foreign designers. They were pretending to still be in mourning for Uncle Thad and Aunt Lenore. I didn't even know they made black sequins and rhinestones until I saw them on Doni's Aunt Cairo and Uncle Sherman. Our armies of lawyers stood between us, a wall of summer weight Italian suits.

"London..." Aurelia Halliday, the matriarch of the clan, had the I'm-holding-back-my-tears-to-avoid-a-public-spectacle-but-can't-you-see-I'm-suffering act down to an art. "My dear child, I hope you won't suffer too much when you realize the mistake you've made. I want you to know that we forgive you for your...your misperceptions. We understand that you have acted entirely out of grief. And when you see the light and want to come home, our arms will be open."

"As long as I'm writing in a checkbook," Doni muttered, and leaned a little closer to Gram. I was standing behind her, so I heard her just fine, but from the lack of reaction on the other side of the elevator lobby, I was one of the few who did. She held hands with Gram and Granddad. The Hallidays had to maneuver a little to see past our protective wall of lawyers to get a glimpse of her.

"I advise my client against it," Mr. Carr said. "Considering the kind of life you live in the spotlight, I advise her to avoid it for her mental and emotional health. And especially to protect the estate she stands to inherit when she turns twenty-one."

"Estate?" Cousin Trevor Halliday snorted. "No matter how much the value appreciates in the next twelve years, I can't imagine Thad's share growing enough to be considered an 'estate' by the time the little twit can access it."

"Yeah, and I'm sure you're already working on taking that away from her," Uncle Jinx muttered. That got a little "hush" from

Gram. From what I could see of her expression, she was fighting not to smile.

"I'm not referring to her father's inheritance at all. I'm talking about the massive--and that's speaking conservatively--" Mr. Carr said, "--massive and geometrically expanding investment portfolio her mother assembled. Lenore was a genius when it came to anticipating the market. She left explicit instructions for buying patterns for the next five years, and put everything in the hands of a trusted family friend. London is quite a wealthy young lady already, and in twelve years...well..." He shook his head, and from the angle where he stood, I could see his face clearly. He looked somber. Until I caught the malicious twinkle in his big gray eyes.

I also caught the dawning dismay on some Halliday faces.

"If only you had been a little kinder," Mr. Carr said. "Remember, London was given the right to choose her trustee and guardians. If you had only *pretended* to grieve her parents' deaths... In time, with a little acceptance and a lot less mockery and criticism on your part, you could have turned this little girl to think like you and give you free reign over her estate. I've never understood the mindset of relatives who attack children and punish them for the so-called sins of their parents, when the smart tactic is to accept and train those children to think like them. But no."

He sighed loudly, covering some of the mutters and sounds of dismay from the Hallidays. Some were looking a little green. A few of the more foolish ones were aiming sappy grins at London. *Puh-lease!* As if she would believe all of a sudden they liked her?

"No," he said with another sigh, "you had to punish her for being like her father instead of you."

The elevators opened up right then, and Mr. Carr whisked Doni and Gram and Granddad into it before Aurelia could say more than, "But London, dear--" Our elevator car got to the ground floor first. We were outside and heading for the parking garage before the Hallidays stumbled out of their elevator.

Our next step was to use our court orders to go into all the Hallidays' homes to search for any property they "confiscated" from Aunt Lenore and Uncle Thad's home. Poor Doni, she had to be there to identify each piece. Mr. Carr made her put together a shopping list of sorts before we even went into any of those homes. He registered those lists with the court and the judge who granted the search-and-seize orders. How could the Hallidays claim Doni was just taking things to punish them, when we were working from a long list?

They tried, though, digging their heels in and lying.

"Oh, but I was hoping to keep it, in memory of darling Lenore, she was so precious to me."

"But I gave this to them for their fifteenth anniversary. It's a family heirloom. Won't you be merciful and let me keep it?" Which was a blatant lie, used *four* times before someone remembered Aunt Lenore and Uncle Thad had only been married thirteen years.

"This is a family heirloom I gave them for Christmas." A lie. The Hallidays never even sent them Christmas cards.

Our best weapon was to offer--no, let's be honest, it was a threat--to speak to the media. My job was to hold the digital audio recorder with unlimited memory that Kurt Hanson had rigged for us. Uncle Jinx had the digital video recorder. Between us, everything the Hallidays said and did, and every item Doni found in their homes, was recorded. All it would take was to push a button, open up a wireless link, and upload the news bite. There were a lot of vicious media outlets who couldn't wait for a juicy bit of negative news about the Hallidays.

We did our snatch-and-grab tour in two days. Granddad and Uncle Jinx were ready to rent two trucks, if necessary, to drive it all home. The sad thing was that the Hallidays had already sold about nine-tenths of the contents of the house, including most of Doni's clothes and toys, and all the books.

Gram, Doni and I got on a plane and came home and left Granddad and Uncle Jinx to drive the rented van home. We had the red-eye flight and I got about three hours of sleep before I had to get up to go to school to start the school year. Gram let Doni sleep, because the elementary school started a day later.

Doni had her first nightmare right after I walked out the door. I didn't hear her shriek and burst out sobbing, but I swear, I felt it. Something just felt "off," all day. And it wasn't just because Miss Lanie wasn't at the sign-up table for the basketball team or in the homeroom for Yearbook and the school newspaper staff.

Doni had a lot of nightmares after that, mostly about walking through an empty house, or having things vanish, including our family. She spent a lot of nights with me, coming into my room with her eyes still half-closed in sleep. Or I would hear her whimpering as the nightmare started and I would go to her room and curl up in bed with her. Just having someone hold her helped end a nightmare before it woke her, if I heard the whimpering start in time. Gram had her share of comforting Doni on those nights when I was gone or out late with school activities. I mean, after all, she was a grandmother, with a grandmother's radar.

The nightmares finally started calming down, after about two weeks. Then the Hallidays commenced their campaign of trying to buy Doni's love with boxes of presents, and the nightmares resumed. It wasn't hard to figure out that she feared, if only subconsciously, the Hallidays would somehow break in and take her away from us. Doni was smart enough to know we had the law on our side, but the subconscious, especially when wounded, doesn't always react logically.

After some long talks with Angela and some exploration therapy at Divine's Emporium, Doni figured out the problem. It got down to her subconscious and the nightmares stopped.

That was a good thing, because *my* nightmares started about then. I thought at first maybe I was subconsciously worried Doni might be won over by the incredible presents the Hallidays sent. Who wouldn't be tempted by all the cool toys? The latest electronic gizmos, the newest movies, CDs, bikes (six), skateboards (eight), and scooters (three), and anything relating to teenage girls in movies. Any Disney princess, all the girls on Disney and Nickelodeon. Regular shipments came every couple weeks.

However, those problems were only irritating, in comparison to the standard weirdness of Neighborlee that bubbled up to the surface and got a little scary.

Like I said, I had nightmares. Those really nebulous, misty, disjointed nightmares where I knew I was being chased. I had to keep moving, because if I slowed down or looked behind myself, whatever it was would catch me. Plus, the nightmares weren't letting me go. As soon as I fell asleep again, I was right back to the point in the dream where I had managed to yank myself awake.

"What's bothering you?" Bethany asked, one morning after some wake-me-up-six-times-during-the-night nightmares.

That was the great thing about having Bethany for my closest friend. We could tell when things were wrong with each other, or when one of us had an incredible secret. I lost count of the times, growing up, when one of us would be thinking about the other, wanting to talk, and the other one would call, or come by the house. Angela encouraged our friendship and said we were good for each other. As we got older, I grew more sure that she somehow helped our link or whatever-it-was grow stronger.

So when Bethany asked me, before I even finished sitting down next to her in homeroom, I tapped my ear, then my wristwatch, our signal for "tell you later--when the mundanes aren't listening."

We went outside at lunch and walked around the high school instead of sitting in our favorite spot under the trees next to the agriculture class's experimental garden plot. It was the only way we could guarantee someone wouldn't eavesdrop. When I finished describing the nightmares, the solid sense of threat but no other details, Bethany didn't even pause before telling me what was only common sense.

"You need to talk to Angela. Have you told your folks?"

"I would have, but you know how crazy it is in the mornings at our house."

Bethany just rolled her eyes and grinned. She had slept over enough times to know that no matter what time of the year, whether it was the weekend or weekday, Longfellows couldn't seem to get our acts together in the morning. We were always rushing around and snatching up things, hurtling out the door and coming back a few times. Usually we raced out the door half-dressed, running late for work or shopping or appointments or school or wherever we had to be that morning.

Honestly, I wanted to talk to Gram and Granddad about my dreams before anyone else. They would listen and understand. They weren't the kind of grownups who listened to psychology books that contradicted what their children knew was going on. I planned on going to them that night, probably after dinner, when all our day's craziness had calmed down.

Going to Angela, however... That might be a better first step.

So we went right after school, Doni and Bethany and me.

Doni slipped her little hand into mine as we sat around the white wrought iron café table in the main room of Divine's. We sipped pineapple sherbet floats while I talked about my dreams. Angela didn't react. Her expression didn't change, except maybe that funny little smile, indicating she knew more than anyone else about what was going on... Well, it didn't quite fade, but it wasn't as strong as usual. She didn't ask me any questions, just focused her big blue eyes on me and listened until I ran out of words. Angela had a way of listening that made me think she heard more than anyone said. It would have been a relief not to say some of the things I had experienced in my nightmares, just picture them in my mind and have them go directly to hers.

I finished my story. We sat sipping in comfortable silence, for a few more minutes. I felt a lot better, like some pressure had been removed. Maybe it would be more accurate to say that having told Angela, I had fulfilled a responsibility I didn't know I had.

That made sense, I realized. Angela and Divine's Emporium were there in Neighborlee to protect it, or us, or maybe... Well, to be honest, sometimes I was sure there were things in our town that had to be contained in our town. So maybe Divine's protected the world from Neighborlee, instead of just the special people, the oddness, being hidden from the world? By telling Angela about my dream, I was helping her to guard us, or guard something else?

"Guardians," Angela murmured. Her little superior smile edged toward a smirk when I flinched at her word, coming so soon on the heels of my thoughts.

Yeah, I could definitely believe Angela read minds.

"Bethany, would you and Doni go upstairs and get one of my moonlight journals from the chest in my bedroom?" Angela reached inside the neck of her dress and drew out a thin silver chain with a long, crystalline skeleton key hanging from it, and handed chain and key to Bethany.

As the two of them held hands and hurried out of the room, heading for the stairs, Angela's smile faded entirely.

"It's real, isn't it?" I whispered. "The things in my dreams." I swallowed hard. "And you don't want Doni to hear what you're going to tell me about fighting it."

"Right, and yet not entirely." Angela took hold of my hand. "My dear Athena... How I wish you weren't so perceptive, that you hadn't inherited your grandfather's gifts and the responsibilities that come with them. And yet I know, from long years of experience, we are born to duties and burdens. We destroy our souls if we refuse them." She took a deep breath, exhaled slowly, all the while gazing into my eyes. "First, I sent them away because there are things I don't want Bethany to hear. I made a promise to her mother to protect her from the very things you must face because you are Ford Longfellow's granddaughter. Until Doni starts dreaming too ... why worry her?"

"Why don't you want Bethany to know?"

"Her bloodline has done enough already for Neighborlee. Her mother was another foundling, just like your grandfather, like Lanie Zephyr and her friends."

"Her mom?" I shivered, the cold coming from deep inside, as I remembered when Bethany's mother died. We were only nine. Sometimes being young helped to make the heavy sadness fade, but other times it just made the impact worse, and last longer.

Then I knew. I understood. Fragments of those sad, confusing days bobbed up to the surface of my memories.

"There was that weird storm. Mrs. Miller... She didn't die of a heart attack, did she?" I whispered.

Angela gripped my hand tighter and shook her head.

Six years ago, there were strange buzzing sensations in the ground for a day or two. Other people didn't seem to notice the electrical tingles in the soil, but Granddad let me curl up on the couch with him, where we both kept our feet off the ground. That day, Bethany and I were at soccer practice with Miss Lanie. Mrs. Miller had left the diner on an errand before lunch and didn't come back. A freak storm had struck, sending people diving for cover, driving rain horizontally. When it cleared up, she was found collapsed in an alley between two stores on the Mall, drenched, cold and dead.

Part of me wanted to yank my hand free of Angela's and run away. If I tried, she probably wouldn't hold onto me, keep me there. Not with her hand, anyway.

"Where are the dreams coming from? There's someone--no, something trying to come up, come out, break through a wall." I shook my head and pressed my free hand against my forehead. "I remember hearing things. You and Miss Lanie and Granddad talking. Mrs. Miller stopped something." For a second, it was like I couldn't catch my breath. "Something that tried to happen before."

"Yes, our enemy tries periodically to shatter the barriers we hold up to protect the world. Stephanie was part of that defense.

Neighborlee has many guardians, each of us picking up clues, warning signs, in different ways."

"So my dreams really do mean something?"

"How I wish they didn't. But be encouraged. Every time the enemy tries to break through, we grow stronger and we learn better how to fight it. Someday, we will defeat it once and for all."

"Break through from where?" I thumped my sneaker-clad foot on the floorboards. "I get the feeling it's underneath the town, but trying to come through a wall at the same time."

"The answer is yes." She released my hand, then leaned forward and patted my cheek, turning it into a caress before that smirk came back.

"Yes, to..." I shivered again. That half-glad, half-afraid, half-stunned, ready-to-burst sensation, when something incredible and unbelievable and should-be-impossible was about to happen. I know--three halves--but that was why I felt ready to burst. "Magic?" I whispered.

My gaze immediately went to the Wishing Ball that had sat on the counter next to the old-fashioned brass cash register for as long as I could remember. It was a metallic-toned dark rainbow in swirling, shifting colors. All the children could see the colors shift, but as we got older many of us couldn't see the movement anymore. I could still see the colors move, swirling around, promising to reveal something incredible someday. The stand was a coiled dragon, holding the Wishing Ball in the loop of its tail. Children in Neighborlee came to Divine's to make wishes. If they were good wishes and not entirely selfish, if they solved problems and helped people and didn't hurt them, those wishes often came true.

"Magic." Angela nodded. "And doorways to other worlds, other levels of reality. Good worlds, strange worlds, dangerous, and so pure and fragile that the doors must be held closed to protect the inhabitants. I am telling you this because you can still see the magic at work here, when all your playmates have grown older and less able to see."

"Even Bethany," I murmured, feeling guilty for leaving her behind.

"Oh, she is very able to see and sense and even hear the magic, the visitors. She has spent so much time here that the magic has soaked into her blood."

"But not enough for her to be a guardian." I thought of Bethany's mother, dead after having battled an invader from another reality. "That's a good thing."

"A very good thing." Angela turned, glancing toward the doorway.

I heard footsteps coming down the stairs, Bethany and Doni returning from their errand.

"Record all your memories of your dreams in the journal. Every time you wake up in the night, write them down. Only you and other guardians will be able to read what you wrote," Angela said, lowering her voice slightly. "When the other guardians feel the enemy moving, we will meet and compare notes, and find the right tactic to defeat him in what we all have dreamed."

"Do you dream about it, too?" I felt a thousand percent better, knowing Angela was feeling the same stirrings or warnings or premonitions or whatever they were.

"I dream even when I am awake." She touched her index finger to her lips, signaling me to silence, just before Bethany and Doni came through the door.

"There should be a book on dream interpretation in the book room," Angela said, taking the journal from Bethany and handing it to me. "Write down what you dream, and look up what the book says, but for heaven's sake, don't accept anything it says without a few grains of salt."

"Enough salt to melt a foot of snow," Bethany said. We all laughed when Angela just wrinkled her nose at her and made a shooing gesture at all of us.

"Don't you hoodlums have homework to keep you busy and off the streets?"

We walked out of the room and down the main hall to the front door, with a side trip to the book room. Sure enough, the book on dream interpretation was visible on the top shelf. I was pretty sure that book wasn't there when we walked in half an hour before.

"If you find anything interesting, Athena, do come talk," Angela said, handing me the book. "I'm always interested in what bubbles up from the sleeping subconscious."

On the way home, we parted company at the first intersection. I had slid the journal into my backpack as soon as Angela gave it to me, but once we had turned another corner and there was no one else close enough to spy on us, I took it out again.

"Major cool," Doni said. She wasn't like other kids. She didn't just reach for something that caught her attention, but she did walk close enough I was afraid we would trip over each other's feet.

She was right. The journal was major cool. It was in a gauzy drawstring bag, with crystalline beads on the string. Both gauze and beads were the same swirling, dark, metallic rainbow as the Wishing Ball. Even if Angela hadn't just confirmed magic was indeed real, I would have equated all of that with something incredibly mysterious and wonderful and full of potential. The material seemed to hum, subliminally, pressed against my palms. The beads sparkled when I slid the drawstring open enough to pull out the journal.

When Angela said moonlight journal, she meant moonlight--it glowed, all soft blues and silvery grays. Slowly moving ripples traveled across the journal cover from top to bottom. The glow faded as soon as sunlight touched the material, but it was strong enough in the dimness of the bag that I could see it.

Three pens were attached to the journal by a braided cord of the same material as the bag, each in its own little sleeve. I slid one out of its sleeve, and it looked like an ordinary gel pen. At first glance. Then I saw the ink swirled around in the transparent barrel, the colors changing--again, the same dark, metallic rainbow as the Wishing Ball.

"You can see all this," I said, glancing down at Doni. She nodded, her pointed little face somber, her white, fuzzy hair blowing in the afternoon breeze.

"It tickles my fingers, just like when I touch the Wishing Ball," she murmured, and ran one finger down the cover of the journal.

"Doni... Angela says you're a guardian, just like me. You're probably not old enough to have the warning dreams."

"Good." She gave me a momentary grin that looked a lot like Angela's smirk when I stumbled for a second, startled by her easy acquiescence. "I bet you wish you weren't old enough."

"You're just too smart, you know that?"

She nodded and linked her arm through mine, which made it kind of hard to put the journal back in its bag and then my backpack. We did it together, feeling silly and giggling a little, and then we marched down the sidewalks back home.

Of course, I didn't have a nightmare that night, and Doni didn't ask me as we hurried through breakfast and out the door to school the next morning.

I paid for it, though, at lunchtime.

The days were still nice and warm, and we were allowed to go outside to eat. There weren't enough picnic tables for everyone who wanted to eat outside, and the natural pecking order meant the seniors had the tables. The juniors--*moi*--got first dibs on the edges of the cement planter boxes and the cement car bumpers in the parking lot, whatever made seats. Everybody else had to make do with stretches of sidewalk. That day, I didn't feel very sociable and I didn't want Bethany asking me if I had any more dreams. So I wandered around the side of the building, where there was a little bit of a slope, down into a drainage area. The grass and ground were dry, so why not sit in the sun by myself and just relax?

Big mistake. The next thing I knew, I stretched out on my back, my eyes closed against my will, and I walked through a misty, warped, funhouse-but-not-fun copy of Divine's. The floors rippled and the walls tipped in toward each other so there was no real ceiling. Doors faded in and out of the walls where doors didn't belong. One door kept coming back, the edges glowing that poisonous color that wasn't quite green or blue or ultra-violet and always made me think of rotting things.

"Athena?" Doni's little hand grabbed hold of my shoulder and yanked me backwards out of the dream.

I opened my eyes and sat up so fast I smacked my head into Doni's. She had bent down to shake me. Her eyes were big with worry and they stayed big, even as she tumbled back and rubbed where my forehead hit hers.

"You had one of those dreams," she whispered.

"Did you see what I dreamed?"

That was a dumb question, and really made no sense on first thought. I was relieved so much I actually ached inside when she shook her head. Then I thought of something else.

"What are you doing over here? Forget it." I stood up and reached for my backpack with one hand and Doni's hand with the other. "You felt something, didn't you?"

"It was like..." She shrugged. "Like one of *them* were yelling your name and saying they were going to hurt you, and laughing about it."

When Doni said *them* with that little nauseated inflection, she was referring to the Hallidays.

"And you came running to protect me, huh? Thanks." I shifted to wrap my arm around her shoulders. We headed across the back of the high school, toward the elementary school, where Doni's classmates were using the playground (lucky dogs) during their lunch hour. But not so lucky, they weren't allowed off school grounds during the school day unless they were going home for lunch. I had to get her back across that foot-wide line of fluorescent purple paint before one of the playground monitors saw Doni.

"What did you dream?"

I shook my head, more focused on looking for an eagle-eyed adult for the moment. As soon as we crossed the border into elementary school territory, we sat down on the railroad ties that formed a planter box for one of the classroom gardens. I opened my backpack to get my lunch. Strange thing about those dreams--they kind of made my head ache, and made me hungry.

The first thing my hand touched was the gauzy bag protecting the moonlight journal. Doni didn't even blink when I pulled it out and put it on my lap, and then went in again for my lunch. I offered her some. She solemnly shook her head and lifted her own lunch bag, which she had been clutching this whole time. We ate in silence for a few minutes. I glanced at my watch to see how much time I had left. Only ten minutes left of the half hour, meaning I had probably slept for at least ten, maybe fifteen. Weird.

"I left this at home, in my headboard," I said, stroking the journal.

"Major double cool."

"More like freaky." I flipped the journal open and jotted a few lines in my own half-hieroglyphics shorthand as I told Doni what I remembered seeing and feeling.

"Think it'd do any good to read the dream interpretation book when we get home?" she said.

The bell rang, summoning everyone back to classes before I could answer. I settled for sticking my tongue out at her.

She laughed.

I felt a little better as I jammed the journal into my backpack and hurried to catch up with the others heading back to class. I wondered if I really had to worry about anybody trying to steal the journal. If the journal *came* to me in the middle of the day, then it could probably hide from eyes that shouldn't see it.

Not that I was going to test that theory and take stupid risks. I grew up in Neighborlee. Understanding the rules of magic and what stupid things *not* to do was kind of bred into us, unspoken lessons.

By the end of the day, I had a tentative plan of action. Doni and I met at the place where the sidewalk from the elementary and middle schools intersected with the sidewalk from the high school, and we headed for the new part of town--meaning the residential area that had been built in the 40s and 50s. Our family lived in the "old new" part--our houses were from the turn of the century, instead of the old part of Neighborlee, which was most of downtown, where buildings went up between the 1840s and 1890s.

"Who are we going to see?" Doni finally asked, when we passed up the last three streets that would take us home, by a roundabout path. If we were going to Divine's to talk to Angela about the dream that ambushed me in the middle of the day, we would have been heading the other direction.

"Miss Lanie."

"Okay." She was silent for exactly twenty-seven sidewalk blocks--I counted--while she processed things. I could almost guess her train of thought. "You think because she got hurt rescuing that guy who stole the city truck, she's a guardian too?"

"One way or another." I caught hold of her hand and gave it a few extra hard swings, earning another grin from her. "You're a pretty smart kid. Don't let the creepazoids give you a hard time for being smart, okay?"

"Nobody really notices me. Other than me being the new kid," she hurried to add. Her grip on my hand tightened a little. I decided not to challenge her statement.

"You've got friends, though, don't you?"

"Oh yeah." She nodded and looked up at me, and her smile seemed more normal. "Some of the kids say I should change my last name, so people know I'm a Longfellow. They say that'll stop some of the bozos. They say I'm lucky, living with Gram and Granddad."

"Hey, what about me?"

She snorted and swung our arms extra hard twice.

When we got to Lanie Zephyr's house, major renovations were going on, turning her two-car garage into an apartment. The ramp for her wheelchair had been built about two months ago, when she was finally able to leave rehab and go home. Granddad and Uncle Jinx helped with that. Most of our church took care of renovating her house to be wheelchair accessible. The apartment was for her friend, Felicity, who was going to be her part-time, live-near instead of live-in aide.

Five mongrel dogs came racing around the side of the house. They ran into a snow fence that spanned a gap where the chain link fence had been taken down between the house and the front wall of the garage. They barked and howled and yapped and kept slamming into the fence, making the wooden slats shake and bow like a hurricane-strength wind had hit. Doni flinched and made as if she would step behind me, then she sort of paused and tipped her head to one side like she heard something.

A lot of bits and pieces of the background weirdness of Neighborlee slipped together into something that actually made sense, while I watched her. Felicity did the same thing when her dogs were around. Some people joked that she should get a job as a "dog whisperer," or go into veterinary medicine. From what I could tell, Felicity still didn't know what she wanted to be when she grew up. She did have a gift for dogs. Most of them were strays that she took home and tamed just by loving them.

Maybe Doni had a gift for dogs?

"Are they saying anything?" I pitched my voice low.

Doni gave me an "are you nuts?" look for a moment, and then she grinned and shook her head. We headed for the ramp coming down from the back door of the house to the driveway.

"You heard something, though, didn't you?"

"Yeah. I don't know what. Yet." She tipped her head and gave me a sideways look.

Felicity came to the door before I could ask any more questions. She glanced past us at her dogs, who instantly settled down. No signals, no dog whistle, nothing. Then she gave Doni that considering look that, when Granddad used it on us, meant he was up to some kind of mischief.

"The boys like you," she said, and pushed the screen door open, standing back so we could come in.

"Please tell me you aren't coming to complain about whoever got suckered into taking Yearbook this year," Miss Lanie said as she wheeled into the kitchen.

I wasn't sure what I expected, seeing her for the first time since she left the hospital. She looked good, but she wasn't herself, either. Her hair had been trimmed short. She looked thinner than normal, and pale, and her collarbone and cheeks looked sharper than I was used to seeing. Miss Lanie was an athlete and always outdoors, so it wasn't like she was ever overweight to begin with.

Before I could finish the inventory, she took over, introducing herself to Doni, and insisting since she wasn't my teacher anymore she was just Lanie now, no "Miss" allowed.

She reached for the glass of deep red juice sitting on the edge of the kitchen table. I could have sworn that glass moved two inches into her grasp. Well, if Lanie was a guardian, maybe she had superpowers?

If I was a guardian, what were my superpowers? Was I waiting to grow into them? According to most comic books, powers manifested in adolescence, which was behind me. Maybe my only superpower was having weird dreams. That reminded me of what exactly we were here for.

"Uh-oh." Felicity had settled down at the table after offering us lemonade and ginger ale.

"What oh?" Lanie glanced back and forth between us. "This isn't about school, is it?"

Doni sat up a little straighter and pointed at me. "Athena is having weird dreams and Angela says we're guardians and..." She shrugged. "You are too, aren't you?"

"Dreams." She and Felicity exchanged looks.

I wondered if maybe they had telepathy and could talk without anyone overhearing. That would be a cool superhero talent to have. It made sense that the guardians of Neighborlee would need instant communication.

"If Kurt were here," Felicity began. "The snake, you think?"

"Athena didn't dream about snakes." Doni frowned, her little forehead getting all wrinkly.

"That's what we call it. We're just going on impressions." Lanie took a long, slow drink, while watching us over the rim of her glass.

"But yeah, we're guardians. I'm sorry, even though it makes sense, with Ford being a guardian. So you're having dreams..."

"Why is Athena having the dreams, when neither of us are? And you didn't have dreams the last time, just weird feelings in the ground and the air," Felicity said.

"I felt weird things in the ground," I had to admit. "When Mrs. Miller died."

"Uh huh." Lanie shook her head. "It could be need, bringing you into your duties now. Someone has to be sensitive enough to step into the gap." She gestured down at her chair.

"You still have gifts. It's not like we've been relegated to the advisory role, without actually going into battle. At least I don't think so," Felicity ended on a mumble.

"We're confusing them. Here's the problem, kids. I'm still getting all the drugs and other junk out of my system. I don't dream. Or if I do, they're so far deep down, I don't remember anything when I wake up. Felicity rarely has the warning dreams. Or maybe it's more accurate to say, dreams that let us eavesdrop on the snake's plans. We figured it was because her brain is kind of hard-wired for canines--"

"What does it say about you, that you can overhear a snake?" Felicity muttered. She winked at Doni, who lost her big-eyed look and giggled.

"Kurt's talents are more toward mechanical things. He definitely couldn't hear anything, but he's got this inborn thing in his head, to feel when people like us use whatever gifts we have. He can feel the vibrations where the snake or whatever it is tries to come from underground. It scared the heck out of us, when he could feel it moving around underneath the town, trying to find a place to come up."

I thought of Mrs. Miller, dead in an alley after a freak storm. What exactly had she done to stop the snake from breaking through into our world? Had the battle caused the storm, or was the storm just a warning the wall between dimensions became weak enough for the snake to cross over? We had to go back and talk to Angela. I had not asked the right questions, last time.

"Please don't tell me it's all resting on me this time around," I said. If Lanie had the dreams last time and Mrs. Miller died, did that mean I wouldn't die? But if not me, who had to give up their lives to hold the door closed?

"There are more guardians, don't worry. Angela said some people don't even realize they're guardians until the time comes for them to do their part." Lanie tried to smile as she patted the side of her wheel, but she looked sad and tired for a few seconds. "I always said this job sucked worse than gravity. We're semi-pseudo-superheroes with no costumes, no cool names, and no invulnerability."

"Maybe the girls are having the dreams," Felicity crossed her arms on the table and leaned forward, "because you can't hear and Kurt is out of town. The energy has to go somewhere, be picked up by someone."

"Only Athena is having the dreams," Doni said.

"But you can feel when I have them," I had to say. "You're part of this, too."

"Okay, time to share some information," Lanie said. "We get to be your advisories. Kind of like in the *Young Wizards* books. The young ones have all the power and the old ones--"

"*Older* ones," Felicity corrected her, earning another giggle from Doni and another tongue stuck out from Lanie.

"Older ones have the experience and questionable wisdom." Lanie nodded, kind of a "so there" gesture.

"*Young Wizards*?" Doni said. If she could have, her ears would have twitched like a horse's, at the mention of the books.

"Ordinarily, I don't loan my books to anyone, but since you're a Longfellow, I know you'll take care of them. Remind me to give them to you before you leave."

Doni's face lit up. Even if we hadn't gotten any useful information that afternoon, it was worth it going to Lanie's house.

We told about my first dreams, going to Angela and getting the moonlight journal. Then I related what I could remember of my dream that ambushed me at lunchtime. Doni told how she felt when it happened and came to wake me up. Lanie and Felicity weren't spooked at all when I told them how the journal appeared in my backpack, managing to escape the hiding place in my headboard.

"Okay, normally we just don't talk about the ordinary, everyday weirdness," Lanie said, "but just as a test ... please tell me that sometimes when you go to Divine's, rooms look bigger, the ceiling is higher--"

"Especially at Christmas," I said.

"And sometimes, you walk past a shelf, you decide what you really want, and when you walk past the shelf again it's there, when it wasn't there before?" Felicity said.

"Why are you asking us?" Doni asked.

"Testing," Lanie said. "It's different. We are Lost Kids, but you're the granddaughters of a Lost Kid. While we're either mutants or space aliens or Nazi breeding experiments, you have some Human blood from your grandmother, so ... it could be different."

"Here's to the Lost Kids," Felicity said, and saluted her with the remains of the lemonade in her glass.

"Granddad says Lost Boys," I had to offer. "Like Principal Wellington and a bunch of others. Like Pastor Rocky."

"What's that?" Doni said.

Chapter Four

"Our town has a tradition of lost children found within the geographic limits," Lanie said. "The kids all end up at Neighborlee Children's Home. Kids nobody ever reports missing. Like your grandfather, and a bunch of others."

"Like us," Felicity said. "And Kurt."

"Call me crazy, but I'm looking forward to seeing how the next generation handles all this weirdness."

"You're crazy." She snorted, grinning.

Then the two of them locked gazes and they went very still. There was this buzzing in the air. They claimed later they couldn't read minds, but I was pretty sure there was some communication, even if it wasn't in words.

"Kurt's right," Felicity said. "We really need to get to the bottom of the whole mystery. Especially if the next generation is being drawn into the guarding work. How many Lost Kids have talents, the kind of talent that gets passed along to the next generation? There has to be a reason why we are the way we are."

"What can you do?" Doni asked.

"Show her," Lanie said with a little smirk. Then she held up her hand. "The safe stuff. I don't need to replace my coffeemaker or my computer, thanks very much."

"You're no fun." Felicity pouted. She leaned back in her chair, closed her eyes, and clenched her hands into fists.

Her hair changed. Her long, gently curled, amber hair went from shoulder-length to past the pocket of her polo shirt in eleven seconds. I counted. Then it tightened up into corkscrews that would have made Shirley Temple jealous. After that the color shifted in visible waves, spreading from the roots to the tips, changing to strawberry blonde, to chestnut, and then to deep auburn, to a red that could only come from a bottle. Only it didn't.

"Major cool," Doni whispered.

"The dogs are part of your superpowers?" I said.

"And EM bursts guaranteed to kill your car, your computer, your microwave, and anything else that will inconvenience you at the worst possible time," Lanie said. "If you really want to hack her off, and destroy something, call her Zap."

"Ah...no thanks."

"The kid is smart." Felicity opened her eyes. She tugged on a few strands of her hair to look at and smirked at the color and curls.

"Not smart enough to figure out what the dreams actually mean."

"You will."

"But if my dreams are real, the snake is threatening Divine's."

"That's not good," Doni said. "If there's magic in the building..." She looked like she would be sick.

"What?" Felicity reached over and caught hold of her hand. "You just thought of something."

"I had a dream, too," she whispered. "I didn't remember until right now."

"It's okay." I scooted my chair over and put an arm around her shoulders. Doni was always pale to begin with, but now her skin looked like chalk.

"You know those eel things in the ocean, that are all teeth and they stick to whales and sharks and things and suck and they're like vampires, kind of?"

"Lampreys," Lanie said.

Felicity got up and opened a cupboard and brought out a box of chocolate bars. One of those assortment boxes, six different kinds of dark chocolate. She pulled out a bar with raisins and cashews, tore it open and put it into Doni's hand, and then she nudged the box over closer to me and Lanie.

"I can't remember anything--anything clear--but walls were melting and something was--" Doni shook her head, and it turned into a shudder through her whole body.

"Something was sucking the life out of something else?" I suggested. Well, she did mention vampires.

"Divine's is the target." Lanie pushed back from the table and looked down at her wheelchair. "My adapted car isn't ready yet, and flying is completely out."

"Because it's daylight and you don't want anybody to see you fly?" Doni guessed.

"She never could fly." Felicity stood and snatched a purse off the counter. "It was more like controlled gliding, levitating. That got broken when she broke her back. Come on, I'm taking you two to Angela, and then you'd better get home."

"I'll call your folks, let them know what's up." Lanie winked at Doni and reached out her hand. Her phone jumped off the hook on the wall and slapped into her hand.

"Major cool," Doni said.

~~~~~

Granddad's truck was parked in the street in front of Divine's when we got there. Angela met us in the hallway as we came in the front door of the shop. She beckoned with a crook of her finger, and we followed her to the main room. Granddad's eyes got big when he saw me and Doni, and for a second there, I thought he might cry.

"Dang," he muttered. He picked up the big mug of coffee that needed two hands, and guzzled it so long I thought he would drown.

"Blood runs true, Ford," Angela said. She sat down and gestured for us to take seats at the table with them.

"They're too young!"

"How old were you, the first time you joined in the battle to discourage the invader?"

"Yeah, well, in my day we grew up a lot faster." Granddad scowled down into his mug for a few seconds, before meeting my gaze, and then Doni's. "You girls gonna be okay?"

"Now that we don't have to keep any secrets from you and Gram?" Doni looped her arm through his and rested her head against his shoulder.

"Your Gram...she's not gonna be happy."

"Charlotte has all the-- Well," Angela corrected, winking at me, "*most* of the common sense in the family. She knew what she was getting into when she married you."

"Is Gram a guardian too?" I said.

"Support squad." Granddad said, and patted Doni's hand. "Okay, how did you two get drawn in?"

"I'm kind of support for Athena," Doni said. "It's more like I get echoes of her dreams."

"She woke me up when I fell asleep during lunch."

Angela's customary mixture of serenity and smugness slipped, just a little bit. More like that flicker that used to happen in the cinemas back when the movies were on reels of film instead of being digital--a warning that the reel was about to run out and it was time to synch up the next reel.

"Spill," Granddad said. "From the top. We're a team now. Forget the X-Men and Superfriends and all that other Saturday morning comic book spandex foolery. This is for real."

"Lanie said something about not having costumes or cool names," Doni said. "If we're a team shouldn't we have at least a name?"

He snorted and shook his head and twisted around enough to press a kiss on her forehead.

"All right, start from the top."

Without any interruptions, it didn't take very long. Of course, part of the speed came from having rehearsed the story a couple times already. Granddad held onto Doni's hand the whole time and shook his head every once in a while. He and Angela kept exchanging those looks that adults always thought kids couldn't read. Maybe I couldn't understand all the communication between them, but I caught enough. This was serious. This was dangerous. Granddad was building up a head of steam over Doni and me being part of whatever had to be done to protect Neighborlee.

"I suppose we should have expected this," Angela said. "Not so soon, though." Her gaze focused on Doni as she spoke, her voice soft, her words slow. "Something must have changed, to catch its attention. Maybe make it desperate enough to strike before it is up to full strength."

"That's an advantage for us, then," Granddad said.

"Not if we aren't prepared."

"Aren't we?" I said. "My dreams--we really are eavesdropping on the snake or whatever it is, aren't we? That's what Lanie called it."

"True," Granddad said. "I have to wonder why Kurt hasn't been reacting to all the build-up."

I could read the look he gave Angela. Essentially, he wanted to know why I was picking up things someone else should have been catching.

"He's out of town," Doni said. "Lanie said she's still getting all that medicine out of her system and she hasn't been having any dreams, and Kurt is out of town doing some security system installation in Houston."

"So we're all that's left to eavesdrop on whatever it's planning?" I said. "Like we have some kind of mind link?"

"I don't like it," Granddad said. "What if this link means that thing knows about my girls?"

"According to Athena's dreams, it is focused on my shop. That is a big, big mistake." Angela shook herself and her mouth flattened a little bit. A chill shot through me, as I got a clearer sense of just what that monster was up against, threatening Angela and Divine's Emporium. She caught hold of both my hands in hers and I couldn't have looked away from her blue eyes if I had wanted. "We always win, and we always defeat the enemy. We grow stronger, we grow smarter, and we're ready."

"Despite setbacks like Stephanie and Lanie?" Granddad muttered, like he didn't want us to hear, but we did anyway. He snorted, then winked at me. "Might as well give them full disclosure. The girls have to know by now, battle means getting hurt. Sometimes the good guys come away with scars." He took a deep breath. "And sometimes we don't come away at all."

We sat in quiet for a few moments, and I think they were giving us time to adjust to that somber bit of revelation. Maybe they were waiting for us to ask to opt out. But could we?

"What do all the melting walls mean?" Doni asked.

"My guess is that it thinks it must destroy Divine's to become free. This shop is like a patch, or one of those paper reinforcement rings on filler paper, to strengthen the spot where a hole has been punched, where many realities meet and allow ease of movement between different realms. All the years of traffic through the shop, the powerful, sometimes dangerous objects that have been entrusted to me for safekeeping..." Her smile returned, smug and sharp and promising pain for anyone who crossed her. "My shop and I may look like a tempting sugarplum, but the sugarplum has teeth."

"Indigestion," I muttered.

Granddad groaned, but he grinned and patted my hand. Angela gave me that assessing look that always made me think she could read my mind.

We didn't talk much on the way home. Everything that needed saying had been said already. Besides, I think Granddad was trying to figure out how to tell Gram what was up. He had gone to

Divine's to talk to Angela about the dream he had the night before. Having helped stand against a couple of breakthrough attempts, he knew what a warning dream felt like.

When we got home, Doni and I went up to my room, and she helped me remember everything, so I could write it down in my journal. There wasn't any yelling or any other noise from downstairs, like the clanging of pots and pans, as Granddad told Gram what was going on. I wasn't sure if that was a good sign, or bad. I had never seen or heard them argue about much of anything, except in fun, but there was always a first time.

"Girls, I need your help with dinner," Gram called, just when the silence got so thick and deep, I wondered if maybe they had taken their argument outside and down to the park, so they wouldn't disturb us.

Granddad was nowhere to be seen when we stepped into the kitchen. Gram had five pots going on the stove--yes, we had an eight-burner stove. Granddad got it from an old manor house that was torn down before my mother and Aunt Lenore were born. Gram didn't say anything right away. We knew what we had to do. I took care of the fresh bread waiting to be taken from the bread machine, and poured the dressing on our shredded veggie salad, while Doni set the table. Gram turned down the flames under all the pots and turned around, wiping her hands on the kitchen towel always tucked into the waistband of her jeans. Her bottom lip trembled, just twice. It was a good thing she got control of herself right away, because I probably would have busted out crying, without even knowing why she was teary.

"Well, it's about time someone showed some sense around here," she said, looking back and forth between us. "If you want something done right, you get a woman. Mind you two do us proud. And you--" She reached out a hand to rest on Doni's shoulder, shaking her a little. "You keep your cousin out of trouble, hear me?"

Doni nodded, big-eyed, a little stunned. I sputtered. Leave it to Gram to get sappy and snarky and make us laugh, all at once.

I didn't have any dreams for three nights in a row after that. Maybe the snake, or whatever it really was, sensed us thinking about it, concentrating on it, and it pulled back. Maybe it figured it would play games with our minds. Like if it got quiet and left us alone, we would let down our guards.

The fourth night, my head was so full of my computer class assignment, I didn't even realize I was dreaming that particular dream until near the end.

I was in advanced computer programming, the only girl. Most of the guys were writing programs to analyze sports stats to predict winners, or video games. I wanted to be different. Jinx had some friends who were architects, and they were complaining about the CAD software that kept rebelling or wouldn't let them do what they wanted. We got extra points in our assignment if we gave the program to someone and they were able to use it without us watching over their shoulders and guiding them through it. Two birds with one stone--and maybe some funds to toss into my college account at the bank.

In my dream, I was building a house in virtual reality, talking the rooms into being. I put up walls and decorated them, changing the paint and wallpaper with just a thought. No foundation, no roof, just walls. At first, it was just a thought. As the dream progressed, I started talking. "Green walls. Mint green. No, striped wallpaper. Coffee brown and grass green. No, that's too dark."

Someone was there in the room with me. At first it was just a feeling. I couldn't see the person, but I could feel...her...yeah, definitely a "her" in the room with me. She didn't respond, but she was there, listening. For a while, anyway.

"Paint the ceiling royal blue and put silver stars on it," she said.

"Huh?" I turned around, looking for her, shivering so hard I fell off my feet.

That was when the snake reared its head, so to speak. I fell through the floor and landed hard in the hallway of Divine's. The walls melted, and the air got smoky.

I had to get out of there, but I couldn't move for a few seconds. The wall directly in front of me glowed like it was on fire.

"Athena?" Doni grabbed hold of my shoulder and pulled. Her hand was on fire, her fingernails were talons, and for two seconds my feet stayed glued to the floor while she pulled me backwards, so I felt like I stretched out a couple yards. Or maybe it was a couple miles. Who could tell in dreams?

I woke up with a yelp. Doni stood over my bed, gripping my shoulder. Her face was pale, her eyes wide, and she gleamed in the moonlight, drenched in sweat. The smell of smoke filled my nose.

"Go check on Granddad," I said, once I could catch my breath. She let out a little whimper and ran down the hall. I collapsed back into my drenched pillow and shivered for a few seconds, from the sensation of my elongated arms and legs spooling back into their normal length. I had never been seasick before, but I had a good idea what that felt like.

The four of us met downstairs in the kitchen. Gram had heard Granddad snarling in his sleep and woke him up, just after the fire started in his dream. She made toast dripping with butter and ginger preserves to settle our stomachs. I was ready to believe she had superpowers, just because she knew what would work best without even asking us how we felt.

We didn't go back to bed, but sat there in the kitchen, playing Mexican Train dominoes, not saying much, waiting for the sun to come up. The dreams had hit about four in the morning, so we didn't have long to wait. Finally when the clock hit 7, Granddad picked up the little plastic train marker and put it back into the tin holding our dominoes.

"Feel up to school today?" He looked at both Doni and me. She nodded and glanced at me. It was Friday morning.

"Are we going to report to Angela before we go?" I said.

"If you need a shower, better get it now."

Definitely, I needed a shower. I still caught the occasional whiff of smoke, and I could swear the smell came from me. I wanted to stand under the hot spray and scrub with the lemon gel until the water went cold, but Doni and Granddad both needed to wash up before we left. He gave us a deadline of 7:30 and headed for his bathroom.

Angela came around the side of Divine's from her garden in the back as we drove up to the curb and parked. Her feet were bare and sparkling with dew and she wore a silvery-gray cardigan over her usual blue smock dress. She opened the gate in the wrought iron fence and led us in silence into the shop. Granddad did most of the talking.

"Well, you staying away all week didn't change anything," she said. "I was hoping that your absence would weaken the link."

"Wouldn't that mean we'd have to *stay* away?" Doni asked.

"No thanks," I said. That earned a smile from Angela.

"We need to change our tactics," Granddad said.

That was how Doni and I ended up spending the weekend at Divine's Emporium. Major hardship, definitely. Oh, the things we put up with for the sake of our town.

Actually, there were a few details we didn't like, such as not telling Bethany what was going on, why exactly we were sleeping over and she wasn't invited. Of course, Angela had the perfect excuse and cover story. My dream computer was waiting on the counter when Doni and I walked in after school. I was hard at work, setting up an inventory system for Angela, when Bethany came in after dinner. I would have preferred that Bethany not come by at all, so I wouldn't have to lie to her, but it was inevitable. I should have been working at Miller's Diner along with her on a Friday football night, so she came to check on me during the lull between the dinner hour and when the football game ended.

The other unpleasant detail was knowing that the more time we spent at Divine's, the stronger the homing signal for the snake. We were, in essence, trying to get it to attack before it was up to full strength. Of course, as Granddad said, how were we supposed to know what "full strength" was for the interdimensional terrorist trying to burst up through Neighborlee like evil clowns burst through paper drums in a particularly twisted circus routine?

Bethany never quite understood my fascination with computers, my passion for figuring out codes and getting the sometimes aggravating gizmo to do things that other people said it couldn't do. It was a trade-off, because I couldn't understand her love of acting, of putting on costumes and makeup and sliding into that "otherness" mindset that let her become someone else, just for a little while. I always had stage fright, to put it simply. Our differences never made a wall between us, thank goodness. So, when she walked in and found me hard at work, installing software and scribbling notes to myself and asking Angela questions, she just grinned and rolled her eyes and didn't even ask the justified question: "Why didn't you tell me?"

We didn't tell her that Doni and I were spending the night. Otherwise she would come back after work. If the snake took the bait, we didn't want Bethany around, demanding explanations. We didn't want her stunned and scared, and maybe even needing to hear the truth about her mother dying as guardian for our town.

"Of course, you know this will lead to quite a few weekends spent here," Angela said, once the shop had closed for the night and it was just the three of us in her living room on the second floor. "It will take quite a long time getting that inventory put together."

"Especially since it's kind of hard inventorying things in rooms that don't exist right now," I said without thinking.

She got very still and slowly tipped her head slightly to one side, and her smug, all-knowing smile got a little deeper, a little more mysterious. That glint in her eye got brighter. Maybe even a little frightening.

"What makes you think there are rooms here that don't exist right now? Besides what you've seen in your dreams?"

"Magic," I managed to say, without too much shaking in my voice, and without hesitating.

"There's such a thing as being too smart for your own good," she murmured.

"She just hopes you'll give her that computer if you don't need it," Doni said. She blushed dark when Angela turned that intent, all-seeing gaze on her.

Angela laughed.

We didn't really want to sleep, and Angela didn't make us try. She settled down with Doni to watch a movie while I pulled out my notebook computer and got back to work on my CAD program design. I was ahead of the schedule I had set myself for creating the program, and that was good. It would give me more time to have friends test-drive it.

Being in Divine's for the night helped me get more creative. Maybe that was just more proof of the inherent magic in the atmosphere. When Doni and Angela finished their movie, I had six more lines of programming finalized, tested, and de-bugged far enough to make some of the graphics change on the main screen. Maybe it was a waste of time and energy, but I had created an avatar who walked (granted, a little herky-jerky) around the room or building, depending on the design project, with a hammer, paintbrush or other decorating or building tools. One tap or slap of the tool, and the change appeared on the diagram. At least, that was the plan.

"I think you're letting your video game friends influence you a little too much," Angela said, when I explained to her and Doni what I had finished adding to my program. "This is cute and clever, but I can't imagine an architect or structural engineer appreciating the time taken away from work to watch your virtual reality person."

"Why couldn't it be a game, too?" Doni said. "You could have people compete to build buildings or houses or something. Or maybe they could sabotage each other, or have to do things to earn the money to add on to their houses."

"Two birds with one stone." Angela's smile widened, and I got that funny, warm, expanding sensation of knowing she approved. "What about for people who want to add on to houses they already have? This isn't just for building from scratch, is it?"

That got me thinking. Maybe we could hook up a video camera to the computer and walk around the house, uploading images of actual buildings into the program, inside and out, to save all that measuring and programming work. I would have to work that out and probably create the algorithm for calculating exact measurements. Doni displayed her brilliance by suggesting that I have a standard measuring stick that would appear in every image whenever I turned on the visual upload program, so the computer could calculate everything. Once I indicated the length of the stick, the program could do the rest.

Angela sent me to dig around in the miscellaneous room on the third floor, which usually held something of a technological nature. Sometimes, I was pretty sure the room only existed for Granddad and Kurt to find all sorts of gizmos and bits and pieces to use in their inventions. That night, I found a video camera, with a brand name and label I had never heard of.

Angela said she thought a tourist had left it behind last summer. If it was left at the Neighborlee Arms or maybe in the Metroparks, whoever found it would have brought it to Divine's. There was no extra equipment, no power plugs or cables to connect it to something else, such as a TV or computer or monitor, and she wasn't even sure it worked.

I was pretty sure she just said that to test me. After all, this was Divine's Emporium and nothing was inside the shop that Angela didn't know about or control. Right?

We kept chatting as I spread my findings out on the floor of her apartment and tried to piece things together. I opened the compartment of the camera to look at the battery pack, and it was like nothing I had ever seen before. The batteries--three of them-- were six-sided. If they were dead, I had no way of replacing them without going to another country, and I couldn't identify that country from the scientific-looking symbols and hieroglyphics that covered it. One of the power cables I dug up did fit in the right plug, and a series of lights flickered up the side of the camera, indicating power level as it charged, from red through orange through yellow to green. Pretty cool. There was no place to insert a memory card or a cassette, so I figured it was hard-wired digital memory.

While I worked, our conversation trickled into other directions and kind of circled around the whole idea of redesigning houses. Angela just laughed at us when Doni started scribbling on one of my scrap paper pads, adding rooms to Divine's. Later, I couldn't decide if she laughed at us because changing the shop wasn't within our power, or maybe because Doni was describing rooms that really did exist, but only when they were needed.

We got silly, probably because we were tired and slightly sugar buzzed with cream soda and dulce de leche floats. We designed a spa room that would give us manicures and pedicures, just by putting our hands and feet into holes in the wall. Of course, Angela did us one better by insisting on a hair design "portal," where we could lie down on a sliding bed that fit our heads into an indentation in the wall. Then there was the greenhouse that doubled as an aviary and apiary and butterfly haven, which went up and down on hydraulic lifts to catch or evade the sun, depending on the weather. And of course, more book rooms.

There was a room for watching movies before they came out in the theaters, that delivered all sorts of gourmet treats through another of Doni's miraculous slots in the wall. Having lived in five different countries since she was born, she had a wider concept of what was gourmet than I did. Angela suggested things that I was pretty sure had been considered delectable maybe two or three centuries before, but made both Doni and me gag a little when we contemplated them. Like roasted swans with their feathers put back on before serving, or hummingbirds stewed in honey.

About that time, I got the camera hooked up to my computer and created a file to take whatever the camera would download. I set up a series of fire walls to protect my computer, just in case the camera had some weird data or files that turned into Trojans, just waiting to invade and attack. I could not afford to lose all the work I had done on this term's project.

Angela got a little too quiet and lost her usual smirk for a few seconds when I actually got the camera to work, and an image of Doni appeared on the computer screen, with about a second of lag time between what the real Doni did and what her image did on the screen. Angela smiled and said that was incredible, and I should think about going into business with Kurt, because I seemed to have the same gift for making things work that shouldn't.

"The problem," she said, with her smirk returning and mischief gleaming in her eyes, "is that sometimes people take things that only Kurt can make work, and they get themselves stranded by expecting his inventions to work when he's not around. You don't want to get yourselves into a jam like that."

We did go to bed around midnight. I was just tired enough to wonder if the guest bedroom was one of the rooms that appeared whenever they were needed, and didn't connect with the reality of Neighborlee the rest of the time. I was too tired to think straight, and it kind of made me dizzy, lying there in the dark in my twin bed, trying to calculate where the room was in relation to the rest of the house. If I fell asleep before Doni, or after her, neither of us could decide.

I dreamed of a room that budded off from our guest room and broke off after sucking Doni into it. My eyes were still closed as I rolled out of my bed, reaching for her, trying to drag her back to safety. Of course, I woke up both of us.

"But I didn't have a dream," Doni whispered, when I told her about mine.

Well, I had to explain why I yanked her out of a sound sleep, didn't I?

"Maybe it wasn't a snake dream, then."

I tried to get comfortable enough to fall asleep again, but I couldn't. My computer, sitting on the dresser next to my bed, seemed to be watching me. That made no sense, because the little power light wasn't even phasing in and out for hibernation mode.

I waited until Doni's breathing grew soft and regular, then got up and picked up my computer and left. Working in Angela's living room was out. Not that I had any hope of doing anything in

Divine's without her knowing, but it just struck me as rude, turning on a light and working while she was trying to sleep. I picked up the bag with the jury-rigged camera and went downstairs to the furniture room. There was a fainting couch that Bethany and I had loved since we were barely able to toddle around the shop. It served as our chariot, our Viking longboat, or our spaceship. As we grew older, it was more often just a place to curl up and dream out loud while winter storms howled on the other side of the wall or rain drummed down hard outside, making us feel cozy and safe. It had never sold, which suited us just fine.

I settled on the couch with my notebook on my lap and got to work on my assignment. First step: calculate what I would need to turn the images from the camera into data my computer could read and translate. There were probably programs out there already that did the same thing, but the point of the class was for us to figure out how to do it without looking at what others did. Definitely, I would need to talk to Granddad and Kurt, and maybe someone in the growing computer sciences program at Willis-Brooks College, too. They would be more likely to have up-to-date equipment that I could borrow.

I had the feeling Angela had been warning me that the camera wouldn't work outside the walls of Divine's. Then again, I had been hearing Granddad and Kurt talk about problems with friends who worked in research, how they had to sign papers giving the patents for whatever they discovered to the research lab or university that they worked for. If I borrowed WB equipment, would they have a claim on whatever I developed?

Heady thinking for a high school student at barely two in the morning. I made notes of things to discuss, including a trip to Carr, Cooper and Crenshaw. I could probably trade some office work for consulting time. Mr. Carr was such a softy. Then I got back to work on my assignment.

I did a sketchy diagram on the screen. Not yet sleepy enough to go back to bed, I plotted out the room I was in, including the placement of the furniture and the lone, shuttered window in the corner, mostly hidden by a china cabinet that Bethany and I had always fervently believed was a companion to Lucy's wardrobe. I heard the top door creak, which jolted me out of my sleepies. Nothing moved in the cabinet, visible through the beveled glass doors, but the little lamp I had turned on when I came into the furniture room cast incredible shadows, so how could I be sure?

Right then, I realized just how stupid I had been, sitting where I was. The fainting couch was positioned so I faced into the china cabinet corner, with my back to the doorway into the rest of the shop. Turning the couch so I could see both the doorway and the china cabinet, and also the window beyond it, was an easy matter of shoving the one end where I was sitting about forty-five degrees to the left. Easy, except that it meant I would have to put my feet on the floor.

Problem: I had always believed since infancy in the monster under the bed. Or in this case, the fainting couch. This was along the same lines of hating to swim in water that was murky or tangled with water weeds badly enough I couldn't see what was underneath me. To be honest, I also hated the deep end of the pool at WB, because it was far too easy to imagine that filter/drain grating at the bottom opening up and letting awful things in, to attack unwary swimmers--piranha, sharks, octopi, monsters from other dimensions, or just the grossness of a sewer backing up.

My imagination was always hyperactive. After the things I had been learning in hints and snippets about other dimensions and realities, it was running on Warp Factor twenty-five.

More creaks, from elsewhere in the shop. Footsteps, padding soft on the hardwood stairs. At least, I hoped the feet were on the stairs and not coming from another dimension, ready to push the china cabinet door open and leap--

"What's wrong?" Doni asked, and startled a yelp out of me.

That got me standing up, feet on the floor, and no attack from the monster under the couch. A few minutes later, we were both settled on the couch, repositioned to let us watch the cabinet and the doorway. I told her what had been going through my head, about the video-to-computer program as well as the china cabinet being a doorway to another world.

"Wouldn't that be major cool?" She snuggled down in the afghan she had brought from the guest room.

Doni brought one for me, as soon as she realized I had left the room. Even though I was the older one, she had a knack for looking out for me, so maybe it really wasn't a joke when Gram made her responsible for keeping me out of trouble.

"Yeah, it would, but with the snake trying to break through, I'm not sure it's so wonderful having an open door anywhere around here. Besides, Narnia isn't there anymore and, like Digory found out, there are a lot of not-so-nice worlds out there."

"True." Doni scooted around so she kind of leaned against the angled back of the couch. "How about if I watch the cabinet while you work?"

"You should be in bed." That was the limit of my token sense of responsibility at this time of the morning.

"Tomorrow's Saturday. Besides, Miss Angela will be down here any minute."

"Just to keep you from raiding the candy jars," I muttered.

Doni stuck her tongue out at me, grinned, and we settled down to work. I asked her to estimate the dimensions of some of the furniture around us. Doni was good at eyeballing things, guessing how far away something was, how tall, how deep, even how fast Granddad's truck was going. With her help, I got the schematics of the furniture room down in no time. Then I hooked up the camera to my notebook again and turned it on. Hurrah, it had retained the charge. I recorded a slow, sweeping image of the room, to compare to the schematics I had made.

Mentioning the candy jars in the main room sabotaged us both. I had a hankering for some of the dark chocolate espresso beans Angela had in a jar behind the counter. These weren't actual coffee beans covered in chocolate, but bits of super-bitter-sweet chocolate flavored with espresso and shaped like beans. I didn't like coffee unless it was half cream and heavy with vanilla syrup, but I loved those beans. Resisting the craving became painful, and I gave in right after putting a doorway in the wall between the china cabinet and the antique green wire baker's rack. I asked Doni if she wanted me to bring her anything. She came with me, since she wasn't sure what she wanted. Maybe her imagination was hyperactive at that time of the morning, too, and she didn't want to be alone.

I shouldn't have left my computer alone for the five minutes it took us to get our treats. But maybe our being in the room wouldn't have stopped or changed anything. Who knows?

Chapter Five

Doni was ahead of me, returning to the furniture room, and picked up my computer so she could sit down in her spot. "Is it supposed to be in color?"

"Color?" That shiver from deep inside made me pause. I stared as she turned my notebook computer around.

Part of the schematic was colored in, approximating the colors of the furniture from the image. Easy to see because I had a split screen set up. This was freaky because I hadn't matched up the images yet. When we left to get our candy, the video camera image showed mostly ceiling, where I had ended recording, while the schematic screen showed the door I had drawn. Now they were matched. The door I had *drawn* now appeared on the video camera image, while the colors were seeping into the schematic. I took my computer from Doni and sat down, mesmerized as colors invaded my CAD drawing.

Dumb to just sit there and watch, huh? Blame low blood sugar, blame weariness, maybe blame the snake? Or maybe blame the unspoken, universal belief I had been raised in, that it was always safe inside Divine's Emporium.

Once everything had color, a "tuning up" started, where textures faded in and little details were refined, like rounded corners on furniture that had been blocky a minute or two before.

Then the schematic started to move, turning, gaining three dimensions. The video camera image moved with it.

"That's not supposed to do that, is it?" Doni whispered.

"I wanted to give it three-dimensional capabilities," I said, "but I only inserted a space in the menu and put in some markers for the different axes for turning the whole thing."

"This isn't like the wizards' manual and Darine, is it?"

It took me a few seconds to realize she was referring to the third *Young Wizards* book, where the younger sister of the heroine had her "ordeal," and her brand new computer took her through the wizard's oath.

"Oh, heck, heck, heck." I got up, my legs trembling. "I am so stupid. Somebody took over my computer--and we've just been sitting here, watching it work!" I put my notebook down on the couch and beckoned for Doni to take my hand. "We have to tell Angela, right now."

"Major mega cool," Doni whispered, ignoring my hand and pointing at the wall.

Right where I had drawn the doorway on the schematic.

An outline glowed in rippling rainbow shimmers as the door drew itself on the wall. In less than a breath's time, a door gleaming in crystalline shades of silver and blue swung open. On the other side, Doni peered out at me. She looked terrified, a thousand times worse than the day she appeared on our doorstep. I shouted for her not to move, and I swear, I crossed eight feet of floor in one step and catapulted myself through the doorway, reaching for her hand.

Two mistakes.

First, I should have turned off my computer, either hit the power switch or closed the lid. Whether it would have done any good or not was a moot point. I should have tried that before racing to the rescue. Maybe it would have closed that door.

Second... Doni was still sitting there on the couch, staring at her doppelganger.

That detail didn't hit my consciousness until *after* I crossed the threshold. Something dull black wrapped around the other Doni's waist and pulled her out of the light. She screamed in pure terror. Well, as much as she could with the sound on mute. I looked back and saw the real Doni getting to her feet and I shouted for her to stay away, to get Angela. But I had been muted, too.

Honestly, I was not and never have been hero material, and if that doorway had still been there, my first reaction would have been to leap back to my own world, dimension, whatever the proper classification. The door wasn't there. Seriously, it was like I was looking through a theater scrim, where in a play the action took place in front of it, seeming to be solid wall. Then, when lights lit it from behind, suddenly was transparent, or almost transparent. I could see Doni, my Doni, looking at the place where the doorway was and her mouth was moving and I could tell she was shouting my name. But no sound.

Maybe I was dumb enough to leap without looking, but I had read enough fantasy books and seen enough movies about stepping into parallel worlds or universes or whatever, I knew what came next. I had to find the doppelganger Doni, rescue her, make right whatever had become unbalanced (besides my brain!) and fix something before I could find the door again to go home.

At least, that was my theory as I raced across the room that was a mirror of the furniture room, except everything was turned around. It reminded me of that episode of *Lost in Space* where Penny stepped through a mirror into another world that looked like hers. Or maybe it was *Warehouse 13*? I really didn't have time to go back through my years of rabid TV watching and get my storylines clear. I had a mirror image of Doni to rescue.

Fear took over my brain: *what if whatever happened to the Doni in this mirror world affected the real Doni?*

I stepped out of the mirror furniture room. No more mirror copy of Divine's Emporium. Just darkness and shadows. I immediately got lost following the glimpses of movement that I hoped was mirror-Doni, fighting the tentacle dragging her away.

Okay, right, it was not smart to just go running into dark rooms. Maybe the lateness of the hour affected my brain. Or something in the air. Or maybe there was no air. Looking back, I honestly can't remember smelling anything, and I can't remember feeling my feet on the floors of the dark rooms I traveled through.

The next thing I knew, I was back in the furniture room, still chasing down that flicker of movement. Maybe I finally started breathing, getting some oxygen to my brain. I stopped and turned around and headed back the way I had come, reasoning that whatever was dragging the mirror-Doni was going in a circle.

A tangle of churning blackness with tentacles going in dozens of directions slid into the furniture room through a door that wasn't there a second ago. It saw me. Don't ask me how I knew that, because that was all it was, tentacles and blackness, like a haze of ink from an octopus swirling through the water. The next moment, it kind of spasmed like a cartoon octopus, the tentacles uncurling.

Mirror-Doni slid out of its grasp and hit the floor. Without a sound.

My Doni jumped through the scrim-screen in the wall. It lit up like a billion theater lights and made the darkness-tentacles monster shriek like a million bad Saturday afternoon B-movie mutant creatures covered in radioactive goo. That first sound in the heavy silence was like thousands of nails and chain saws scraping across a thousand blackboards.

Mirror-Doni staggered to her feet and turned into a whirling dervish, pummeling the darkness-tentacles monster. It staggered away and shattered into splatters and shards and oily clouds. The room got wobbly, like the light spilling in from the real furniture room diluted everything. Or maybe like someone spilled paint thinner on a painting. The monster shrieked louder as it dissolved and shredded from the outer edges inward.

My Doni grabbed hold of me. More light flared, coming from a rope tied around Doni's waist. It went through the scrim. I grabbed onto it. Something pulled, and we staggered toward the screen. With each tug of the rope, the scrim grew more transparent. I saw Angela on the other side, pulling on the rope. Granddad was behind her, and Jinx and Kurt. Three more tugs and we stumbled through the scrim, with a cold scorching sensation drenching me. I really expected to find my pajamas burned off me, or maybe both of us covered with slime like in the first *Poltergeist* movie.

"Close it," Angela said, in that sharp, intense tone of voice I hoped never to hear her aim at me.

Kurt let go of the rope and held down the power button on my computer. It let out that little powering down whine and I looked over my shoulder to see the dimensional doorway in the wall flash and vanish.

I was right--I should have turned off my computer. But who could think clearly when Doni was in trouble, already on the other side of the doorway? Or at least, what I thought was Doni.

Funny, but Angela and Granddad agreed with me. Always better to leap to the rescue, to follow my instincts, than to stop and reason things through and waste vital seconds. When it came to magic and all the things that conveniently slid under the label of "otherness," often logic worked against the valiant knight errant.

Just to be safe, Kurt opened up my computer and took the battery pack out. Angela walked through the house, every room, inspecting the walls. What she saw or didn't see, wanted to see or not see, she didn't tell us. After what we had gone through, Doni and I didn't really want to know. Kurt and Jinx went outside and conducted their own inspection. They never told us what they were looking for, either. Granddad sat with us on the stairs, waiting until

Angela told us it was safe, and then we gathered in her living room for a late night/early morning... well, pig-out and gabfest, to be totally honest.

In the proper sequence of events: Kurt had come back to town from his installation job around dinnertime. Lanie and Felicity told him what we had told them. Kurt had kind of an inner divining rod that let him know when something nasty was creeping around, so he spent the night driving around town, waiting for that creeping sense of threat to go off the meter. Granddad woke up about the same time I had. He'd also dreamed about Doni getting sucked out of Divine's. He figured it was a threat, but the safest place to be was with Angela, so he didn't panic.

Plus, he had enough experience with weirdness to be hesitant about interrupting whatever we might be doing, disturbing our concentration. He and Angela and Kurt gave each other those "looks" that adults used a lot and thought kids didn't understand what they were silently communicating to each other. It was kind of funny, but Uncle Jinx got left out of that "conference glance." Still, it wasn't fair. If Doni and I had been drafted as guardians, we had a right to know about the history of some of the battles.

So, to get back to the story: Granddad woke up Jinx and they came to the shop and stayed outside, standing guard. When Kurt showed up, they only needed to talk for about five minutes before they decided to come inside.

About thirty seconds before they stepped on the porch, outside forces took over my computer and used my half-developed program to create the doorway. When Doni shrieked for Angela and raced up the stairs, the men heard her. The front door opened before they even thought about breaking it down. Nobody was sure who saw the coil of rope and picked it up, but they had it when Doni and Angela came down the stairs and headed for the furniture room. The scrim opening was shrinking in size, so only Doni had any chance of fitting through when I put the brakes on and turned around to wait for the monster to come up behind me.

Funny thing. Doni saw her doppelganger, but everyone else said they only saw a vague, shadowy shape that could have been a person.

If that was the next attempt to break through, if we had drained enough energy from the snake to keep it quiet for a few more years, only time would tell.

Granddad and Kurt were both interested in my CAD program and promised they would work with me to set up an interface with a normal video camera, to help with redesign and renovations. The camera I found at Divine's didn't even have a power reading when I took it outside. After what had happened, I was more than happy to leave it behind, locked up in the attic where Angela put things of questionable safety. Better to do things the hard way, with "dumb" equipment that had to be told every step to take.

Kurt warned me to be careful to keep my CAD program away from Freddie Grandstone when I eventually took it to local architects. He was trying to make a name for himself as an architect. His brother Reggie was a lawyer at Carr, Cooper and Crenshaw. That just made it easier for them to follow the family tradition of trying to rewrite reality and claim things in Neighborlee that had never been theirs. Easier, but they still never succeeded. Mr. Carr made sure of that.

I asked once why he let his firm hire Reggie, and he laughed and admitted that Reggie was a good lawyer as long as he wasn't focused on himself. Plus, it was always wiser to keep possible sources of trouble close enough to swat them back where they belonged whenever necessary.

When my mother was in elementary school, the Grandstones had tried to take our house. They claimed it had once been their rental property, and they never sold it to the family who sold it to Granddad and Gram when they got married. The Grandstones also claimed the antique furniture in our basement and shed had been left there in storage, but Gram had all the receipts from when and where she bought every single piece. The easy explanation was that the Grandstones realized what a good living Gram made, finding and selling antiques to collectors. They tried to get their hands on it all by claiming everything had been stolen, including the house. The Grandstone/Longfellow feud officially started around that time. I would be a target if Freddie heard about my CAD program.

So we were ready for war.

I learned that the enemy would never strike when we were prepared for it--at least, not the enemy we expected, and not in the avenues we expected. Without the weird, foreign video camera, I was essentially back to square one with designing my video-to-

CAD program. That was fine. I didn't delete the files, but I did set up more firewalls around them. I considered moving everything off my computer, just to make sure it couldn't get any energy and activate, but I couldn't find anything that I considered secure enough, outside my notebook computer.

Funny thing, though. The video file of Doni that I took that night just seemed to evaporate.

The nights and days went past and fall slid into winter and the holidays came. I got an "A" in my computer programming class. Jinx showed my CAD program to his architect friends, who thought it was pretty good. They gave me a lot of suggestions for improvements and making my program unique and ultra-user-friendly. Kurt and Granddad hooked me up with a patent lawyer friend of theirs, to start preliminary work for filing and protecting my intellectual property. The snake didn't make any effort to return, not even a flicker of a bad dream to disturb me or Granddad or Doni.

The Hallidays, however, did.

Make efforts to return, and give bad dreams, that is.

They sent glitzy presents for Christmas, and invited Doni to go with them to Europe for a ski vacation over New Year's. We figured it was a trick. If Doni went on the trip, they would never let her come back to the country. Or, they could try to claim that when Doni called to respond to the invitation, she was calling them to come rescue her. We didn't need that nightmare to start all over again. So Doni didn't respond. We all pretended like the invitation never arrived. The Hallidays could just call if they really wanted to make contact.

Then Gordon Priebe walked into our Star Trek club Christmas party and announced that someone was following Doni and me around town. Gordon was also a Neighborlee cop. He could have dressed as Bigfoot for Halloween every year, but he was more like Legolas in his powers of observation. He'd noticed rental cars gliding around Neighborlee. Nobody ever got out of the cars, and they only stopped when a member of our family went into a store or other building. Gordon figured something was going on.

He knew about the Hallidays trying to get their grubby hands on Doni's trust fund. We found out later that the Hallidays had gone to the Neighborlee police and tried to claim we had kidnapped Doni, when they realized how much money had slipped through their fingers along with her. It didn't take much thinking to figure the outsiders in town in their rental cars, watching our family, were either private investigators for the Hallidays or part of preparing to kidnap Doni. Either way, it didn't matter. Foreigners were harassing Neighborlee's own. One way or another, the town was ready to close ranks and stand against the threat.

That night at the Christmas party, Gordon followed us home. Then he strolled down the street to have a talk with the man sitting in the black SUV, under the Picarelly family's gigantic weeping willow at the bend in the street.

That was Saturday night. Sunday afternoon, Grandmother Aurelia called to let Doni know she was sending her tickets for the family ski trip. Did Doni need a limousine to take her to the airport? She couldn't understand why Doni didn't feel safe to respond to her invitation, why Doni wouldn't want to spend time getting to know her loving family. (Yeah, they loved her money.) Doni had the speaker turned on and we were all listening in on the phone call. I caught a loud gulp and a gasp, when Doni told her grandmother that she had been silent on advice from her attorney. Mrs. Halliday definitely remembered Mr. Carr and the good dressing down he gave the whole miserable, greedy clan.

That didn't last long. Aurelia was back to her feelings being hurt when Doni said she didn't want to ski, and she preferred to spend Christmas with her family and not a bunch of strangers. The Halliday matriarch then bemoaned the "misunderstanding" that led Uncle Thad and his "darling daughter" and "adorable, brilliant wife" to miss family holiday events. Doni let her have it. I was so proud of her, with her calm voice. She told the nasty old dominatrix wannabe she didn't appreciate the spies dogging her steps, and if the P.I.s didn't leave Neighborlee soon, the police would start arresting them.

Gordon reported the rental cars vanished the next day, but that didn't mean the spies had left. Anybody who would work for the Hallidays weren't the kind who picked up their toys and went home. They were the kind who tried to take everyone else's toys. Mr. Carr agreed. The Hallidays were getting ready to either kidnap Doni or try again for legal custody.

"Don't worry," Angela said, when we told her what we

theorized. "Neighborlee takes care of its own."

The Hallidays returned to long-distance bribery. They regularly sent Doni invitations for cruises and ski trips or world tours. They sent her fashionable clothes and jewelry and makeup. If we didn't use the extravagant, glitzy, revealing, much-too-mature clothes for costumes for science fiction conventions or Halloween, she kept them for dress-up games. We had the best time turning ourselves into totally unrecognizable fashionistas and glamour-chicks. Uncle Jinx had given me a digital camera for my birthday, and uber-expensive software for morphing digital images. After we took dozens of pictures of ourselves, we spent a couple hours playing with them, making ourselves look older, changing our bone structure, our skin tone, our hair. Major fun.

Doni turned it into a new hobby, dividing her time between that and helping Gram with the garden and turning herself into quite an herbalist. She had a knack for homemade cures and potions that would have had her burned at the stake as a witch four centuries ago. The rest of the time, she altered those clothes into the most insane outfits and costumes for her school friends.

They were the smart girls, the shy girls, the ones who spent more time thinking and dreaming and reading than they did trying to turn thirty before they turned thirteen. She had lots of friends, and no enemies. Maybe people didn't gather around her like bees to honey, but when someone mentioned her name or asked about her, everyone in town could say, "Oh, yeah, Doni Halliday. The Longfellows' granddaughter. Sweet girl. Smart. She made an herbal oil that healed my..." Or "She found that little reference in an old book from 1895 that got me my 'A' in history class." Or "She should go into dressmaking. You should see what she did with that old bolt of cloth my grandmother had sitting in the basement."

Everybody loved Doni, once they remembered who she was.

~~~~~

I graduated from Neighborlee High, and spent that summer working for Carr, Cooper and Crenshaw, expanding their computer network and fixing a legal search program that cost far more than it was worth. That turned into a side business of helping people with their computers. Between my scholarships and the computer programs I designed, I was set for my college bills. That CAD program sold to a boutique software company that customized programs for customers, and I had an invitation to submit anything I could think of. Gram and Granddad had been saving for me, too, because they weren't penniless by any means. If the Longfellow clan in general had a superpower, it was the ability to make money. My computer sideline work took care of the extras, the fun stuff, like movies and pizza and the all-important college survival items: three-pound bags of M&Ms or gummies for those study-until-three-in-the-morning cram sessions.

Willis-Brooks College regulations required that freshmen lived on-campus, even if they were locals. That made sense. But there were a lot of nights I went home for dinner and to do my laundry, and weekends when I slept in my own bed at home. I didn't really have a "gang" of my own until the second semester of my freshman year. Mostly because I was still trying to figure out where I fit in, who was my "tribe."

I found them in the computer classes, naturally. All of us tended toward the brainy, somewhat naïve computer geeks stereotyped on TV and in movies. We weren't malicious. We just got so caught up in things in our digital world that we didn't think through the real-world consequences.

I took most of the ordinary, required freshman classes. But I tested out in anything relating to computers and programming, all the fancy languages, the technology, the hardware and software. I had taught myself a lot, and Granddad had encouraged me to read all the magazines and books available. We went to technology shows, and experimented with motherboards and chips, expanded memory, and lots of fun toys.

The results of those tests were posted after Thanksgiving. After that, I skipped a lot of classes, and ended up in the advanced classes. Masters and doctoral-level classes. I was the youngest in a group with an age range from nineteen to thirty-seven.

We had people in our classes who planned to work for the Pentagon and think tanks at the Ivy League schools. Others were working on the next killer video game or improving on what passed for virtual reality--as in science fiction-level tech that hooked directly into the brain, recreating all physical sensations without needing gloves and goggles, or environment suits postulated in some futuristic books.

My sophomore year started with a year-long experimental

class in the advanced computer track. The trio of professors teaching our class came from the computer sciences (Dr. Bowman), psychology (Dr. Khalif) and social sciences (Dr. Floyd). They were quite honest with us from the beginning: they were doing research for a book. Heck, they *had* to be totally honest with us. Their publishing contract required everyone in the class to sign off, giving permission for their comments and findings and names, even histories when necessary, to be included in the book, to be turned in about two months after the school year ended.

I wasn't sure who felt the most pressure right about then, them or us. Of course, the ones who had some experience with the marketplace in the real world (and had been burned enough to be litigious and/or mercenary) asked for changes or addendums to those permission forms before signing. They wanted to be free to pursue any line of investigation they came up with during the course of the class, without having to fight with the professors or publishers over who owned the intellectual property rights. They also wanted the right to have their names, images, and comments stricken from the record and never published. The first two weeks of class covered very nebulous subjects while we waited for the legal department at the publishing house to agree to the changes and send back the new forms to sign.

Our class was called "Studies into the Online Effect." The first half of the first semester, we studied and discussed the statistics and case studies of how online rumors, the social media phenomenon, and online dissemination of news impacted how people perceived the world. Even when, maybe especially when, people knew the online information was skewed or entirely false. The smart ones started doing private research, planning ahead for the project that would take up the second semester and be eighty percent of our grade. Problem: all their preparation work could only be based on the hints our teachers gave us. All three of them had wonderful futures as politicians, the way they dodged our questions and avoided giving away anything.

The second half of the semester, we discussed theories for how we could sway people's perceptions, influence them toward a specific action, and how we could get people to get online and read the information we created when they were Luddites. Either that, or they were lunatic fringies, convinced that everything posted online was a lie or a conspiracy meant to brainwash the general population of the world, or monitor our thoughts and actions.

Just before Christmas break, our profs told us to create teams to work together second semester. No less than four and no more than ten. Over the holidays, we had to come up with a project for second semester. Our grades second semester depended on those projects--the concept, the execution, the results.

My team was made up of locals. We had seen each other around town, and had a nodding acquaintance even if we had never spoken before we met up in class. Some of us had had classes together. Of course, I missed out on a year's worth of basics because of testing out of an entire level. We had one big benefit from the start: we could meet during Christmas break, instead of communicating over the Internet or by phone. Less chance of being spied on by those who from day one adopted an "us against the universe" attitude toward the class, the project, and their grade. Even before we knew what the second semester project would entail.

Chapter Six

Our team:

Simone, Alvin and Theo--I'm not kidding, those were their names. What made it even funnier, or weirder, take your pick, was that none of the three knew who the Chipmunks were. Simone was a big girl more suited to Wagnerian opera than geekdom. Granted, she did have a stainless-steel corset, but she was into SCA activities during the summer. Theo (Theodora) had braces constantly clogged with purple bubblegum, and hair like hay because she was constantly dyeing it, bleaching it, and re-dyeing it. She could have joined the track and field team as the javelin. Alvin was an adorable little old man, great-grandfather to about fifty kids in Neighborlee, and balder than a cue ball. He went to my church. I didn't even think he knew what a computer was, until I saw him in class. After that, we were constantly meeting up at church and trading computer magazines we had finished reading.

The three of them were a trio from the beginning of class, looking out for each other, and constantly whispering and cracking up in the upper corner of the amphitheater-style lecture hall.

Then there was Wallace. We tried calling him Wally, but it just didn't stick. His uniform was a dress shirt, sport coat, and slacks, all color-coordinated. By the second week of class, I decided he wore the spiffy-geek persona as a disguise, along the lines of Spider-Man or Green Lantern. I suspected there was something underneath Mister Spit-and-Polish, because he sometimes ripped off these dry, sharply witty comments in response to our teachers. I got proof that Wallace had several different people inside that GQ shell when I ran into him at a role-playing game marathon over mid-term break.

I just went to observe. Doni invited me, because some friends from the herbology club were involved and they got her hooked. Nope, that didn't make any sense to me, either, until she explained further. Some of these role-playing guys went to extremes, kind of like the historical re-enacters who became their characters, right down to the language and social structures, food, and underwear.

The current popular game was medieval quest/warfare, and they had to be authentic to the nth degree, cubed. That meant using real, legitimate medicine appropriate for the time period. Hence, going to the herbology club for information on preparing and using natural medicines.

One thing led to another, and the club members who attended some meetings so they could understand what the role-players wanted got hooked, either playing or observing. Doni begged me to come along because we hadn't been able to spend much time together, between all her clubs and my living on campus.

Wallace was there, a totally different guy, even when he wasn't fully into his medieval commando-slash-assassin-slash-terrorist-slash-makes-Alexander-the-Great-seem-warm-and-fuzzy persona. Jeans, slippers that looked like they belonged to Bigfoot, a LarryBoy T-shirt, three-days' growth of beard, tangled hair. Topped by a funky hat holding four soft drink bottles with long, flexible straws that fed into one sipper tube that circled his neck twice. He stopped just short of being a filthy slob. He dropped all classroom restraints and roared laughter. That was how I got my first glimpse of him-- this big, rolling rumble of laughter spilled across the main gym at Eden, where the gaming marathon was set up. There was something compelling and totally unfamiliar about that laughter, so I had to turn to look.

Of course, I didn't recognize him at first, because he just wasn't the Wallace I was used to. But then someone called him by name (he was still *Wallace*, despite the get-up) and he said something that was specifically Wallace, as only he could say it: Funk-a-dee-ell-ick, with the extra syllable.

He recognized me when he came over to the herbology gang to ask for a judgment on a dispute. Were cobwebs sufficient to coagulate a particularly vicious wound caused by a knife with three edges and poison in the center bore of the blade? Yeah, they really got into details like that. To be honest, I found it kind of fascinating. I was hooked from that point, just like Doni and her friends, who were all younger than me. Of course, we had been playing *Star Trek* with Lanie and her gang for a few years by that time, so it wasn't that much of a step.

We had costumes and makeup, fanzines, newsletters, and the yearly quest to come up with believable, non-alcoholic Romulan ale. I even worked with Kurt and Granddad to create tricorders, communicators, and other equipment with lights and sound effects. When we took them to conventions, we always cleaned up in the dealers' room.

"Minerva!" Wallace cried when our gazes met. He went down on one knee, giving me the Roman salute: fist slapping his breastbone and then arm straight extended. "You grace us with your presence, oh Goddess of Wisdom and War Craft."

Of course, Wallace bellowed that just as loudly as he did his laughter, and people actually quieted down and looked at us.

For clarification: Wallace had insisted from the first day of class that my "proper" name was Minerva, because the Romans had overthrown the Greeks and Athena the Greek goddess translated into Minerva in the Roman pantheon. Anyone else, I would have been tempted to punch his lights out or just avoid him at all costs. Wallace... I couldn't be angry with him. Maybe because he was so funny, claiming that I was suffering amnesia.

And okay, he kind of looked like Stuart Granger. Who wouldn't put up with some silliness from a cute guy who knew the origins and history of my name and could tease me without humiliating me in the process?

Some of Wallace's lunatic fringe friends insisted that I had to join their role-playing club, since I was a goddess of war craft. He protected me from them, to some extent. After that mid-term break, he made a point of sitting either next to me or in the row in front in the lecture hall. That let him turn around and make comments during class. He kept me updated on the latest activities and campaigns of his club. That meant I knew a lot about role-playing without even trying. And yes, I sometimes sat in on some games when I didn't have anything to do, or I just needed a study break. Especially when there was pizza or gummy worms.

The last member of our team, besides me of course, was Cosmo. No, that wasn't his name (it was Sherwood), but he got the nickname because he was constantly stealing issues of *Cosmopolitan* and other gossipy fashion magazines from the girls' dormitory lounges. Why? Who knew? I never asked and he never explained when someone did ask. However, those magazines became fodder for our project later, so it was a good thing. Cosmo was this quiet guy who was almost invisible all through high school. I know because he was in my graduating class. He had red-brown hair in a buzz cut, enough freckles to almost qualify as a year-round tan, a nose like an Olympic ski slope, and the most gorgeous blue-green eyes. He had an amazing talent for web page design and supported himself solely by creating web pages and untangling code for other designers. The urban legend surrounding him was that once he touched a page, it was un-hackable. His online name among the hacker community was Anthrax, because anyone who tried to break into something he had worked on usually ended up in major trouble. Equipment failure. Unending processing loops. Or Trojans that dumped their most dangerous data into the hands of someone with the most reason to hate the hacker. When the time came to divide into teams for our class project second semester, everyone tried to recruit Cosmo.

Almost from the beginning of the class, the lecture hall had been pretty much divided up into cliques or camps or social groups. Sure, there were some who floated from one side of the lecture hall to another, depending on the day of the week, the weather, what door they had come through, and how late they got to class. The floaters were on the edge of the social strata, or hadn't really discovered their area of interest within the world of the Internet and computers. The fact we were locals, more than any interests in common, had cemented our group together even before we had to create our official team.

When we were given the assignment to form our teams, and forbidden to choose our project until we were on Christmas break, our teachers gave us the remainder of the lecture hour to "clump."

Cosmo was sitting two rows above me. He got up on the table and kind of jump-walked down the levels to get to mine, and plopped down in the seat next to me. Simone, Alvin and Theo moved down together, ignored by the other groups, to the row below me. As one person they turned around the chairs attached to the tables, sat down, and looked up at Cosmo and me with big, let's-make-some-trouble grins.

"What?" My jolt of panic didn't make any sense at first. I was distracted watching everybody scrambling around.

Okay, I was really tired. I had been up until 2am, observing and kibitzing with Wallace's role-playing gang, and our class was first period. As far as I knew, Wallace hadn't shown up for class.

But was that any excuse for not making the connection that, duh, I should be moving around and trying to find a team? Or maybe, as Cosmo quietly pointed out when we met that evening, we already knew, instinctively, who our team would be? Or maybe what panicked me was this sense they were waiting for *me* to initiate the process. Why? Cosmo and I were the youngest members of the team. Simone was twenty-four, Theo was twenty-two, and Wallace was twenty-five.

"We're a team." Alvin usually spoke for Simone and Theo.

"Yeah?" I grinned back at him. "Shouldn't you guys think about it for a while?"

"We have. For weeks." He winked and leaned forward to rest his bony elbows on my table. "We overheard the Terrible Trio planning this back before Thanksgiving, and we've been thinking strategy ever since. The loco-locals need to stick together."

"Really?" As soon as he made his statement, something inside me let out a quiet little cheer. I had that sense of rightness that I often let guide my actions and decisions. "Just how did you overhear the profs making their plans?"

"They have a bug planted in Khalif's office, where all of them meet. It's the only room big enough," Cosmo said.

"And you know this how?"

"He helped us iron out the transmission problems." Theo blew a kiss at Cosmo that made him turn bright red.

"Hey Cosmo!" The guy who ended up being the leader of the Politics project came bounding down the stairs of the lecture hall. He slammed his hands flat on the table at the end of the row with enough force I felt it two tables further down. He had that grin I always equated with used car salesmen. The ones who thought they were doing you a great, personal favor by allowing you to buy a car that would fall apart in all the areas not covered by warranty half an hour after driving off the lot.

"Hey, Milton." Cosmo looked at me with this sort of pleading look, and right then I knew yes, we were on the same team.

Alvin was right: the loco-locals stuck together. Besides, I liked Cosmo, sort of as a semi-clueless little brother who needed help tying his shoes and closing the cereal box. Which made no sense, considering what a creatively dangerous genius he was.

"Buddy, you have got to be on our team. What do you say? All the meetings will be at my apartment, so all the triple espresso mochas you can drink."

Cosmo physically wavered. A little shudder from one side to another, like a heavy wind had pushed him. He had a publicly known addiction to triple espresso mochas, the kind that were so thick the different ingredients created three layers in the big clear glass mugs the Sipping Post used. Hot fudge on the bottom, a black espresso syrup layer in the middle, and latte coffee on top. Legend said Cosmo created them when he worked at the Sipping Post in eighth grade.

Cosmo looked at me with an expression I could almost call pleading.

Steffani from the Dating project just about flew down from the nosebleed section of the hall, all in a fluttery panic as she declared Cosmo had to be on their team. She repeated herself three times, her voice rising in pitch until it was ready to cross over to the range only dogs could hear. The rest of her team followed her down the stairs, eight girls and one other guy; all what Angela called the "pretty people," in their in-fashion clothes and perfect hair and teeth and makeup. Even the guy. How could they move that fast, wearing those stiletto shoes? (Even the guy!)

Cosmo swallowed hard, and I thought for a moment he would declare his allegiance with them. After all, hanging around with all those girls, chances were good he could get at least one date without humiliating himself too badly. I already knew that underneath the geek, Cosmo had a strong sense of justice, even chivalry. The problem was, he was the proverbial awkward adolescent when it came to people interaction.

Steffani and Milton got into an argument, every once in a while turning to Cosmo and offering him other incentives to consider their teams. It didn't take long for the other semi-coagulated teams to notice the argument and who was at the center of it. They came trooping down to throw their hats into the ring, so to speak.

I would have gotten up and out of the noise and congestion, but I was surrounded. The one time I tried to sidle out, Cosmo gave me this absolutely panicked look, like he might start screaming. So I stayed. Simone, Alvin and Theo got up and stood leaning against our table, giving physical support.

Out of the chaos, Wallace's quiet, in-class voice startled me.

Somehow he got to the row below mine, stepped up next to Simone, and rested his elbows on my table, without anyone noticing.

"What's the hub, bub?" he said, in a reasonable impersonation of Bugs Bunny--if a guy with a deep chocolate baritone voice could manage that sound.

Our gazes locked and I could see in his eyes he had a plan, just like he had last night during that interminable game I should have left three hours sooner.

Wallace reached out to slap Cosmo's arm and get his attention. "You're not thinking of jumping ship, are you?"

Cosmo jumped like someone jabbed him with a cattle prod right in his belly button, kind of folding in protectively on himself. He glared at Wallace for about three seconds. The arguing recruiters caught on that they had lost him even before I realized it. Quiet spread out all around us while that big mischief-making grin spread from Wallace's face to Cosmo's.

"Give the word, Captain," Cosmo said.

Someone groaned in the back of the crowd behind me. Someone else started to swear, and someone else protested.

"The word is given," Wallace said. "Second star to the right, and straight on to morning." He hooked his thumb over his shoulder to the left side of the lecture hall, ground floor, and the closest door.

Cosmo jumped up on the table and walk-ran down to the floor of the lecture hall in about six seconds flat, and vanished out that door. We still had about ten minutes left of the class period.

"What are we waiting for, team?" Alvin said.

Wallace snagged my notebook before I could scoop it off the table and into my backpack. That was considerate of him, I realized, as I looked around at all the unhappy faces surrounding me. I stood up, sat on the table, swung my legs over the top, and slid down to the next level. Not at my most graceful, but nobody was judging us on grace. If anything, our profs were watching and noting the speed of our reactions and our common sense.

Right then, common sense, gut instinct, and that sense of rightness screamed for me to get out of there before I got lynched. Even though technically Wallace had stolen Cosmo and his Anthrax talents from the other project teams, I was part of the team that got him and I was the only one accessible. So I fled, almost running over Simone, Alvin and Theo, who were scrambling to get down to the stairs to follow Cosmo and Wallace out the door.

Our first team decision was to split up, reasoning that multiple, singular targets would be harder for the disappointed rival teams to catch. They would likely try to further recruit Cosmo, with lots of euphemistic carrots, while the rest of our project team would undoubtedly get different versions of the "stick." Either threatened or real.

We realized then what a plus it was to be the loco-locals. This was the last day of classes for the semester. Lots of our fellow students had already run for home, or had their cars packed and ready to break the speed limit out of town after their final classes. We didn't have to go back to our dorms and pack up before we headed home. Some of us could even walk home. That prevented the really ambitious "convincers" tracking us down in the parking lots. Whatever we needed, we could come back during the break and retrieve it from our rooms after our opponents had vacated the premises.

Wallace, Cosmo and I walked Simone, Alvin and Theo to the parking lot where Alvin had left his car. He offered all of us a ride, but the guys and I declined. Mostly because with Simone in the back seat of Alvin's VW bug, maybe Cosmo could fit in, but Wallace and I would have to ride on the roof. The girls lived on the other side of town and needed that ride. At the edge of the parking lot, the rest of us each went a different direction. We would regroup that evening at my house. It was the best place to meet. Central to all of us, and guaranteed lots of snacks and plenty of couches for lounging while we thought.

I went back to my dorm room. First, because I had some provisions from studying for exams that I did not want to leave for my roommates to confiscate. Second, because I had laundry to do and my bed wasn't made and my notebook computer was there. I couldn't live without it, not even for one day. My other three roommates in our suite were all members of the computer class, but that didn't make me nervous. I wasn't afraid of them ganging up on me, because I had already noticed we were all on different teams. The way I figured it, they wouldn't do anything to upset the balance by trying to convince me to set Cosmo free of our team.

The reception I got wasn't what I expected.

Dorinda was the first back to our suite after me. She posed

dramatically in the doorway and shrieked, "How did you snag Wallace on your team?"

"Me? Snag Wallace? You have got to be kidding." Any other guy on campus, I would have said that he probably didn't even know I was alive, but that was a lie and she knew it. Wallace had been to our suite a couple times to ask what we thought of an assignment, or to borrow notes from the day he had to take his great-aunt to the hospital for some outpatient surgery.

Shaunda lifted Dorinda's arm from where it was braced against the frame so she could slide inside. "If you remember, he drafted her. Right in front of everybody. Smart move on his part. Nobody can hate you for snagging Cosmo."

"I didn't--" I sighed and resumed packing up my notes from class, and slid a few packages of dark chocolate bars, gummy worms, and my last bag of Turkish delight into my computer bag. I would have to make a stop at Divine's and find out if Angela had received another shipment, because dark chocolate and Turkish Delight were my "thinking" treats. Gummy worms were my frustration and energy treats.

"Somebody would think Cosmo had a crush on you." Dorinda finally came into the suite. She dropped down on the couch that we were sure had been there since the 50s. The cushions were so old and thin that we had invested in long sheets of foam rubber from a craft store to build them back up. We wanted to be able sit down for more than five minutes without being inoculated by the springs.

"More like safety in numbers. Familiarity. We went to school together." I shrugged and slung my computer bag over my shoulder to go into the closet-like bedroom I shared with Celeste.

All I was taking home, for now, was my bulging laundry bag. Gram didn't mind my bringing laundry home, as long as I processed it myself, immediately. She had established that rule when Uncle Jinx went through college and made a bad habit of bringing laundry home and dumping it somewhere, still in the laundry bag. Usually he would forget he had even brought the laundry home until a few weeks later, when he needed a particular piece of clothing. Like most men, apparently, his favorite tactic was to just buy more underwear, jeans, and T-shirts. And laundry bags. The ones that sat for three weeks with dirty laundry in them just couldn't seem to get the stank out of them. Yes, past tense, because it was a dead-and-gone smell.

I unmade my bed and put the sheets in the laundry bag. It waited by the suite door with my computer bag. I was hooking the plastic rings holding the last two cans of my six-pack of ginger ale to my computer bag when Celeste finally strolled in.

Celeste was working her way through school as a fashion model and had a great future as a benevolent dominatrix. She favored pastels, but somehow always projected a mental image of shiny black leather from head to toe, and ten-inch stiletto heels. I loved her dearly, because while she couldn't seem to get out of bed without putting on makeup, she never gave me any grief over my insistence on living in jeans and T-shirts, and refusing to wear any makeup whatsoever. She let me be me.

"You've got a lot of guts," she announced, once she had sauntered over to the shelving where we kept our entertaining supplies: mugs, boxes of tea and hot chocolate, cookies and crackers. She snagged a plastic fork out of the box and settled down on the big green floor pillow. Without needing to smooth her long skirt under herself. Celeste's clothes cooperated with her as if she had mental control over all the fibers.

"Guts?" Dorinda looked up from the papers she had spread over the couch. She blinked like she had just emerged from a dark room, then laughed. "Oh, yeah."

"Guts for what?" My mind was already on the shopping I wanted to do, and wondering if I should run home with my laundry, get my car, then shop. Or shop, run home in time for the meeting, and come back tomorrow for my laundry and the rest of my gear. I preferred not to have to pay for the parking fees on campus, so I left my car at home and walked everywhere. It saved on gas, and I got exercise without having to go near the gym. That was fine, except when the snow was wretchedly high.

"Showing your face on campus while the others are still steaming about Cosmo." She opened her double order of lo mein noodles and paused to inhale the steam.

Celeste had the infuriating ability to eat six full-size meals a day and not gain an ounce. Dorinda and Shaunda loved/hated her. I had learned to keep my extra eating away from them, as well as the color of my dining hall pass--blue with gold stripes, indicating I had unlimited eating privileges. Only the athletes had those passes, and I definitely wasn't an athlete. Everyone else had to get tallied or they were limited to specific cafeterias across campus, depending on the meal plans they had bought. According to Lanie, I had a superhero metabolism, even though I had yet to demonstrate any powers other than being able to understand Kurt when he talked gizmo-ese.

"If you haven't noticed, I'm in the process of getting off campus." I slung my computer bag over my shoulder. "When are the rest of you flying out? Do you need rides to Hopkins?" I felt not a bit of guilt that my trip home would take, at the most, half an hour of walking. And that was if I got detoured on the way home and did some window shopping.

The other three were set. Dorinda and Celeste had rides from their current boyfriends. Shaunda had a car and was driving home to Pittsburgh.

"I don't suppose the rest of you want to give me hints what your teams are doing, so we don't do the same thing?" I said, after we had exchanged hugs.

"If none of us knows what the others' teams are doing, then we can't be accused of spying." Shaunda rolled her eyes and leaned over to snag a couple noodles from Celeste's box with two fingers. "We're going to get more grief about being roommates than you'll get about having Cosmo on your team. If leaks develop in any of our projects, we're going to be the ones accused of spying."

"Meaning you've already been warned?" Dorinda groaned.

"Tell you what." Maybe I was making empty promises, but these were my friends. We had chosen to be roommates when we realized all four of us had been invited to participate in the special class last spring. "If you can convince your team leaders that we're trustworthy, and not give us any grief, I'll ask Cosmo to give free help to your teams."

"Won't that make Chasity Boah blow a couple O-rings?" Celeste said, and snickered.

Chasity Boah claimed to be *someone*, dropping large hints that she had diplomatic privileges. She laughed at us when we didn't understand any of the Nigerian words she threw into conversations. She and Celeste appeared to be rivals for fashionistas and who could be the slimmest female on campus without dying of starvation. The only problem was that Celeste wasn't trying to win any competition, and any time Chasity tried to declare a challenge of some kind, Celeste walked away.

That didn't mean Celeste didn't care that Chasity was out to get her. She simply chose to ignore anyone who tried to stir things up between them. It was common knowledge that Chasity had to beg, nag, harass, blackmail, and use up every favor she and her supposedly powerful parents and diplomatic friends were owed, to get into our experimental computer class. That included hiring people to dictate all our textbooks into MP3 files so she could listen to them as she put in her two solid hours of exercise every day. Common knowledge, which Chasity denied loudly--and foully--on a regular basis.

"It's a deal," Shaunda said, and stuck out her hand in a fist. Dorinda laughed and rested her hand on hers. Celeste got up from the pillow and put her hand on theirs, and I finished it. Our ritual for a solemn, binding promise.

Anything to totally rile Chasity and her team of clones and sycophants.

I got out of there soon after that, and hurried home through a threat of snow. Doni met me halfway there. She was on her way to the campus to eat dinner with me, because Gram, Granddad and Jinx were out helping deliver Christmas trees and baskets to the families who were having a hard time during the holidays. She had a cold and Gram didn't want her riding around for hours on end, getting out into the cold and then riding in a warm car. Doni should have stayed home, but she decided that walking to my dorm wouldn't aggravate her cold.

What could I say? I had made some pretty silly decisions of my own when I was her age, that seemed entirely logical at the time. I didn't scold her, because honestly, her congestion was gone and her color was good. I was a little disappointed that I couldn't help out with the deliveries, but on the other hand, it was a good thing. My team would have the total privacy of the house until about ten or eleven that night, if the regular distribution ritual stayed the same as always.

With Doni to carry things, we took a short detour through town and bought provisions for the meeting and our dinner, instead of going home first to drop off my laundry. I explained to her what we were doing and the reason for the meeting. She knew all my classmates because she came on campus at least once a week to eat with me or just sit in the suite and talk.

With Doni asking all sorts of questions about our assignment, I was able to clarify a few things in my head by the time we got home and made dinner.

Another package from the Hallidays waited at the front door. Doni waited until after we ate and cleaned up from dinner before she opened it. She was still unloading the shipping box in the living room when Simone, Alvin and Theo showed up. Cosmo was coming up the sidewalk from the other direction, and he called out to us before I closed the door. Wallace showed up about ten minutes later with pizza and wings, and it took a while to put out the provisions everyone had brought--soda, bottles of lattes, M&Ms, three different styles of peanuts, cheesey corn, and a rainbow of licorice-type chews.

Something was odd about Cosmo. I kept watch on him as we settled down in the living room with our snacks and our notebooks and computers, prepared to brainstorm. It was the way he locked gazes with Doni that clued me in. That, and the way the both of them got sort of starry-eyed and then blushed neon for about a ten-count, then looked away.

However, they kept stealing glances at each other. Even locking gazes whenever they caught each other looking.

Cosmo stayed standing until Doni chose a seat. And of course, she hesitated, because she was watching to see where he would sit. It was kind of cute. I almost felt jealous, but Cosmo had been somewhere between a brother and a pet in my affections, so it wasn't like there could ever be any rivalry between Doni and me. I was kind of glad for her, because I did like Cosmo, and I knew he would treat her right.

"Here, Doni." I pointed at the sofa with only two spots open. "Better stay close to the tissue box."

She grimaced, as if I had mortally embarrassed her by pointing out that she had a cold. Then she saw the empty spot next to her as she dropped down into the end seat. Cosmo zeroed in on it like he was a heat-seeking missile. I winked at her and she blushed again, and snagged the tissue box off the end table, to hold it on her lap like a shield. Probably to keep her hands from shaking.

Yep, they were hooked on each other. I re-thought all the times

Cosmo stopped by the suite or looked for me in the cafeteria to talk about class. And all the times Doni showed up on campus. Especially on the days she didn't have school, and she wanted to sit through my computer class with me.

Well, duh, I wasn't the attraction. I was just the common denominator.

That, and the fresh-popped popcorn liberally sprinkled with chili powder, which was Doni's specialty. She kept a bowl of it on her lap, and Cosmo ate it, one kernel at a time, with the rhythm of breathing. I watched them as they crunched almost in unison and stole sideways looks at each other. If it weren't for the fact they both contributed to the discussion, I would have thought there was no one else in the room for each other. It was cute.

Wallace started off the meeting by discussing the other teams, their members, their talents and interests, and what he had heard them discussing as their possible projects.

That explained why he hadn't shown up right away when we started putting the team together. He had walked the perimeter of the room, listening to the discussions and watching how everybody divided up. It was kind of sneaky of him, and pretty smart. Everybody was so busy making sure their teams had people with the same ideas and priorities, they didn't notice they were being spied on. They also didn't realize how loud they were talking, and how much information they were giving away. They just assumed everybody was too busy plotting to spy on them.

That wouldn't last long once classes resumed. If we met in each other's homes rather than on campus, we would be fairly safe from spying attempts. I had some ideas for how to protect us when we couldn't get off-campus to talk and plot. Kurt had a white noise generator that ran on batteries, that I knew he would loan us. We agreed never to discuss our project via text or email or phone calls. That would frustrate the classmates who had wonderful futures working for the CIA.

"Okay, so we have a good idea what the others are doing. The best way to stay safe from anyone sabotaging or borrowing our work is to do something nobody else is doing," I said. That was obvious, but nobody had said it yet. I had learned that sometimes important details got missed if people ignored the obvious.

Chapter Seven

"We could do a fashion focus," Simone said. She waved her hands to silence us almost before the groans left our throats. "But sarcastic. Track the really stupid trends, how long they lasted, maybe work up a pattern and figure out how the stupid trends got started, and try to predict what's going to come up next, based on political and economic and weather patterns. Or something like that," she added, her voice dropping to a mumble and her face going red.

"That kind of sounds like fun." Alvin grinned. He earned squeaks from a few of us when he popped his dentures halfway out of his mouth and sucked them back in again with a loud *slurp-clack*. On anybody else, it would have been just disgusting, but his dentures were currently purple from the fresh wad of gum Theo had given him.

"Fashion?" Doni put down her half-decimated bowl of chili popcorn. "You want stupid fashions?" She wiped her slightly greasy fingertips on the paper towel Cosmo held out to her and stepped over to the big shipping box she had kick-shoved into the corner of the living room when everybody showed up.

She explained about her snooty relatives constantly sending her packages full of useless things, trying to win her over, as she dragged the box into the center of the room. Everybody laughed as Doni pulled out shoes no human without bone surgery could walk in, purses that wouldn't hold more than a credit card, scarves in nauseating color combinations and patterns, thong underwear covered with glitter, boxes of makeup, and four dresses.

"Paris wore this to a party in San Francisco last month," Cosmo said, holding up a long nude-toned dress that seemed to be all elastic and beads and fringe.

"Put it on?" Theo said. She had something like awe in her eyes as she picked up one end of the dress and fingered the material. "I would really love to see a real person wear something like this."

We giggled at the implication that Paris wasn't a real person. Doni agreed and picked up the dress to take it into the little bathroom around the corner from the living room. Cosmo insisted that she had to wear the scarf and shoes and hat that went with the dress. The fact that he knew all those details proved he did read those fashion and gossip rags, instead of just stealing them.

"Wouldn't it be funny," I said as Doni disappeared into the bathroom, "if we found out that Paris wasn't a real person, but CGI or a composite of people? And all those people who claimed they were her best friends and went to parties with her, they were just hallucinating or they had been hypnotized or something?"

"Or something." Wallace's voice went soft and thoughtful, and that mischief-making gleam got brighter in his eyes.

"It was a major blow-out," Cosmo said. "It was supposed to be a charity fundraiser, but the gossip was that people spent five times more on their clothes and the food than they raised for the charity. And nobody could agree on what cause they were supporting."

"Typical," Alvin said with a snort. He levered himself out of the couch where he had been sitting with Simone and Theo, and scurried back into the kitchen to refill his plate.

"You know..." Theo narrowed her eyes and stared at some spot mid-air in the middle of the room. "There are a lot of similarities between your cousin and Paris."

"Keep insulting Doni like that, and you're out of here," I growled. We all laughed.

"No, I'm serious," she continued, after Alvin returned to the living room and we told him what we had been laughing about. "The hair color, the cheekbones, the snooty relatives. The big difference is that Doni doesn't want the spotlight. And if she looks as good as I think she will in that dress... Maybe that's why her weird relatives want to get their hands on her. I mean, think what a sensation she'd be. Like bookends or something. Just mention to the right person that Doni Holiday--"

"Halliday," I corrected without thinking.

"Sorry. Mention that she could be Paris's long-lost half-sister..." She grinned.

"It'd start a firestorm in the gossip rags that wouldn't go out without a nuclear bomb," Cosmo said, mirroring her grin.

"Oh--man--" Wallace got up and took big steps, circling the living room. "Oh--man--like--man!" He clapped both hands to the top of his head and kept walking, moving faster. "That's it! Yeah, that's gotta be it." He nodded, still with his hands on his head, and walked even faster.

"What's it? Convince people Doni is an evil twin?" Cosmo shook his head. "You don't want to do that to her. Nuh-uh."

"Not Doni *Halliday*." Wallace let out a bark of laughter and came to a stop in the middle of the room. He nudged the shipping box with his foot and bent to pick up a couple pieces of clothing scattered on the floor. "London Holiday."

Doni appeared in the doorway at that moment. "Huh?"

I never had any use for the excessive, sometimes weird world of fashion. Especially the unspoken rule that a woman could only be glamorous if she looked like she had just survived ten years of the African famine. But even I could see that Doni looked good in that ridiculous dress. She looked about ten years older, even without the makeup. I understood what Wallace was talking about, even if I couldn't put it into words.

"You look incredible," Cosmo whispered. For a second, I thought he would drop to his knees in front of her and propose.

"London Holiday. A totally made-up person," Wallace said. He stepped back, studying her, framed in the doorway.

I swore to myself that if he put up his hands like those stereotyped Hollywood directors, framing her like in a camera lens, I would bop him one.

"A computer person. Someone to rival the rich and useless. Someone to point out what the wasters and fashionistas are doing, and how ridiculous they are, *without saying it out loud*. We put our made-up girl on the web, all the networks and social sites, and see how long it takes for people to realize she isn't real."

Simone raised her hand. "Umm, what about the Terms of Service? Even if some of the sites don't say outright that you can't put up a false person, there are enough stories out there about people who created false personas to hurt others. If anybody found out what we were doing, we could get in major trouble."

"Okay, that's a problem. But not a big one. Not one we can't handle." Wallace nodded. His gaze focused on Doni, as he backed up and settled down in Granddad's big new armchair.

"What if she's semi-real?" Cosmo said. "If we're using Doni's name, why not her face?"

"It won't be my face," Doni said. She turned around, showing off the dress. "It won't be my clothes or my hair or anything. And it's not really my name, is it?"

"So you'd do it?" Wallace stayed perfectly still, but it was like he had just pounced on her. Like a used car salesman only halfway to his monthly quota, and hyped on triple espressos.

"Do what?" Alvin asked. Granted, he had been busy shoveling down the snacks, but hadn't he caught on to anything anybody said for the last ten minutes?

"We'd have to create a totally new site, so we don't violate anybody's TOS," Cosmo said. "London will be the hostess, so she's right up there, but it's like the first friend you get when you join some social sites--you know the guy isn't real."

"She'll be the face and the voice of the next big social media site," Wallace said.

"Just make sure you're not infringing on any copyright or intellectual property, or at the very least copying what the other sites do," I said.

Sadly, that was the only caution I spoke for the rest of the evening. Then I got caught up in the fun of it--because it was *fun*.

Looking back, I wonder if this was how Dr. Frankenstein got started. Did he ever reach a point when he realized he was in trouble, but he had put in too much thought and effort, took too many risks, so he just couldn't back out or walk away or shut everything down?

We met almost every day of Christmas break, at the Sipping Post, Miller's, Eden, and each other's homes, throwing ideas back and forth, arguing, laughing, and generally convincing our families and the people sitting near us that we were insane. We pooled our money and bought a computer to serve as the hosting site, and paid for domain name registration, Internet access, and backups so the site wouldn't go down. We named it FlopDrop.

To be safe from possible sabotage, we went to Darbyville, where a friend of Wallace's family let us rent the studio apartment over his garage for the rest of the school year. There we set up all our equipment and created our Fortress of Solitude. Only, since there were at least four of us there at any one time, it wasn't really solitude, was it?

We had three battery backups and Cloud backup, so if the power died or something tried to crash the website, we would have enough time to make repairs before everything went down. We also had alarm systems set up to notify us if anyone tried to break into the apartment or if fire broke out. Wallace, Cosmo and I collaborated on a program that would automatically dump all our data and control programs and applications into the Cloud if that happened, with a notification to be sent to the whole team so we could uplink and download everything before it got lost. No way was sabotage or accident or the stupidity of human beings going to ruin our project.

We went to all the social media sites we could think of, even in other countries, and signed up London Holiday for membership. Everything we put in her profiles was false, yet based on facts. For instance, Doni and London's birthplace and date were the same, but not the years. We made London nine years older than Doni, who was thirteen going on fourteen. We made up lots of brothers and sisters for her, and false names of schools she attended. Then we got nasty and named all her Halliday relatives--listing them as Holidays, of course. We switched ages and relationships. Grandmother Aurelia was now a baby cousin, age three, for instance. We talked about what wonderful people the entire clan was, coming together to raise London and her siblings after the tragic cruise ship death of their socialite parents.

So many lies should have set off a big flashing red light for those who considered themselves guardians of social media. But they didn't.

We used all those pictures of Doni that we had taken and modified through the years, showing her in all those frivolous, outrageous clothes the Hallidays had sent her. They were everywhere on the Internet, not just on the pages of FlopDrop after we launched the site.

Cosmo and Wallace got into the program I used to alter the photos of Doni, and added a vocal synthesizing program they created (just for fun!) and synthesized videos of London talking about social events around the world, describing world leaders she had (not) met, the rich and infamous she had (never) partied with. She said outrageous things about them. Insulting things, and the truth, whenever we could manage it. Wonderful thing, the Internet, allowing the invasion of privacy with the eager assistance of the victims who valued notoriety over truth.

By the New Year's Eve official launch party for our site, London had pseudo-interviewed two movie stars, a couple rock stars, some professional athletes, and a cruise line mogul—owner of the fictitious cruise ship her parents had supposedly sailed on when they died. Those podcasts were posted on the day of the launch party.

However, two days before the launch, we realized something. London was essentially alone. She needed a BFF, a sidekick. Theo was pretty close to her in size and shape, and she liked all those ridiculous clothes Doni was playing with. So we put her in the same clothes, slathered her with makeup, altered the images and put her in some new videos with London and named her Adora.

"Can't we animate this?" Doni asked, when the guys had created a slideshow of the two new BFFs clowning around together.

"What, like cartoons?" Cosmo said.

"Could start a nifty new trend." Alvin was nodding enthusiastically.

The studio apartment had become our hangout. It was a good thing all we had for furniture was folding tables and lots of folding chairs and floor pillows; otherwise, I think we might have ended up having sleepovers. Right then we were sitting on the floor, gathered around the wide screen Wallace had plugged his computer into. He had a suspiciously bottomless supply of equipment that made me wonder if he had blood ties to Microsoft or maybe someone high up at Best Buy.

"No, I mean move around. Remember how we were talking about having us show up at some parties, superimposing us walking around?" Doni said.

"That was the late hour and too much chocolate talking," I said.

"No such thing as too much chocolate," Simone said. That got snickers from most of the gang.

"But you did that--or you were going to." She gestured at my notebook. "Remember when you were playing with the video camera to tie into that drafting program you made in high school?"

"Hey, yeah," Cosmo said. "I remember that. You got an 'A' in that class. What video camera?"

Granted that everybody in our team lived in Neighborlee, and they had all passed the Divine's Emporium test, I knew better than to just spill the entire story of that weird night when I went into an alternate dimension to rescue Doni's doppelganger.

"What?" Wallace had been lounging against three neon purple floor pillows. He sat up and reached for me, like he might hold my hand. "You kind of looked like you might hurl for a second."

"Need some fresh air in here," I muttered.

"It was so cool," Doni said. "Angela let Athena use this weird video camera somebody from another country dumped and she used it to record the room so she could use it for her drafting program, but before that she recorded me and put me in her computer and--" Her eyes got wide and she kind of cringed. "But the camera doesn't...doesn't work anymore...because...something happened and...the battery doesn't hold a charge, so we can't even take it out of Divine's. You know how some things just don't work anywhere else."

"But that's an idea," Cosmo said. "That was what, three years ago? Technology advances so fast. I bet we can find a camera now that will work. Do you still have the original program you used to take the upload?"

"Uh, yeah, but..." I shrugged. "I'm not sure if it's still usable."

Wallace made a noise that in someone about forty years older would have come out as "pshaw," or maybe a *hack-spit* combo.

"What the boy means is that we know how you put things together," Alvin said. He was the only one sitting in a chair, which put him above the rest of us. "Anything you design, it'll be usable when the glaciers come back."

"I don't know if that's good or not." My face felt hot.

The others joined in with flattery and teasing, overruling my first instinctive reaction to refuse to take down those firewalls that isolated the video camera-to-computer program and the recording of the furniture room that merged with my schematics drawing. But that didn't mean I was so caught up in the fun of what we were doing, and how that program would help our overall goal, that I wouldn't go to Angela.

I called Kurt and asked if he could meet me at Angela's, that it had something to do with the snake. I left a message on his answering machine, and then headed over to Divine's.

He was waiting outside by the gate when I arrived. We stood outside talking, just long enough to give him a good idea of what we were doing with the team and our project. He thought it was cool, but in a lot of ways he was like Granddad. Gizmos were more his interest, rather than programming. He understood more, and expressed some reluctance to let the video camera leave Divine's, if Angela would let it leave at all.

"You're not asking me to come over and convince it to work, are you?" he asked, as we headed up the path to the front door.

"I think if it won't work outside the walls of Divine's, that means it probably isn't safe. My concern is taking down the firewalls. What if I reactivate something that shouldn't wake up?"

"The snake is asleep," Angela said slowly, after I had explained everything, in more detail, and we had finished a cappuccino each. "The magic inherent in these walls was integral to what happened that night. Outside these walls...well...not to downplay your programming genius, but did you think it might not work now?"

My mouth dropped open and for a few seconds I couldn't even breathe. Kurt snorted. Then a few seconds later we all laughed. We agreed that chances were very good that whatever connection my computer had made with the other dimension, it wouldn't re-establish, because the failed attempt had drained the snake of its power, and my computer wouldn't be inside the walls of Divine's. In fact, with the rental apartment more than ten miles away, the chances of magical influence on my computer were nil. I wanted the reassurance of "less than nil," but negative values really only existed in mathematics.

Having permission from Angela eased a lot of my qualms about taking down those firewalls and updating the program.

It also helped that when Wallace and Cosmo got a look at it, they were impressed. It took the entire team, however, and multiple trips to electronics stores until we got a configuration of equipment and software that would do what we wanted, giving us a file we could easily rewrite and augment.

Theo and Alvin were responsible for the program that let us change colors in the clothes, but allowed textures and the angle of light and contrasts to stay the same, and also erase elements and fill in the blank spots with a logic algorithm so it didn't look like a patch. That let us change the backgrounds and the clothes of our puppet versions of Doni and Theo, and insert them in new surroundings. Which meant from just a few videotaping sessions, we could create a lot of new videos. If we needed them.

We did three videos, of London and Adora shopping, clubbing, and touring the Cleveland Metroparks Zoo in the winter. Doni and Theo never went into the clubs. We used video from a PR piece that a new club in downtown Cleveland had on their website. They did go shopping, though, and we had a blast going through the zoo in the winter, with hardly anyone around us. Once we had the videos, our teams went to work, adjusting and changing and stripping off layers and creating something totally new and unrecognizable.

During the launch party for FlopDrop, we sent London and Adora touring four different clubs in New York. We cobbled together backgrounds and surroundings from movies and TV shows and inserted them. All the other people appearing in the videos were sufficiently blurred that we wouldn't get sued for copyright infringement. We figured if famous actors and background people weren't recognizable, we wouldn't get into too much trouble.

According to the stats mechanisms Wallace adapted, we had a lot of hits, but nobody said one word about London and Adora socializing in places that weren't real. Just before the official launch, Simone uploaded London and Adora's first blog posting. Then we activated all the social media site memberships, invited all the new friends on those sites to come play on FlopDrop... and sat back to watch the fireworks.

A lot more fireworks than we expected, even projecting from the stats and counters and other feedback Wallace and Alvin collected.

Initially, we got a lot of "Huh?" looks and reactions when it was our time to unveil our project in class the next week. Alvin was our spokesman and the PowerPoint projector/connection was messed up, so we couldn't hook Cosmo's laptop into the system and show the class FlopDrop from the start. Alvin stood there at the bottom of the pit of the lecture hall with our three profs sitting to one side, their arms crossed and giving reasonably good imitations of Simon ready to snark at the latest wannabe Idol.

The whole time, Cosmo and Wallace muttered and fussed and pressed buttons and kept popping up from the control board to look at the screen, which still didn't show anything, not even the little blue flashing light that meant PowerPoint was playing hooky.

All that noise and waves of anxiety coming from the side of the classroom had to be distracting. To everyone but Alvin, at least.

I had to hand it to him. He was gung-ho for the project. Every once in a while, he paused from reading the basic proposal/report that everyone had to hand in, glanced around the lecture hall, and gave everyone a big grin. The kind of grin that said, "Ain't this the greatest thing you've heard of since the invention of the wheel?" He wasn't wearing his contacts or his tri-focals, so Alvin had no idea of the spatters of scorn on our classmates' faces. It was just a big blur to him, as he told us after class.

Then a huge spark erupted from the corner of the room and Wallace staggered backwards from the control panel. I ran to check on him and Cosmo, sure I would find the other half of the projectionist team stretched out on his back, scorched. He wasn't, though he looked a little unsteady for a few seconds, kneeling there on the floor. A little grayish-blue smoke rose up from the equipment, but at that very moment light splashed across the projection screen and the music Wallace had written as FlopDrop's theme song blared through the room. Yeah, Wallace wrote music, among all his other talents. Sometimes I could really hate the guy.

But not that day.

The muttering among our classmates died instantly. The lights went down in the lecture hall and Cosmo got to his feet to stand over his notebook. The advertisement for FlopDrop currently posted on YouTube zipped across the screen. Cosmo let out a yelp and pointed at his screen. Wallace and I leaned closer, barely able to read the little statistics bar because his finger kept going up and down, hiding it.

Several *hundred thousand* people had viewed the video since Cosmo posted it at midnight of January 2nd.

"Check the blog," Wallace whispered. We saw the stats from London Holiday's first blog about ten seconds before the blog went up on the screen for the class to see. At a rough estimate, nearly a third again as many people had visited the blog. A lot of them left comments.

It was a good thing we listed London Holiday as being a resident of New York, because among the dozen or so comments I scanned, three were invitations to parties that coming weekend. One of them sounded like the invitation had been posted several times. Another guy offered to drive by London's penthouse (when had we stated she lived in a penthouse?) and take her skiing for a week. At least he thought she lived in New York.

I had the awful feeling that if we had said she lived in Neighborlee, the guy would fly a private plane into Hopkins and either show up at Gram and Granddad's front door in a limo, or a rented Ferrari. With bodyguards.

"Whoa," Cosmo whispered. "We gotta warn--"

"She's not real, remember?" Wallace said.

The video feed switched again, mercifully stopping the automatic scrolling through the messages London had received in the last ten hours, and went to the FlopDrop site. We had started off simply in constructing the site--or so we thought. There were "rooms" we labeled *pads*, where people could set up personal information and program the levels of access and what was available to everyone, to those who had chosen the same key characteristics of interests, jobs, education, geography, or visible only to close friends. Then there were *clubs*, where people could go to chat online about interests, to get involved in civic activities such as fundraisers and petition drives, or where people could hook up for parties. We only put the last in because it fit the personality we had created for London Holiday.

In the *Coming Attractions* part of the site, we claimed we would eventually have a "shopping mall," where London and Adora would discuss what they had seen and either loved or hated in that week's shopping trip, and then offer links where people could find those items online. That is, we would do that if our profs gave us the green light, because we worried about legal action.

What if London--and us, as her creators--could be sued for slander if she said she disliked or refused to buy something and sales immediately dropped off? Then there was all the legislation and proposed bills governing Internet sponsors and so-called free advertising, where we had to say if someone gave us a free copy of a purse or book or tickets to a movie or a thousand other things in return for a review about the object or experience or service. We had only scratched the surface researching all the legalities. This class project had already turned into more work than anyone anticipated.

At this point in our presentation, it switched from prearranged and programmed to interactive, meaning our profs and anyone else who wanted to could come down front of the class, get on the computer, explore FlopDrop, and interact with London's page. We had a prototype robot program Wallace and Cosmo brainstormed, to act as hostess, the face and voice of FlopDrop. It let her respond to messages people sent her and even make suggestions for places and people to visit, both within FlopDrop and across the Internet.

"Uh, you know, you could get sued for copyright infringement," Chasity said. She was the second person to explore FlopDrop after each of our profs.

"Yeah?" Wallace leaned back in his seat and crossed his arms over his navy blazer with the maroon paisley tie. He crossed one leg over the other, clad in gray flannel trousers with razor sharp creases pressed into them, and waggled the toe of one glossy black loafer. Talk about lazy, GQ confidence. "Where, exactly?"

"You can't take Paris Hilton's face and put a new name on her and claim she's working for you. There's no way you can get away with it." She gestured at the screen, where images of London in at least a dozen different outfits created an overlapping frame for the current interactive message board.

"That isn't her," I said, while the others burst out laughing.

The truth was that we had taken extra care to search the Internet and gossip magazines, to identify all the outfits Doni owned that indeed did match Paris's. Then we made sure that all London's poses were in outfits where Paris *didn't* take that particular pose. We made sure all the backgrounds in no way resembled any place where the real girl had been photographed. Which wasn't hard, since she had never been to Neighborlee, and Doni had never been anywhere but Neighborlee since the day she climbed out of that taxi. It was a lot of work, but we were careful to make sure that we could refute every accusation.

If such accusations ever came.

Honestly, we didn't think FlopDrop would take off as quickly as it did.

To be accurate, it was more like a nuclear explosion, launching our site out of the galaxy. Just during the time it took to make our initial presentation in class, the membership of FlopDrop increased another twenty percent. We had witnesses, our entire class, with the visitor counter spinning as everyone watched.

"I'm not Paris Hilton," London Holiday said, all her images speaking in unison. Oddly, by the time she got to the end of the sentence, there was just one voice speaking and she sounded only vaguely like Doni. Her voice had an almost metallic sound, like it had been synthesized.

Wallace and Cosmo must have done some extra programming when the rest of us finally gave up, exhausted and blurry-eyed, after one of our until-two-in-the-morning plotting sessions.

"Oh, very clever," Chasity said, her nose wrinkling up and her mouth turning into that sneer that made me wish her mouth would freeze in that position. "You have it programmed to say that, because you know people are going to accuse you. That just proves how dumb you all are. Making preparations like this just proves that you are, in fact--"

"I can hear you," London said, all her images turning to glare down from the big screen directly at Chasity. "Who's the dumb one, to make accusations without any facts? You're an arrogant snot, Chasity Boah, and that's being generous."

The class erupted, most of it in applause, but not loud enough to drown out Chasity's shriek of outrage. She turned and pointed at Wallace and Cosmo. Both held their hands up, gesturing that they weren't doing anything to the image on the screen.

My computer was closed and sitting on the table in front of me, in hibernation mode, waiting to be a backup if there was any problem with Wallace and Cosmo's equipment. Now, though, it hummed, vibrating quietly under my hands. The power light flickered, which it shouldn't have done. I took my hands off it and nearly swallowed my tongue in an effort not to shout.

My computer should not have turned itself on without my permission--or at least my cooperation.

We should have taken that as a warning sign right then and there.

"Hi, Athena," London said, turning to look at me, on the far side of the room. "I do like you, but you're too protective, you know? I'm a big girl now, so let me have some fun, okay?"

"Depends on what your idea of fun is." Dr. Floyd stood up and moved to the center front of the lecture hall.

"For right now, running FlopDrop, stretching my legs." She

grinned. "Metaphorical legs. Learning to speak. Learning about the big, wide world. I don't need a visa to go all over the world. But there are limits. I'll figure them out." She turned her head, looking over her shoulder. "I have to go to work now. But I'll be watching. Especially you snots who think you're better than everybody just because you have a lot of money. Athena is richer than most of you, with money she earned herself, instead of getting it from her parents, and Wallace has royal blood."

Wallace jerked halfway to his feet, and that was all the proof I needed--really, by this time, did I need more proof?--that this wasn't something he and Cosmo had programmed just to have fun with the rest of us. For a few seconds there, I half-consciously hoped that maybe Theo had gotten together with Doni and played a trick on all of us, rigging cameras and microphones so she could interact with us, but I was pretty sure nobody knew about Wallace having royal blood. At least, nobody who hadn't done a lot of research and run genealogical searches on him Anyway, Doni would never ruin things for me by mentioning my money.

London giggled. That wasn't Doni's giggle, by any means. There was something crystalline about the sound. Chilly. Enough to make me feel like I had worn one of my summer dresses without any underwear, and took the long way from the dorm to the lecture hall in sandals. In the snow.

"Ta ta," London Holiday said. All her images in the frame waved in sequence and blanked with a pop, re-lighting a moment later with the FlopDrop logo. The message screen in the center displayed the cartoony logo Simone had created, with the impression of a body spread-eagle in a huge pillow. While the class erupted with cheers and applause, the pillow cycled through the spectrum all in neon colors. We hadn't programmed that, either.

I had to get out of there--but I stayed nailed to my seat because I didn't have the faintest idea what I should do, where I should go. To Granddad? But what could he do about a computer/Internet problem? He didn't even play Solitaire on the desktop computer. Gram only bought it to take care of bookkeeping and inventory for their antiques business. To Kurt? He wasn't into computers, either. Angela? She didn't touch the computer I set up for her inventory. The high school girls from Neighborlee Children's Home who clerked part-time handled that for her.

I couldn't get any help from the people who knew what had happened that night at Divine's when we played with that foreign video camera and...did what? Loaded a copy of Doni into the ether? Created an artificial intelligence?

Besides, there was still a good chunk of class time left. I had enough self-preservation skills to know that getting up and fleeing would attract the wrong kind of attention and generate speculation we didn't need. I had to sit there and pretend I knew what was going on and face the reactions from our classmates and professors.

This was probably the equivalent of the Id monster from *Forbidden Planet* being released into the World Wide Web. Then I mentally tripped over a horrifying realization: I hadn't been able to find the video image file that I had made of Doni that night at Divine's when we fought the snake/tentacle monster. I had searched my computer every way I knew how, and it was like the file had been wiped. Subconsciously, I think I had hoped that the firewalls I built around the software had also been enough to imprison the doppelganger.

Obviously not.

Had London Holiday escaped into the Internet that night? Had that been a real, growing person, who broke free into an electronic dimension the moment she fought back against the snake?

If so... Why had she come back and put on the costumes Doni wore in the images we uploaded, and why had she chosen to interact with us? Could artificial intelligences need homes? Had we created a place for her to live on the file server that hosted FlopDrop, maybe?

A dozen episodes of Classic Trek flashed through my mind as questions went around the room, and our profs gestured for our team to come to the front of the lecture hall. All those episodes where Kirk took a metaphorical hatchet to a supercomputer that had gained sentience. Was that what I had been reduced to?

Could I?

Should I?

Would I end up getting kicked out of school, scorned by my teammates, maybe committed to a psycho ward? Who would believe me? My family would, and Angela would. For all I knew, she had decades of experience dealing with similar situations. Yeah. I would wait to talk to Angela and figure out what we needed to do, what we could do, and how. No need to rush into it.

Besides, it was kind of cool seeing the envy on all those faces, hearing the applause and whistles, being nearly deafened by the questions and comments ringing off the lecture hall walls.

Within two hours of class letting out, we were a phenomenon on the WB campus. Everywhere we went, someone was calling up the FlopDrop site on their smartphones or tablets or using the computers in the Student Center to check out the site. It was like we had miniature Goodyear blimps floating over our heads, with flashing signs that told everyone we were the creators of FlopDrop. We were flooded with questions and suggestions--some usable, some utterly stupid, even vulgar. A lot of people wanted to be introduced to the real London Holiday.

"Hey, guys, she's an AI," Wallace said. Repeatedly. With many expanded variations.

I was stunned the first time I heard him say it. Did he know? *How* did he know?

Chapter Eight

Maybe Wallace had set up an interactive program after all, and hadn't told us? I wasn't sure if I would strangle him or bow down at his feet in worship. If he had done such a thing, he should have told us, just to save me from several hours of feeling guilty for the possible future destruction of civilization.

"Okay," he said, when we escaped our admirers and instant groupies by splitting up and then reconvening at the apartment in Darbyville for a very late lunch. "Which of you is the genius who set up a feed to Doni? How did she get away with it at school? Athena, did you get her to stay home from school?"

I must have looked so shell-shocked that it convinced him I had nothing to do with London Holiday's brilliantly timed put-down of Chasity. He went on to interrogate the others, while I caught my breath and managed to sit down without collapsing. It was kind of draining, to be offered some hope that I hadn't created a monster, then have it dashed a short time later by the one person I thought capable of saving me.

Theo was everyone's nominee for co-conspirator, which she loudly denied. Everyone believed her, because her defense consisted of, "If we set up a live feed to the class, I would have pretended to be sick, and I would have been right next to Doni as Adora. Where London goes, Adora goes."

We didn't have time for arguing. The others were flying so high from the success of our presentation, there was no chance of our team splintering over secrets and steps taken without group consensus. We devoured our lunches and then wiped out all the snacks we had stored at the apartment, in an excess of adrenaline and celebration. We had work to do before we headed back to campus for our afternoon classes. FlopDrop had already grown enough to require regular maintenance and administrative actions.

Questions had come in via communication boxes and the email programs, demanding answers. Why didn't London Holiday answer those questions, since she had decided to interact with our detractors? There were requests and suggestions for new features on the site. We had built a conference "room" just for people to discuss what they would like to see, while strictly demanding that the chat area not turn into a "bash everyone who disagrees with me" forum. We had requests for advertising rates, which was encouraging. And kind of frightening. Advertising meant people thought FlopDrop was a going concern and would have enough influence and visibility to make it worthwhile promoting their products on our site. People requested an address to send their products for London and Adora to evaluate. They wanted to pay for the BFFs to endorse their products online--only five days after London Holiday had officially been born!

That evening, when I made a dash through the dorm to drop my books and grab necessary items for a sleepover work session at the apartment, Doni was waiting. She practically glowed, like she had fallen into a vat of radioactive goo. More than half her class, and what felt like a third of the high school--staff, faculty and students--had visited FlopDrop and recognized her, despite the wacky outfits and makeup. She had eight date offers for the Valentine's Day dance, more than a month away! Instead of being traumatized by all the attention, she thought it was great fun and laughed at all the people who wouldn't believe her when she said she was just a face, a body for the costumes, and didn't control what London Holiday said and did.

Okay, I was glad that I hadn't hurt Doni, but her excitement kind of frightened me. Shouldn't she, at least, have been the voice of reason? My roommates descended on the room about then, and their excitement over FlopDrop just added to the insanity. It was great that they had always treated Doni like she was a little sister, but it kind of irritated me how they squealed and hugged her and started spilling suggestions for more outrageous costumes. Doni just sat and grinned, chugged the cream soda Shaunda gave her, and soaked up the admiration. She wasn't visibly floating a good foot off the ground, but I heard and felt the thud when Celeste congratulated her on blasting Chasity during the presentation.

"You know..." My brain went into overdrive, scrambling for how to cue Doni into the deception without my roommates catching on that she, in fact, did not know what had happened in class. "The hidden two-way camera and microphone, that let you see how everybody reacted to the presentation. When Chasity started spouting off about how we were going to get in trouble with the real Paris Hilton--"

"That inbred twit has to prove *she's* real, before she can sue anybody for infringing," Dorinda said with a sneer. Can I say how grateful I was that she interrupted, granting a few more seconds for my hints to register? "Besides, Doni is a whole lot cuter than her. No copyright infringement at all."

Doni just gave me that wide-eyed, deer-in-the-headlights look that made me feel like I had thrown her off a cliff into a circling school of Halliday-faced sharks.

"We need to get going." I snatched up my half-packed bag. If I had forgotten any of my supplies for the overnight work session, I would just have to stop at a store on the way and buy them.

Fleeing was a smart move. I could finally breathe. Doni followed me without a word as we hurried down the stairs. Once outside, I got out my cellphone and called Wallace, who was supposed to meet me and Cosmo at the grocery store. We had the job of provisioning the apartment for what would be many long, hungry work sessions. FlopDrop was growing faster than we were prepared to handle.

Doni's expression relaxed and the subliminal tense chiming she gave off faded, once I told Wallace to meet me at Divine's, that I had some errands to take care of before we headed to the apartment. Holding hands, we hurried down the snowy sidewalks to Divine's. I told her what had happened in the presentation.

Doni was stunned by my theory: her doppelganger had escaped the video files of my computer, gotten into the Internet, and now had come to roost in the persona of London Holiday and the FlopDrop site. She was silent for the last two blocks of our hurried journey, her mouth pressed flat and those little creases forming in her forehead and between her eyebrows. A sigh escaped her as we reached Divine's.

"You're right," Doni said. "What are we going to do about it?"

"Well, it'd be nice if we could figure out if London is going to play nice, or if we've created a monster. First step is to tell Angela. She might have some ideas of what we need to do, and how much trouble we're really in."

"Yeah." She hurried up the sidewalk to the front door of Divine's with me. "The last thing you want to do is get caught keeping a secret from Angela."

A shudder washed over me, so I almost lost my balance. Who would be stupid enough to try to hide anything from Angela? That was equivalent to suicide. I felt just a little nauseous, imagining what sort of punishments people who did try something that stupid had faced through the decades.

Nope, first rule of survival was to always be honest with Angela, even if we had to keep secrets from everyone else.

That brought me to another thought, as I pushed the door open and we stepped into the warmth and the scents of cinnamon and pine candles filling the air. If we were going to do anything with computers to track down London Holiday and keep her from causing trouble, try to contain her (*could* we put the genii back into the lamp?) I would need to tell our team.

Would they believe me?

I asked exactly that, after I had spilled everything to Angela, but that didn't happen right away. When we walked into the main room, she had a gaggle of middle school girls in front of the counter, dithering and giggling about a selection of teen dolls and all their accessories. She looked at us and her smile didn't exactly freeze, but it was like she put the entire world on pause. I was ready to believe right then that if she couldn't exactly read minds, she caught images from our thoughts. With a return of her usual smile, she beckoned for Doni to take over the counter and help the girls make their selections. Then she hooked an arm through mine and led me upstairs to her apartment.

"Of course they'll believe you," Angela said without hesitating. She poured tea from the pot she had fixed while I stumbled through a hurried, highlights-only explanation of what had happened in class and my theory. "They're your friends, and they all have lived their entire lives in Neighborlee. While they might not have been exposed to the full reality of what this shop protects and controls, it is in their blood and spirits."

"I keep thinking about what I should have done differently, that night," I said, while holding the enormous, soup-bowl-sized cup in both hands. The warmth felt good, showing me just how cold I had gotten during the narration. "Or maybe what I shouldn't have done at all."

"Hush." She gestured for me to put the cup down, and tipped

up the creamer to spill in a generous amount. It was tinged creamy brown, and I caught the aromas of cinnamon and vanilla as the cream mixed with my spicy-sweet tea. I recognized one of Angela's private blends that she only brought out for special occasions.

I wondered if disasters qualified as special occasions.

"What you did that night was necessary to the battle to defend Neighborlee. Sometimes, yes, there is fallout--repercussions--from the steps we take in performing our duties."

A flicker of sadness touched her eyes. I knew she was thinking of Bethany's mother, Stephanie, who had died in her duties as guardian. I was glad Bethany was at least safe, then a second later I felt even more sick, because hadn't I put Doni in danger by fooling around with that weird video camera in the first place?

"What if Doni was hurt, when I recorded her and put her image in the computer? What if that video camera stole part of her? If we shut down London Holiday, do we hurt Doni?"

"Hmm, that is a consideration that hadn't occurred to me." Angela didn't look worried, just thoughtful. Not a wrinkle in her forehead or around her eyes as she raised her cup with the butterflies embossed all over it and sipped at her tea. "How do you know London Holiday is evil?" She put down her cup and leaned back in her chair, and watched me while my thoughts spun and sparked and tangled over this new possibility. That tiny smirk returned to one corner of her mouth.

I felt stupid, but I also felt better, because Angela wouldn't be even faintly amused by my obliviousness if there were the least bit of danger. If the doppelganger was a threat to Doni, she would know. Angela knew things, and even if she did keep secrets and make us stumble around until we figured out the answers for ourselves, she would never let us get hurt. She would never let Doni be in danger.

A rap at the door startled me. Angela reached for the third cup, painted with gold and blue dragons, and poured.

"Everybody is gone," Doni said, coming into the apartment. She grinned as she dropped into the third chair at the table. "Everything is sold, too."

"Thank you. Maybe you'd consider a part-time job after school?"

"Major cool." She bounced a little in her seat. Then she looked at me, and her grin faded so fast I could hear the subliminal whine as it powered down. "Are we in trouble?"

"I don't know," I said. "I mean, we don't have any evidence that London--that your evil twin is evil at all. That's what you were telling me, isn't it? We should wait and see what London Holiday does before we shut her down."

"That, and find out if you can shut her down at all," Angela said, handing Doni her cup with one hand, and the plate of chocolate-dipped shortbread with the other. "The first order of business is bringing your teammates up to speed. If any of them have questions, or if they doubt you, send them to me. Not that I would expect any of them to doubt you. Whatever you do, do not let anyone go near the mere idea of using that video camera to upload yourselves into the digital world."

Doni stopped in mid-bite. I put down my cup before my hand started shaking.

"Maybe we should try to...I don't know...destroy it?" I said after a few seconds, while that new concept spun through my head. It was getting painfully crowded in there, after the day I had had. Why did Angela have to suggest it?

"I have learned, sometimes the hard way, it is often best to leave magical things as they are." Angela picked up her cup and gazed into its depths. "Whatever power, whatever curse or potential resides in the material form... That is often the best container, the best way of controlling it. Destroy the camera, and we have no way of knowing what will be released." She glanced upward. "There are a number of paintings upstairs that I would prefer burned to ash, to remove the possibility of accident, but who knows what could be released by destroying the container, or what could be done with the ashes that remain?"

We had a lot to think about. Wallace showed just how smart and observant he was, when he met us at Divine's and he didn't bombard me with questions about the change in plans. He let me sit and think on the drive over to the grocery store to meet Cosmo, and he shushed Cosmo a few times when he razzed me about not participating in the provisioning chores.

The rest of the team was already at the apartment when we arrived. Simone had set up the folding tables with pizza, salad and wings, ready for us to dig in as soon as we walked in the door.

"London Holiday isn't--wasn't Doni today," I said, after everyone had loaded their plates and settled down on the floor pillows to eat. "I don't know what to call her, artificial intelligence or an invader from another dimension or what, but that wasn't Doni sassing back at Chasity this morning, and it wasn't any of us showing off with some fancy programming."

The team looked around the room, meeting each other's gazes, silent questions colliding with grins and confused frowns and shrugs. I could almost trace their thoughts as they flip-flopped back and forth between believing me and thinking I was making a really confusing joke.

"What does that have to do with your trip to Divine's?" Wallace asked after a few minutes, perfectly timed as Alvin opened his mouth to speak.

"It started three years ago," I said. "I was working on my CAD program and Doni and I had a sleepover at Divine's. We were having dreams about a monster trying to break through dimensional barriers to get into our world." I paused, assessing their reaction to that first bit of weirdness.

Maybe they were all just tired, after the long, busy day we had. Maybe they were all flying high from our success, and unwilling or unready to come down with doubts and questions. Whatever the reasons, they listened and didn't even flinch or blink much, as I went through the story of that strange night of defending our town almost by accident. When I admitted that I hadn't been able to find the video file of Doni, and that I had hoped I had locked it up behind firewalls, Cosmo and Wallace got those "Oh, okay," grins on their faces and nodded to each other.

My breathing got easier by about two hundred percent at that moment. They not only believed me, but maybe they had some ideas that would solve our problems?

I finished the story with what Angela and Doni and I had discussed just a short time ago. Silence for about ten, fifteen seconds. Then Alvin got up and went to the serving table, dumped the last of the wings onto his plate, and turned to face us.

"Somebody want to make a Twizzlers run for me? We're gonna be here a while."

Simone and Theo laughed, and it took me a second to catch up. Twizzlers were Alvin's "thinking food," as he claimed. He had gone through at least thirty pounds of them, all flavors, while we were brainstorming and designing FlopDrop. He only ate Twizzlers when he was excited and in a good mood.

It was a good thing we planned to be there overnight, because we had a lot to do. Everyone had questions, going into greater detail about what had happened that night when London Holiday had, essentially, been born. Cosmo had examined my initial programs already, but now he wanted to dissect them, looking for something that could explain the germinal spark that turned a video copy into a sentient being. I wished him luck, and then reminded him that we had a website to run.

Simone and Theo took responsibility for trying to make contact with London, along with their other chosen chores for FlopDrop. How exactly would they contact her without going public with their attempts? Did we hope that London was everywhere, looking through every camera, listening through every microphone around the world? Was she the embodiment of Big Brother and all the other bleak futuristic visions of a totalitarian world? What if she could only be contacted when *my* computer had power? If I let it run out of power, would she fade away, maybe "die"? Could a digital sentience die, or would she morph into something else?

Too many questions, and we had a lot of work to do maintaining FlopDrop. We started all this for a grade, after all.

We decided to follow Angela's advice, to wait and see what London Holiday would do, and prepare for the day we had to take measures against her. Then we tried to revert to what we wanted the rest of the world to see: college students with a big, ambitious project that threatened to get out of control, even without an artificial intelligence lurking in the shadows.

We reached eighty thousand members by the end of the second full week of being live. Doni and Theo as London and Adora took turns posting on their blog and on Twitter. That translated into our first unanticipated expense. Maybe we were all subconsciously sure that FlopDrop would...flop. All the things we planned on London and Adora doing, we hadn't really *expected* to do, because why follow through on all those plans, those promised activities, if no one was watching?

Problem: None of us cared about the things that our computer-generated people focused on, such as fashion, makeup, shopping, socializing, the club scene, modern music, etc., *ad nauseum*. Doni was too busy with school, and she had an ingrained aversion to all those things, thanks to the pressure the Hallidays put on her.

So, we had to hire people to search online for new, trendy things and the activities of the "in" crowd, and then write about them. Cosmo and I were too busy dealing with hacking attempts, while Wallace handled the deluge of queries from corporations that wanted to advertise on FlopDrop. Simone, Alvin and Theo were a triumvirate researching new outlets to advertise the site and thinking up new clubs to offer people who joined. They were also handling the monitoring and gathering of statistics required for us to get a grade for this science-project-turned-Blob-That-Ate-Neighborlee. Once we paid off the consulting fees for Carr, Cooper and Crenshaw to make sure what we were doing was legal, and we paid off the people doing research for us, we started making money.

Our ability to turn a profit within a few weeks validated our project, but it was up in the air whether that same profit would secure or destroy our grade. Our profs thought monetary success said a lot about the appearance of validity for FlopDrop, but they weren't sure college rules allowed us to *make money* off what was essentially our term paper. It went in front of the college board, the regents, the heads of all the departments, and the legal counsel.

Cosmo's cousins, Brittney and Cybele were classmates of Doni's. She verified them as trustworthy and levelheaded. We hired them to buy and read every gossip magazine and supermarket tabloid they could get their hands on, to learn the lingo and figure out trends. They also came on board to help with Doni and Theo's costumes and makeup and props when we needed new images for the site. (We still hadn't made contact with London, to find out if she wanted to interact.) They had fun, they were making money, and Doni liked working with them. A win-win situation, as far as I was concerned.

London and Adora were invited to attend a big party near Phoenix, with a who's who of jet setters, party girls and high-fashion models. This was the next test of FlopDrop and London Holiday. Wallace and Cosmo had a great time, dreaming up the software to convince people that, despite the evidence of their senses, London Holiday really was attending the party.

Our research and communication people shifted from tweeting and scanning the gossip sites to researching the location for the party, the guest list, the sponsors, the caterers, and the media reps who were expected to show up. We assigned people to friend and link and do whatever was necessary to gain access to live feed the day of the party, to anyone even remotely connected with the party; workers, suppliers, observers, and guests. The most difficult item on our to-do list was to finagle access to security cameras, the wireless feed from all the cameras, and social links. In theory, at least, there wasn't a square inch of the party venue where we couldn't see and hear what was going on.

We revealed the location of the garage apartment to our profs, told them what we hoped to do at the party, and invited them to drop in and observe. We prepared to record everything we did, the reactions of the people at the party, and anything that might appear online during and after the party.

Our profs arrived half an hour before the party was due to start and settled in to watch and make notes. In the background, I could hear them talking to each other, but they never once interrupted us with questions or suggestions. I was too busy with my assigned chores to get stage fright.

After about fifteen minutes of live feed, the biggest question on my mind was how anyone could say they were *enjoying* the party. Everybody was busy updating their status and reporting what someone had just said or done, or uploading videos and photos or sound bytes. How could they interact with real people, when they were so focused on electronic communication?

"Makes you wonder who the real people are, doesn't it?" Alvin quipped, when I spoke my thoughts aloud to the room.

Wallace and Cosmo were too busy to respond. They handled four computers between them, preparing for the first "sighting" of London and Adora. The rest of us took turns posting on London and Adora's blogs, commenting on others' blogs, tweeting, uploading videos or photos everywhere else on social media, or commenting on what someone else had just posted.

"Cue entrance team, " Wallace said, at the twenty-minute mark.

London Holiday was about to enter the party.

The puppet teams had scripts, created by Simone, Theo and Alvin, to keep their comments and uploads coordinated. At various points, our tweeters, bloggers, and fake paparazzi would change their accounts and online names, so anyone paying attention wouldn't realize the same core of people were the only ones talking about and testifying to London and Adora's presence.

Ever since we learned about the party, we had been busy in the college's video lab, creating video footage of Doni and Theo, in costume as London and Adora, walking and turning and sitting and gesturing in front of green screens. At the right time, we would insert them into the environments we picked up from the actual party, to make it appear that they were there, in real time.

The big question was how long it would take for people to realize that although they were looking at the same scenes where London and Adora walked around on video feeds, they weren't talking to anyone, weren't sitting at the tables, weren't eating the food they talked about, weren't dancing with anyone.

I think we all subliminally hoped that tonight's big party would blow FlopDrop and London Holiday out of the water, totally shred the façade we had created, and by Monday morning our project would be over. It was a lot of work!

We all kept working, doing our multiple assigned tasks, but constantly watching for the "Huh? Wait! What the heck?" moment.

"And the Partycrashers have arrived," Cosmo murmured.

"Huh?" Doni's voice startled all of us. "But I thought I was allowed to come watch."

I looked around, yanked out of my computer screen, where I monitored five security screens from the party venue, watching for a likely piece of feed to patch over to Wallace and Cosmo. Doni stood in the doorway, a stack of pizza boxes in her hands and a cloth shopping bag bulging with bottles of soda and tea hanging from her shoulder.

"Not you!" Cosmo had the most amazing look of panic on his face. His mouth worked for a few seconds as he waved at his computer screen. "They're a group of hackers. They call themselves the Partycrashers because that's what they do--crash big blowouts and post footage until it looks like they're about to get caught. And then they run for it."

"Can we hook into their link?" Wallace said. "They're right there, and a lot better at stealth than we are. Maybe we can even make contact and team up with them."

Cosmo stared at him, and that panicked look slowly slid into a troublemaker grin. In unison they got to work, playing their keyboards like a third-grade duet team would slam out "Chopsticks."

Doni's presence, and Cosmo's fear that he had insulted her, were already forgotten.

I took the pizza boxes. "You're more than welcome. If you want to sit in and pretend to be London, that's fine. Have fun!"

Doni just laughed at me. She sometimes claimed that my passion for computers and the cyberspace world sort of negated any interest in or talent for computers that she might have, so she avoided them. She got more fun out of just seeing what we were doing to the people who lived and breathed cyberspace, the whole masquerade, than she would if she tried to participate. In some ways, Doni couldn't stretch her incredible brain far enough to see the Internet as a world unto itself.

Who was to say she wasn't the smart one in all this?

Cosmo tried to make contact and hitch a ride on the Partycrashers' live feed. Wallace took over coordinating the planned insertions of London and Adora walking around the party. I found six good segments of possible footage and their coordinates on our map of the party venue. After all, it wouldn't be good if London walked across the southwest corner of the room, and two seconds later walked in through the doorway from the restrooms in the northeast corner.

Brittney let out a shriek, and immediately turned red when most of us looked up from our computers and other gizmos.

"This flake just claimed she talked with London Holiday!" She waved her smartphone, where she alternately posted and monitored the social chatter from the party.

"Yeah, and what did I say to her?" Doni said.

"You think her dress is marvy--her words." Brittney scooted over to the table where Doni was filling a plastic serving tray with cups, and showed her the screen of her phone.

"Oh, yuck. I wouldn't say marvy--even if I would use such a flaky word." She giggled with Brittney. "Theo, look at this horrid dress she's wearing!"

By the time I found another video spot, checked the coordinates and sent them on to Wallace for his use, Brittney had showed the image and post to the other girls. They disagreed about Doni's assessment of the fashion status and value of the dress. But they all did agree on one thing.

"Definitely, you gotta call her on it," Cybele insisted. "Don't let those skanks put words in your mouth."

"Somebody tries to put words in your mouth, honey?" Alvin tottered over to the refreshment table, his gaze focused on the box of green pizza--green pepper, green onion, green olive, with pesto sauce. "You gotta bite their fingers right away. If you don't, they'll just keep doing it."

I pulled one of the spare notebooks out of hibernation mode. We had three ready and waiting, in case one of our devices froze up and we needed to fix a problem fast. I logged Doni in as London Holiday before handing it to her. The other girls coached her. She didn't flat out call the twit a liar, because honestly, weren't we all lying? Doni instead commented on how she tried to be nice to a total stranger who had asked about her lime green dress with a fish scale pattern and hot pink marabou trim. That got the twit for claiming London Holiday as her newest BFF.

The twit responded to the comment less than ten seconds later. This just revived my question about who could possibly be enjoying the party if they were busy posting and reading each other's posts. She snarked about someone wearing the same dress she had bought from the designer and daring to harass her BFF.

"She must be three sheets to the wind already," Alvin said. He tossed the crust from his first slice of pizza over the table, into the trash barrel, and moved down the line of boxes. I was relieved when the next slice he took was the Hawaiian. I had voted against ordering one of those and Alvin had insisted. As far as I was concerned, he could eat the whole thing.

Our strategy changed then. I fed images from the party to Doni and her team. Brittney and Cybele tagged the images, so she knew who she was talking about. They kept up a running commentary on the clothes each person wore. It amazed me, how they could tell apart the designers and even discern the *years* and design lines that went with each name, just from squinting at the security camera and online video feed--eight screens now, with a total input from twenty-plus locations, rotating every ten seconds. After listening to half an hour of the girls' snarky and yet totally amusing comments,

I decided they had to be part of the whole London Holiday persona. They were her "fashion voices."

"Sounds good to me," Wallace said, after I had moved over to the table where he worked with Cosmo, and told them my idea. "What do you think? They're your cousins, guess you're a little in charge of them."

"Huh?" Cosmo blinked slowly as he raised his head from his screen. He looked over at the girls, huddled together, sitting against the wall, on a line of floor pillows. Doni was in the middle, her fingers flying over the keyboard, while all three giggled like demented Munchkins. "Oh. Yeah. Sounds good. Aunt Tiff will be glad. Keep them busy."

Like they weren't busy already?

The girls all squealed and flooded us with ideas when I made my proposal to them. From then on, London Holiday made comments like, "The fashion voices say," or "My fashion voices are currently in argument right now, which is a pretty good bet that this (fill in the blank) isn't a good bet. Avoid it unless you like taking risks. One girl's tiara is another girl's mud pie."

About ten minutes after the girls officially became the "fashion voices," talking over each other and bouncing on the pillows, Cosmo announced he had made contact with the Partycrashers. He and Wallace had decided to ask permission, rather than try to piggyback on their feed and stay unnoticed. They were hackers with all the resources and drive of groups like Anonymous, and we had no idea if they had a sense of humor. We were taking the integrity of our computers and online presences into our hands, even *asking* if we could hitch a ride on their far vaster skills and experience. Why commit suicide by employing the totally stupid attitude of, "Easier to ask forgiveness than ask permission"?

The Partycrashers had been around for about three years by that time. They were paparazzi on the move, armed with gear that would make James Bond jealous, physically infiltrating parties without being detected, getting up-close-and-personal video and audio recordings. They focused on people making fools of themselves, while skirting the edge of exploitative vulgarity and sexism, like the jerks who made the "Girls Gone Gonzo" videos. Those sleazeoids got girls drunk or drugged them, and then insisted the girls *wanted* to be abused and humiliated. The

Partycrashers instead targeted people who voluntarily poisoned their brains with drugs and alcohol and acted like idiots. They were just there to record the evidence. If they made any impact on the rich-and-useless, revealing their excesses, maybe encouraging them to change their lifestyles or at least cut back... Who knew?

We didn't get a response to Cosmo's initial message. That made sense. The 'Crashers had to figure out who we were. They had to figure out how we had broken through their disguise, their defenses. We were only college students working on an assignment. Granted, we were in an advanced class, but we weren't online legends. For all we knew, they were prepared for such attempts and Cosmo had been routed into a dead-end, to wait. For hours. Or worse, they were already infiltrating all our computers, preparing to steal all our data and shut us down.

Good thing we had decided to be super-cautious and have nothing whatsoever on our computers except what we needed to run the party infiltration. FlopDrop was on a separate server.

Had we done enough to protect it, in case the 'Crashers decided to circle around us and attack where we weren't keeping watch?

We were too busy to talk about our fears as the minutes passed and no response came, with no signs of any impending disaster. Occasionally, we would look up from our screens at the same time, share crooked grins or widen our eyes or wipe our foreheads in not-so-feigned stress, and go back to work. Despite that, we were riding high and having fun. When we weren't having panic attacks because the party had shifted around us and we couldn't figure out where London was supposed to "be" right at that moment. Or something happened, but our cameras and microphones weren't picking up anything other than confusion and noise.

After the first back-and-forth with the twit in the green fish scales and pink marabou, more people reported seeing London Holiday. We waited twenty minutes after the first person reported talking with her before we posted a picture of what we had decided London would wear that night.

Just to test how observant people were, we changed London's outfit every twenty minutes. Nobody called us out on it. How could people who ignored the physical world so they could devour what was on their screens *not* notice that?

Oddly enough, the ones who did notice the change in

wardrobe seemed to feel some compulsion to make up a story to explain what was happening, and why. One bozo claimed he had spilled a beer on London and she slapped him before running off to change her clothes. Two girls reported they had been in the women's lounge. One claimed London had been in tears as she stumbled in, peeling off her soaked dress. The other one retorted about thirty seconds later that London wasn't crying, but laughing, and remarked that she liked that particular brand of beer, so if someone had to spill it on her, it wasn't so bad.

Doni immediately responded that she didn't like beer at all, she wouldn't be caught dead drinking moldy, rancid grain liquid, and she only drank one kind of beverage at any party she attended where she wasn't the hostess.

The first reaction was for about fifty-some people to immediately beg for invitations to her next party.

The next was for the two twits from the lounge to get into a cat-fight, on Twitter, about how neither one had seen the real London, only someone tacky enough to wear the same outfit.

Doni and the "fashion voices" launched an online discussion, asking people for input on what she should wear next. She posted three more pictures, giving people a choice, implying that the first "costume change" had been planned.

Through all this, not one person spoke up and said she was in the lounge and *didn't* see London Holiday come in.

Not one person asked where all her spare clothes had been stored. In her car? In the lounge? Did she have an assistant to bring the clothes to her?

Right about then, Theo let out a shriek and slapped herself on the forehead a few times. She had been having so much fun just watching what Doni and the "voices" were doing, she had forgotten all about moving Adora through the party. She settled down on the pillows with Doni, Brittney and Cybele, and set Adora patrolling the party, making comments about clothes and drinks and bits of overheard conversation. Just to stir the pot, she made comments about how nobody seemed to see her or hear her, and she was feeling peeved enough to start kicking people.

Chapter Nine

"She kicked him!" Simone reported, with a bark of laughter. She held up her tablet for monitoring several feeds about the party.

"Did not," Theo retorted.

"Well, according to this guy, Adora bumped him as she slid past, and didn't see him because she was busy with her smartphone--"

"He got that right, at least," Cosmo said.

"And he spilled his drink. So he said something to her. And she got mad and turned around and kicked him in the shin before she stomped away." She shook her head. "You ought to see the responses spilling in. People calling him a liar. People saying they saw it, and Adora was going for his nuts." She snorted.

"That does it," Theo said. "We're at war."

"Theo, honey--" Alvin settled down next to her. "--why don't you take a breath and think about this for a second?" He offered her a big blue plastic cup of soda.

"He's telling lies about me!"

"He's telling lies about *Adora*," Doni said. "Adora doesn't exist, remember?"

"That doesn't mean he has the right to--to--to violate my copyright! Or is it my patent?" Theo frowned for a few seconds, lips pursed, eyes narrowed. Then she giggled. "Whatever, he's lying, and there are enough people there who say he's lying--"

"We're all lying," Wallace said.

"We're interfacing our virtual reality version of the party, and our virtual reality people, with the drunken, drugged, over-dressed, half-deafened by loud music, egocentric idle rich," I said. My mouth felt slightly scorched from the venom passing through my lips. Okay, so I had had some bad encounters with the Grandstones through the years, but that was no reason to assume that the rest of the glitterati were just as bad, was it? After all, the Longfellow clan was nearly as rich as the Grandstones, but we didn't assume it made us entitled and better than everyone else. "Is it our fault that they're so eager to be on stage and be part of the 'in' crowd, they lie as naturally as breathing?"

"Got some issues there, 'Thena?" He crossed his arms over his chest, and leaned back in his borrowed swivel chair.

From the corner of my eye, I saw movement along the wall where our professors had been enjoying the show. They quietly tapped away on their computers, making notes and muttering to each other. Oh, great, we were giving them material for a psychological paper, not just our online project testing what people perceived as reality.

"Doesn't matter," Alvin said, after wrinkling up his face like a walnut with the force of his concentration. "Get the lousy scumdogs!"

He gestured like a Cavalry commander aiming his troops at enemy forces across the battlefield. Some of us laughed, but we all got back to work with renewed vigor. Well, at least I know I did.

The argument with the guy who said Adora kicked him lasted about ten minutes. It died out once the vote over London's new outfit ended. I immediately picked up the image, switched it over to the profile on her Twitter feed and her blog, and fed the image over to Wallace and Cosmo, to show London coming out of the women's lounge.

Strangely, the people who applauded her new outfit were the ones who had voted for *other* outfits. Almost to a person. I kept track of such things, whether we would ever need the data or not. Weird. Had they damaged their brain cells from so much partying they couldn't remember from one minute to the next what they wanted and liked?

"Sucker-uppers," Wallace said, when I mentioned what I had been thinking.

People posted invitations to London to leave and go to other parties with them. Others caught onto that and suggested she go on ski trips next week, or spend a few weeks in Florida or the Bahamas or crash for a few days at their condo in Hawaii. Shortly after that gained momentum, we lost control.

"Guys!" Cosmo gestured at the flat screens we had borrowed to display where London would appear. None of us had really been paying attention, busy with our various chores.

The biggest screen flickered from an image of the wall where the long buffet tables were set up (the plan was to have London go over there next and rave about the food) to show the dance floor. We had no intention of sending her or Adora anywhere near the dance floor, and not just because Doni and Theo didn't want to dance, or even try to give us some video images of them dancing.

London Holiday appeared among a crowd of dancers. She stood on the edge of a red-tinted spotlight, her arms raised over her head, doing a shimmy with her hips and making her short-short skirt peel upwards on her hips like a magician was levitating it.

Let me restate this: even if we didn't have any animation programs running, we did *not* have any video clips of Doni dressed as London doing *that*. She wouldn't move like that, even if we put a gun to her head and threatened to set all her books on fire. I glanced at Doni. She was just sitting there, her mouth dropping open, her eyes getting wider than the bottom of her plastic cup.

"Where is that coming from?" Theo asked, when the rest of us just stared for about five seconds.

"Partycrashers." Cosmo bent back over his keyboard, tapping away so fast it was a loud hum. "I guess we got their answer."

"How are they doing that?" Wallace stood up so he could see over his notebook and watch the big screen while he worked. His fingers competed with Cosmo's for speed and the buzzing/tapping of his keyboard.

"What can we do?" Simone asked.

"Get her off the dance floor as soon as we can," I said.

"Do we have to?" Doni looked a little pale, but she managed to smile. "I mean, as long as I'm--as long as London is on the dance floor, I don't have to tweet or blog or anything. My fingers are kind of tired."

The other girls agreed. I was ticked for a few moments, because I had been working just as hard as them, doing the coordination work, making sure they could see the people they were supposedly reacting to and interacting with. Then it kind of hit me that none of us had anticipated this much work, this strong of a reaction, to London Holiday's first "public appearance." When the girls got up to graze at the snack table, I moved over to join Wallace and Cosmo at their long worktable. Alvin joined us.

"We all need a break," Cosmo said, nodding. His gaze focused on Doni. Which made sense, of course.

"Yeah, but is it permanent?" Wallace said.

Alvin gave him a confused look.

"He means, when the dance is over, do we get control of London again?" I said, guessing what was in Wallace's somber expression. "Or do the Partycrashers keep moving her around the party? Do they destroy the image of her that we've created so far, by having her do things we don't want?"

"Well, heck, we gotta do something. We can't let them hurt Doni like that. She's just a kid," Alvin said, glancing over to where everyone but our professors were snarfing down room-temperature pizza.

"It's not Doni. London Holiday is a construct. A virtual person," Cosmo said with just a little more heat than I thought the situation warranted.

Then I got a good look at the expression in his eyes. He was worried about Doni. Was it more than just a crush? Like, was Cosmo in love with my cousin?

I liked Cosmo, really. Despite his obsession with those fashion magazines, which he still hadn't explained. In those few seconds that I let myself think of something besides the Partycrashers hijacking our party girl creation, my worry was if he knew enough about the real Doni for his feelings to be real. In a kind of warped symmetry, just like all those party people were falling over themselves to meet and talk and party with London Holiday-- falling for the virtual person--Cosmo might be falling for an image he had created that wore a Doni Halliday mask.

Did that make any sense? Maybe I was so tired by then, I was borrowing trouble and making connections where there were none.

"We gotta do something," Alvin insisted.

"What do we do?" Wallace said, looking at me. "Like 'Thena said before, we can't accuse them of lying, of putting up a fake London, because only we know she's fake."

"We counter their lies with more lies of our own, then," I said. Definitely, I was tired. Words like that shouldn't have come out of my mouth. Gram and Granddad would have been disappointed. Even if, at the same time, they laughed, shaking their heads at the foolishness of all of us, scrambling to keep control of the unreal person and situation we had created.

"What kind of lies?" Cosmo shot back.

"Time stamps," Wallace said, snapping his fingers. He winked at me and bent back over his keyboard.

The dance was ending, anyway. That meant our break was over and we had to go back to work.

And we did work. Hard. So hard that cold, dry pizza and room temperature ginger ale with hardly any fizz left tasted like ambrosia at 2am, when the party ended and we could collapse.

Wallace took care of time-stamping all the images of London Holiday we sent out. He became our orchestra conductor, feeling his way through the maze that had been complicated by the Partycrashers playing with our Barbie doll.

"Uh oh," Cosmo muttered, as another song started and we braced for a fight to keep London off the dance floor.

He glanced over his shoulder at the Terrible Trio. Fortunately, they were taking a snack break, chatting quietly with Simone while Doni and Theo settled down in their nest of pillows and got back to work "being" London and Adora.

"What?" I whispered, and scooted my notebook over a foot to see what was on his screen.

He had a dialogue box on the side, with the font set so small I couldn't read it. Maybe I didn't want to, because Cosmo looked green, and it wasn't the reflection from the big screen glaring at us from three feet away.

"The 'Crashers want to know what program we used to make London move like that. As far as they could tell, it was live feed. They couldn't find any seams." He pitched his voice low enough nobody at the food table three feet away could have heard us.

A dialogue box opened on my screen. My computer wasn't set up for instant messaging.

Hi, Athena. This is lots of fun. I've heard about parties, but I haven't been able to go to one until now.

"Good morning, HAL," Wallace muttered over my shoulder. He had moved around behind me without my noticing.

Well, that was understandable, considering I was ready to swallow my tongue.

As one, we all turned to look at Doni, giggling with Theo, both of them busy with what we called "dueling keyboards." London and Adora rattled out the silly, snarky comments so fast no one else at the party could get a word in edgewise.

Please, London, don't let the others know you're here, okay? I typed.

Don't scare Doni.

I crossed my fingers, and for good measure crossed my toes inside my boots and prayed really hard. *Please, please, God, don't let her say that she's part of Doni. Or that she's the real Doni. Please don't let it be like that Alice episode in* Warehouse...

That would mean my cousin Doni had been trapped inside the computer or virtual reality world and a copy had been running around in her body for the last three years. Not good.

I like Doni. Promise. No scaring. Just don't make me leave?

Sure. Have fun.

"Just don't do anything I wouldn't do," Wallace muttered. He patted my shoulder and started to go back to his seat.

What wouldn't you do? London asked.

Cosmo let out a few choice Klingon curses--at least, I thought they were curses. He and Pete Zephyr had an ongoing contest to see who could speak the most fluently in Klingon. For all I knew, he was just saying our grades were in the toilet.

"She can hear us," he said in English, his voice strained. Probably with the effort not to shout.

Yep. ;-)

"Just don't do anything that would make Doni upset," Wallace said.

Where do you want me to go next? Where don't you want me to go? London asked on all three of our screens.

From the others' lack of reaction, we were the only ones she communicated with. Fair was fair, I reasoned. If London behaved, then we should let her have some fun.

When Brittney reported that someone had gotten sick and stumbled into the lounge, Doni tweeted that London was going in to help her. Wallace darkened an image of London bending over and patched in an image that could look like someone bending over a toilet. London took over, animating the imagery and showing us the real girl from several angles. Probably her so-called "friends" had followed her into the bathroom and were vulgar enough to show everyone via the cameras on their phones.

In ten seconds, we had a dozen people reporting that London Holiday was making like Florence Nightingale. It was strangely amusing, and surreal, when the person who got sick reported that she would have been in big trouble if London Holiday hadn't held her hand. Other people washed her face, brought her water to drink and made her lie down, but London Holiday got points for being sympathetic and "not hurling" like two girls in the lounge had done.

I would have held her hand if I could, London said.

For the remainder of the evening, until we had her exit the party, London remarked to me and Cosmo and Wallace that she had a hard time understanding how people could report that they had talked to her and sat next to her and saw her talking to other people. This was vaguely reminiscent of various SF TV shows and movies, where the Artificial Intelligence gained enough awareness to interact with the Humans, and then got so tangled with warped Human reasoning that it blew a circuit.

Funny, but I didn't want London Holiday to blow any circuits and vanish. She turned out to be kind of cool.

When she asked about the food and the people in uniforms taking care of refreshments and cleaning up messes, we decided to educate our friendly little AI. We got into the security cameras for the venue and showed shots of the staff working like mad in the kitchen, putting together trays of hors d'oeuvres or refilling buckets of ice, and later hauling enormous urns of coffee out to the refreshment tables. That gave us an idea. Soon, London "walked" through the kitchens, posting shots of the staff at work. She talked about the members of the staff. That took some fancy footwork on our part to pull up information on the people on staff that night, and share personal details.

A flood of appreciation rolled out, after London and Doni, working in unconscious synch, talked about appreciation for the people who worked behind the scenes to make the party great. Someone emptied out one of the enormous crystal bowls that held ice, and set it up by the main doors for people to throw in tips for the kitchen and wait staff, after London speculated, three times, about whether it wasn't just right but a moral imperative to tip the workers, who were "going above and beyond," in her viewpoint. I saw at least one fifty-dollar bill in the pile that threatened to overflow after about twenty minutes.

The day after the party, Doni decided London Holiday and Adora should do a blog about the "unsung heroes" of the party scene. The people who did all the setup and planning, who took care of the sick and blitzed and just plain nasty, who called for taxis and ambulances and made sure broken furniture and torn draperies were repaired and replaced. Cosmo gave her video feed of people dropping money into the tip bowl and worked hard to clear up images so that famous faces were clearly identifiable. Adora mentioned on her blog and her page on FlopDrop that she wasn't sure who had taken care of the collection and making sure that the workers got the money, but could he or she speak up and give a tally of how much was collected?

Did that sound like we didn't trust the party people to make sure that the workers actually *got* the money collected for them?

Absolutely.

We still hadn't recovered from the effort of that very long night of intense activity when we reported on the party to our class. Alvin and Simone had documented us at work, with four cameras and microphones set up to get a full panorama view of the room and hopefully catch everything. Every reaction, every word of discussion, every argument, every snarky remark, every spilled cup and dropped cracker, and the giggle fests when the hour got very late and we turned loopy from exhaustion.

If I hadn't loved Alvin before then, I was in love after he shared the rough cut edits during the first fifteen minutes of class. He was kind, to put it simply. He didn't embarrass Cosmo and Doni by showing every longing look. He switched views whenever someone scratched. He did a masterful job of stringing together tiny clips of us hard at work when things got frantic, such as when we thought the Partycrashers hijacked London Holiday. He made us look like we not only knew what we were doing, but we were a well-oiled machine, working smoothly in enviable coordination.

London scrubbed every scene that showed Wallace, Cosmo and me talking with her through our computer screens, adjusting our pretense of being puppet masters, so she could enjoy the party. Who was the puppet master here, and who was the puppet? I don't know if I was relieved or worried by how she behaved herself. Was this AI a nice girl inside her electronic world, or was she so smart she knew just how to play us, to ease our worries?

Yeah, like that consideration didn't raise my sense of impending doom a few notches higher on the Richter Scale of panic?

We had other things to think about. For one thing, Chasity

Boah was not happy with our report. She protested that what we had accomplished just was not possible without expensive help and technology way beyond our reach. Well, she was partly right, but we weren't about to admit it. She was so intent on proving she was right and we had somehow cheated, she ignored one important point: our three profs were there the whole long night and testified that what appeared on Alvin's video really did happen. Each time she expressed her disbelief, one of them would simply say, "It happened. I saw it."

After that fifteen-minute video report ended, it was time to get grilled. Our professors had pages of notes, asking why we had done something or reacted in some way, when they had seen other options. They expressed some reservations over getting high school girls involved, yet admitted that part of the flawlessness of the "performance"--one even used the word "deception" a few times-- was that the language, the reactions, the opinions being expressed were real ones, from real girls. The mask separating London Holiday from Doni Halliday was so thin, few suspected it was a mask.

We went overtime discussing the technical issues. The profs discussed the hijacking episode with the Partycrashers. During the next class period the entire class discussed how to predict when a hijacking might happen again, how to prevent it, and defensive as well as offensive measures we could take. Interestingly, Chasity's group brought up the offensive measures, as in punishing hackers. The others were more concerned with defense, prevention, and learning from the Partycrashers, so they could try it themselves.

Wallace, Cosmo and I kept silent, letting everyone else talk, because we certainly couldn't admit the 'Crashers hadn't done anything except watch. They had been just as flummoxed as us when London Holiday started dancing and interacting. I kept checking the screen at the front of the class, waiting for her to show up and laugh, tease us, maybe even chew out Chasity. How long, after all, until she wasn't satisfied with playing in the background and decided to tell the world she was a "real" person?

Near the end of the discussion, Wallace's phone vibrated. He sat up a little straighter and slapped his pocket. That much movement caught my attention, in time for me to glance over and see him look at me. What? Did he think I had buzzed him or something? He shot our profs a look, but they were on the far side of the room, listening to a discussion of possible changes that could be made to CGI, based on what we had done with the party.

"Oh...heck," Wallace whispered. Our gazes met, and he looked a little queasy.

We were supposed to turn off all electronics during class, unless we specifically needed to do something on our computers or tablets or other gear. We also weren't supposed to be looking at our gear while our profs were talking to us. That had been part of the rules we agreed to when we signed the documents about rights and proprietary information and releases for research purposes. So what was Wallace doing?

"Partycrashers want to have a conference," he whispered, so softly I almost had to read his lips as he leaned over, close enough to me I could feel the warmth and smell the cinnamon on his breath.

Conference? I mouthed, and turned my attention back to our profs. Murphy's Law of Classroom Disasters dictated that the teachers would always see me looking away and talking to someone else at the worst possible time.

"I wouldn't trust them if they were sitting in a room shielded from all electrical signals, reduced to doing everything with paper and ink," Alvin said, when the six of us met over lunch.

"Well, yeah, that's a given." Wallace slouched back in his seat. Not easy to do with the stiff folding metal chairs the cafeteria stocked.

We had chosen the cafeteria because it was crowded and noisy and the tables were narrow enough we could lean in to talk and keep almost everyone from reading our lips. It felt like a bad spy novel. Wallace's move kind of spoiled that advantage, and I really wanted to slap him. Or at least kick him under the table. But he was sitting next to me and my leg just didn't bend in that direction.

"What do they want? What did they say?" Simone said.

"Why did it take this long for them to find you?" Theo added. "And you and not Cosmo, since he was the one making contact? Why not send a message through FlopDrop?"

"Maybe because I wrote to them after the party." Wallace's grin got wider.

"What did you do that for?" I demanded.

"I figured it was only polite, after they were so nice to us."

"Nice?" Simone snorted. "After hijacking London?"

"They gave her back," I said. Cosmo, Wallace and I met each other's gazes and rolled our eyes a little. After all, we knew that the Partycrashers never *had* London in the first place. They were just as confused as us.

"How come they waited so long to get back to you, then?" Alvin said.

"They've been investigating us further." He nodded to Cosmo. "They figured you're the maestro, want to hire you, whenever you're ready to move up in the world. Their words, not mine."

"Hire me for what?" Cosmo said. "Forget it. I'm not leaving."

"Who says they want you to move? Virtual world, remember? That's what they're working up to, by the way. At least, that's what their messages say." Wallace brought his phone from his pocket and held it up so we could see the screen filled with headers for text messages. It looked like he had been carrying on quite a conversation, just in the time we left class, took care of errands, dumped books in our dorms, and reconvened in the cafeteria.

"You let them text you. Is that...smart?" Simone said. Her voice had always been sweet, in comparison to her build, but she had never sounded weak and delicate before. Maybe she was scared?

"If they wanted to put a bunch of time bombs and self-destructs in all our computers and crash FlopDrop, they could. I figure, if they're texting, they're basically showing they want to be friends."

He had a point. The Partycrashers were proving they wanted to play nice by being polite and...well, yeah, playing nice. They could have just slagged everything we had done like some terrorist hacker groups would do, and then told us to stay out of the big kids' playground. They were being nice. Which meant they wanted something, and wanted to work with us, instead of giving orders.

Unless of course they had tried to hurt us, sabotage us somehow, and London had already stopped them? Maybe that was the delay between Wallace's communication and their response? They had been fighting London, who had defended us? Now they were scared and wanting to make friends?

I hated knowing I would have to get Cosmo and Wallace alone to voice that theory, almost as much as I hated the theory in the first place. Besides, the longer we waited to tell the rest of the team that London Holiday had been the one dancing, the angrier they would be that we had left them in the dark. And yet she had only contacted the three of us during the party. Why did she leave the others out of the conversation?

We sat and thought and talked it over and our cafeteria food got cold. Well, all except Cosmo. He ate everything on his tray and started eating off ours before we told him that was gross. Then he got up and got seconds. We had to break up to go to other classes, and that evening we met in the apartment and discussed the proposal more, along with all the best case and worst case scenarios we had come up with in the meantime.

It felt even more like a bad spy novel as we arranged for the conference. We agreed Wallace would be our voice and the only point of contact. We agreed on a phone conference, nothing by computer, nothing on the Internet. We would have a speaker phone, so we all could hear, and then instant message him, so our contributions and questions and answers would show up on the screen in front of him, to respond to the Partycrashers.

We took our lives and our grades in our hands and told our profs what was up. They could decide we had gotten in over our heads, pull the plug on our project, and tell us to shut it all down.

Funny thing, but as we discussed the possible outcomes of the conference, the problems, the threats, the dangers, the obligations and responsibilities, we discovered that we didn't really care if FlopDrop survived. We had gotten into this for the challenge. None of us were into the social media scene. Once we had proven what we could do, the thrill was gone. Yes, we felt some responsibility for the people who were drawn to what we created. Five thousand-plus more members joined within twelve hours of London and Adora attending the party. The advertising money didn't really attract us. Sure, we could have replaced all our equipment, twice over, but did we really want all the hassle?

We had better things to do with our lives. Graduate, for one thing. Figure out how to study while following the Indians, with Spring Training starting in a few weeks. Of course, there was the allure of frustrating Chasity Boah and her clones...

The point was, we took a big risk going to our profs.

We shouldn't have been nervous.

They were fascinated with where our project was taking us, the things we were learning about the online social world. It turned out they were fans of the Partycrashers, each from his own unique academic discipline perspective. The Partycrashers weren't like other hackers who seemed to derive so much joy from causing mayhem and destroying what others had created. The selfish brat jerks who felt that no one had any right to privacy, or to control what they had created. The ones who went after anyone and everyone on the Web with self-righteous indignation--as if *their* rights were being violated when someone didn't want them to have access to every detail of their lives.

The Partycrashers, as far as Internet legends went, didn't *hurt* anybody. They didn't destroy websites, didn't hijack email or blogs or Twitter accounts. Didn't upload viruses everywhere they went. Didn't get online and post rants and make threats and declaim that privacy was illegal--all while wearing masks and using voice-masking technology and hiding their ISP address to protect their own privacy. The Partycrashers were out to have fun while uncovering the stupidity people committed against themselves.

Our profs helped us, borrowing a speaker phone from the college administration. We set up in the apartment with equipment to record everything said, our reactions, our notes to Wallace, and of course plenty of food. Because of the time agreed on for the conference, our profs couldn't be there. They had families and real lives, after all. They had the option of linking in and sending us questions if they wanted. If they woke up. The conference was set for 2am. I wondered if the Partycrashers were on the West Coast, or maybe in another country, to pick that time. Alvin suggested they were all second shift workers in Silicon Valley. For all we knew, they worked for Apple or Microsoft, and that time of the night was the only time they could get together during the workweek without the big bosses having heart attacks and accusing them of espionage.

~~~~~

"Captain Taggert, it's nice to finally meet you and your crew." The voice of the rep for the Partycrashers was nice, tenor, and very clear. If they were employing any software to disguise his voice, such as make a woman sound like a man, there was no distortion, that I could hear. Alvin had the job to run analyses on whatever came through the phone, and make sure the recording caught everything, including muffled background noises.

Just because we were willing to talk to the Partycrashers didn't mean we weren't going to try to backtrack them and arrange as much protection for ourselves as possible.

Captain Taggert? The question popped up on my screen, coming from the profs. So they did get up early in the morning to observe over the Internet. Nice to know they were as fascinated by all this as the rest of us. Or maybe they were just worried about the book they hoped to get out of our class.

Why did they ask me, specifically, about the name Wallace used online? I guess they expected me to know all the quirky little details, since I was nominally second-in-command. I hurried to explain Wallace's screen name was taken from the character played by the actor Jason Nesmith, who was played by Tim Allen in the movie *Galaxy Quest.* Essentially, it was about a bunch of actors in a TV show much like *Star Trek,* who were still going to conventions twenty years after the show went off the air. They got drafted by aliens, who didn't know it was just a show, to help save their universe. I had been amused and somewhat pleased to learn that was one of Wallace's favorite movies, because it was one of mine, too. We often shot quotes at each other in the middle of conversations, trying to stump each other, and irritating the rest of our team.

"Nice to meet you too, Captain Reynolds," Wallace responded.

Malcolm Reynolds is the captain of the starship Serenity, *in the movie of the same name,* I explained, before the profs could ask.

The fact the leader of the Partycrashers knew about the movie, and the TV series *Firefly,* and chose that screen name, kind of gave me a good feeling about this meeting.

"Okay, let's cut through the bull and get down to business. I imagine you aren't too jazzed about staying up so late, or taking time off work," Reynolds said.

Five points to my theory, Simone wrote. Wallace stuck his tongue out at her.

"What's your proposition?" Wallace asked.

"We're getting to that." He chuckled, and it was a nice sound. Kind of warm, smooth, like caramel. "We're really interested in getting some answers. Your team did an incredible job. If we hadn't been physically there, covering every square inch of the party, we would have been ready to believe London was a real girl."

"She is." He glanced over at me and I crossed my eyes and stuck out my tongue at him. Wallace choked for a second. "She just wasn't physically at the party."

Depends on what you want to call real, Cosmo wrote on the messaging screen he had set up for just him, Wallace and me. Maybe it wasn't cool to keep the others out of the loop, but we needed to be able to confer on what to say or not say if questions and speculations got too close to London Holiday.

I crossed my eyes at him and he stuck his thumbs in his ears and waggled his fingers at me. Simone sighed, but she looked amused by our foolery.

"Her name isn't really London Holiday, is it?" Reynolds asked.

"Hmm, to protect the privacy and general security of a minor, we can't confirm or deny that theory."

"Uh huh. I think we're going to have fun working with you, Captain Taggert."

It was so loud and dark, with so much flashing light and special effects, and smoky and crowded, how can they be sure London wasn't physically there? I asked.

"We had enough of us to cover the place, believe me," Reynolds said, when Wallace passed on my question. "We were the only ones in that whole crowd, including the servers and musicians, who weren't drinking, smoking, and popping pills. We identified every scene you inserted her into. It was definitely special effects, and not a real girl there. Have to admit, you had us going for a while, making us wonder if there wasn't something nasty in the air."

Essentially, the Partycrashers wanted to know how we created the persona of London Holiday, made her look so real, and had her moving so fast, doing so much, people thought they had "just missed her" when they looked around and couldn't find her. They were in awe of us. Especially when Wallace admitted it was a college computer class project.

I lived in terror for about ten seconds, when they talked about the dancing scene. Wallace, Cosmo and I had yet to agree on what to say to our team if the Partycrashers said they had not made London appear on the dance floor. Fortunately, they never said enough for Alvin, Simone or Theo to catch on and start asking questions we couldn't answer.

Then again, London Holiday might just decide to speak up in

the middle of things and "out" herself. I suspected if she wanted to, she could take over that high-tech speakerphone and join in the conversation.

The Partycrashers wanted to work with us. They would coordinate with us, to get London and Adora into more parties, have them up on wall screens, creating the illusion of them being there even for those few who weren't on their smartphones during the whole party. They wanted to share the fun.

"Why?" Wallace asked, after the proposal had been laid out and our profs had even made some comments, asking for clarification.

Chapter Ten

"It was the thing you did with the tips for the workers. We liked the part where London called them the unsung heroes," Reynolds said. "It just never occurred to us to think about them, what they go through at those parties. We started out doing it for the thrill-- record people destroying their brains with drugs and proving that white people can't dance, post it on the Internet, and keep from getting caught. Then it kind of turned into a crusade, pointing out the excesses and..." He sighed. "We figured right then, you were our kind of people."

That was Doni all the way, not us, I wrote. *Confess.*

"Yeah, well, maybe some of us. Not all of us," Wallace said, after reading the screen, frowning at me, then finally shrugging. "The girl who is our model for London decided to do that. She kind of hijacked it at that point. We're hoping with all the money those people ponied up, London and Adora won't be invited to any more parties. Nobody likes to sober up and realize they emptied their wallets for the benefit of the invisibles, you know?"

"Ain't that the truth? Well, we want to help you do it better, again and again. What do you think? Nobody will be able to keep London and Adora out, no matter how exclusive the party is. Nobody will be able to throw them out when they show up uninvited. It'll be a hoot."

Honestly, it sounded like fun. And a lot of work.

Most of the work would be pretending to run things when London got busy. What if she decided to do something that was flat-out impossible for our level of skill and technology?

If we were lucky, the social reform comments we would put in London's and Adora's mouths would irritate enough people that no one would want the two BFFs around anymore. Maybe London would become *persona non grata*, so we could take down FlopDrop when the semester ended, and no one would wonder or complain.

"One more thing, before we sign off," Reynolds said. It was just past 4am. I did not look forward to sneaking into the suite without waking my roommates. "We think London or Adora should get a boyfriend, or a guy friend, at least, to go to parties with them."

"Why?" Wallace said.

"Protection, mostly. Yeah, they're virtual people, but there's safety in numbers when you go to parties like this. Two girls going to parties all alone, all the time, they're just asking for trouble. Having a guy or two around, always with them, that'll halt a lot of the scum-of-the-earth types who will go to the parties specifically to look for London and Adora. If they don't come hunting, they won't attack other girls when their targets evade them. Know what I mean?" He sounded tired as he said it.

I wondered if he had some experience with that kind of situation. Someone he knew, something he had witnessed, or hadn't gotten there in time to prevent trouble. I didn't ask that question, though.

"If we can discourage the slimedogs looking to make physical contact, that delays the time when people put the clues together and realize London Holiday was never there."

"We'll think about it," Wallace said.

We did more than think. We created a twin brother for Adora, who palled around with her and London. We named him Adonis, and got one of the guys who modeled for the life drawing class to be his "foundation." Doni and Brittney brought in two guys from their class who they vouched for, in intelligence, wit, maturity, and the ability to keep secrets, to be the "voice" of Adonis and post on his profile on FlopDrop, Twitter, and the blog.

We were turning into a full-time operation. It was a good thing we had the advertising income, to pay salaries to the people who made our virtual people come alive and give them personalities. We trusted them to keep quiet for their own protection, so we didn't worry about word of this leaking to the so-called real world. Our only real fear of being "outed" was if one of the rival teams in class decided to get jealous and blab.

Honestly? We *wanted* that to happen. We wanted FlopDrop to fall apart and free us, even as we met on Friday and Saturday nights and put London, Adora, and Adonis through their paces.

Wouldn't you know it? Even Chasity Boah and her clique abided by the agreement they signed on the first day of class and kept the whole thing a secret. What was the world coming to, when the class snot didn't live down to her reputation?

We debuted Adonis a week after the meeting with the Partycrashers. It was a fast job, but we had streamlined our process. That didn't mean we didn't have new worries. One night, I even had a nightmare of someone getting hold of that foreign video camera at Divine's Emporium. What if they hooked it up to my computer with the original software, creating Adonis and Adora doppelgangers? And then set them free in the Internet to get together with London Holiday and have fun?

The Partycrashers contacted us about an Ivy League frat sending out messages on all their bulletin boards to invite London and Adora to their party. The dummies didn't contact them through FlopDrop, meaning they wanted the whole world to know London was coming. Meaning they were aiming for their fifteen minutes of fame.

"They need to be taken down," Simone said, when we discussed all the possible motivations for such public invitations, and what the frat boys hoped to gain.

The frat brats promised a hotel room, limo service, transportation on a private plane, the works. Were they trying to figure out where London lived? Did they just want private access to her from the beginning? Control over her every move? What should we do about the frat boys and their questionable motives?

Celeste came up with the answer, when I grumbled to my roommates about the conundrum. Wasn't it kind of weird that we wondered about the frat party being "safe" for virtual people?

"I hate to say this," Celeste said, after all three of my suitemates expressed their sympathy for the plight.

That was really nice of them, considering that we were all competing for the top grade in the class. That was what made my roommates so great. We left the competition behind in the lecture hall. Most of the time, anyway.

"Say what?" Dorinda said, when Celeste just frowned and stared off into the distance for a few seconds too long.

"I'm actually borrowing a page from Chasity's book."

"Uh huh. Nasty or arrogant?" Shaunda muttered. She was lying on her back, staring at the ceiling, doing one of her modified Pilates routines. I really hated her, being able to even figure out how to do Pilates, let alone doing them in front of us.

"Both. Mostly arrogant. Queen of the planet attitude." A giggle broke from her. "Have London respond to the invitations. Thanks, but she prefers to stay with personal friends, and her own transportation options. Privacy and security reasons," she added, her voice sliding into a la-de-da tone. "Plus there's the insult to Adora and Adonis, not inviting them. And she is seriously considering not coming, since they dissed her BFFs so badly."

"Too ready to grab private time with the celebrity of the hour," Celeste said. "That's what all the fuss is, offering her freebies, just to attend their party. They figure if they arrange for her hotel and plane and all that, it gives them a private audience."

"Or--" Shaunda grunted as she rolled onto her side and propped her head up on one hand to look at us as she spoke. "Or they're just as much a bunch of pervs as you see in the movies, and they're rigging cameras to catch London in the shower. For all you know, the complimentary champagne is laced with ruphies."

"Yick." I swallowed down a few choice cuss words Granddad sometimes used when he was really pissed. He didn't get infuriated to that point very often, and when he did, he spoke in foreign languages. Gram said he looked up those words just so he could cuss without us knowing specifically what he said.

When London responded publicly to the invitation, we found out Celeste was spot-on. The Partycrashers had hacked into the frat boys' accounts and linked to the cameras and microphones already installed in the frat house. The pervs had a sulk fest, grumbling about the time they had wasted, lining up the cameras and recorders, the wine and the drugs. They were hoping to separate Adora and London, and distract Adonis so he wasn't around to protect them. They already had bets on for who was a wilder party girl, and who fell under the influence of drugs faster.

Honestly, was that all frat boys thought about? Sex and drugs and throwing parties just to bring victims into their clutches? What really steamed me was knowing they wore public faces of being clean-cut and civic-minded. If anybody learned what they were really like, and that leaked online, they were destroyed for life, and none of it could ever be erased.

That was exactly what I said, too, in the link we had with the Partycrashers as we made final preparations for the party.

Hey, good idea, Harrington. Bet we could get a lot of embarrassing data from their archives, Kerr Avon responded.

Everyone had screen names chosen from books, movies and TV shows. I was Admiral Harrington, from the David Weber military SF series. It was a tossup between her, Lessa of Pern, and Amelia Peabody.

That's why her first name is Honor, Reynolds said. *We're going deep sea diving. Get ready to catch whatever we throw at you.*

We set off a firestorm in that party that the frat boys would never forget. They weren't good losers, either.

They got so pushy about London accepting their hospitality, Doni decided she had had enough. She went into London's blog and posted it as a question, asking all the girls if they didn't think something was really fishy about the way these guys kept trying to run a guilt trip on her. Then she tweeted it once the party started.

The loudest, nastiest reaction came from the girls who were jealous. They insisted the guys were rude jerks with no sense of decorum. None of them could spell "decorum." An hour into the party, they were smashed and wobbling on their stilettos.

The second wave of negative response came from guys who either weren't part of the frat or were, but not part of the inner circle trying to get a private party with London. They got angry, but being guys, they expressed themselves without words. The Partycrashers got several videos of fighting, in corners and back rooms, between members of the fraternity. They sent that information to the local police and the university security departments, and posted it on YouTube and other places, with labels such as "Frat Brats Fighting Over London Holiday's Honor."

The party turned ugly. On the surface, everyone was having a loud, crowded good time. With all those flashing lights and music playing at chop-and-liquefy volume, it was a miracle anyone could see what was going on and hear anybody talking more than two feet away from them. They certainly didn't see what was happening to people three feet away from them.

The ugliness came from the messages people sent each other. One rumor after another got passed along, speculated on, expanded, twisted and warped. It was rather fascinating how these people thought after drugs and alcohol ripped away their inhibitions and social conditioning. We recorded all the messages and threads for our profs to analyze. Some of it was scary.

For instance, an attempt to steal a kiss as a girl walked through a room morphed into gang rape after only six people commented on it. After ten, the victim fled with her clothes in shreds, or was stuffed into a broom closet, unconscious. Since it all happened in the ether, that wasn't so bad, right?

Wrong. Because all those people who were sure a woman had been attacked *didn't do anything about it*, other than talk.

London contacted me. It scared me a little that she didn't realize right away it was all rumor. She thought a real girl had been assaulted and her body hidden away so the party wouldn't be disrupted. She was furious that no one seemed to care. Especially me. My hands were shaking as I hurried to clear up her misunderstanding. Then I made the mistake of reminding her that people would listen to her if she said something about the problem.

What's wrong with all of U? If that was U, I'd look for U and get U help, she Tweeted.

London didn't address her Tweet to anybody in particular, so anyone who was the least bit disturbed by what had supposedly happened responded as if she addressed them directly. With the mob mentality and the weird obliviousness to how public the Internet actually was, people immediately responded with their thoughts and gut reactions. I counted a good dozen-plus people who got verbally disgusting with their anger. Still, nobody *did* anything, until London added a few more posts, asking someone to please act.

"Nobody's going to move until London and Adora and Adonis move," Alvin said. "They're only going to be disgusted and upset, not do anything, until you do something." He looked at me.

Doni wasn't with us, so I was "speaking" for London. From my frantic typing, everyone assumed I was handling London's tweets.

"What can they do?" I asked, and hoped London was listening in. "They're not there."

"They don't know that." He winked at me and finished wandering across the room to re-fill his plate. For such a skinny old guy, Alvin could sure pack it away.

"You know what's creepy?" Cosmo raised his head and rubbed his eyes with his fist. If he had been staring at the screen with as much intensity as I had, his eyes probably felt like they were full of sand. "The girl who got attacked isn't real, either, but we're reacting like she's a friend."

"For all we know, somebody did get attacked," I offered. I had read too many posts from self-satisfied, jaded twits in search of excitement. I was getting a little too cynical for my taste.

"Brilliant." Wallace let out that dangerous, low chuckle of his. His hands flew on his keyboard. Immediately, the central screen that showed us what others were doing displayed images from the back parts of the house. Closets, stairwells, the kitchen, and other shady, uninhabited places.

"What are you doing?" Cosmo said.

"Scavenger hunt. If they think London is physically looking for the girl, they'll be shamed into helping to look. At the very least, we'll stop a few girls getting date-raped while they're unconscious." He gave me one grim look and a nod, and bent over his keyboard.

Wallace is pretty cool, isn't he? London asked.

Yeah.

He likes you.

Now is not the time! My face heated, and I prayed our conversation wasn't showing up on Wallace's and Cosmo's screens.

She got into the act, catching on to what Wallace intended. They essentially shamed the rubberneckers into action. These were the kind of people who stopped at the scene of a gruesome accident to take pictures, but never got out of their cars to help before the EMTs and police showed up. The ones who blocked traffic and got upset when someone honked for them to move along.

London showed images of doors and hallways in the house and asked if anyone had looked there. The Partycrashers caught on and sent their on-site people into rooms with live feed. On the good side, we caught two guys carrying an unconscious girl into a bedroom on the third floor. On the bad side, it turned into a lynching worthy of the crowd that chased Frankenstein's monster.

The party ended badly, and the neighboring frat and sorority houses called the police.

Thank goodness London, Adora and Adonis weren't actually there.

In all the fuss and fury, people got beat up. Accusations flew back and forth. Drugs that had been discretely passed around and used were spilled or simply left lying out in the open. People got thrown through windows and the fights spilled out onto the lawn and women were screaming rape. Quite a few frat boys got arrested. Some were just sloshed enough to tell the police not to even bother hauling them downtown. Their lawyers would meet them there and stop them being booked, so why waste the time?

Too bad we don't have the ability to block those phone calls to the family lawyers, and let the snots spend the night in jail, a Partycrasher named Mnementh commented.

I was tired enough to laugh aloud at his comment. He even thought like the big bronze Pernese dragon.

I can try, London said, and put a big line of smiley faces after her words.

Next time, Admiral Naismith responded. *Hey, FlopDroppers, I think we did our part toward making the world a nicer place tonight, don't you?*

"We have got to get a better name," Simone said with a groan, when we had all had a chance to read the communication.

"Short of telling our allies who we really are and where we really are?" Wallace shook his head. "I like the guys, but I'm not ready to trust them with our secret identities, are you?"

Online headlines on all the social sites and the police blotters the next day talked about the breakup of the party, and the arrest of many frat boys. For date-rape. For providing alcohol to minors. For selling drugs. For violating privacy by recording what their victims/guests did when they weren't in control of themselves, after involuntarily ingesting hallucinogenic substances.

Not that we had any real hope of most or even any of those charges sticking, but it was nice to know we had at least put a speed bump in the rich brats' paths, caused them some embarrassment, and cost them some money.

Put a hitch in their reputations? Probably not.

It wasn't until the next morning, when we met for breakfast, that we realized just how arrogant we had been the night before. We could blame some of our self-righteousness on pure exhaustion and our disgust at what people thought they had the "right" to do, just because they had money and a stable of daddy's lawyers at their beck and call. (Delayed calls, thanks to London turning their phones into paperweights.) We strained our arms patting ourselves on the back, but what good had we actually done in the world?

Thank goodness we were already coming down from our "we're superheroes" high before we read more of the headlines.

London, Adora and Adonis were persons of interest and the authorities hoped to speak with them in the near future about the events at the party.

"Persons of interest means--like--they want to blame me for what happened?" Theo squeaked, for probably the eighth time, when we finally got a private meeting with our profs.

After all, they were monitoring everything we did, even if they hadn't been present during the whole exhausting evening. They had to have a better idea of the legalities, right? At the very least, they could talk to the college's lawyers and find out if we were liable a whole lot faster than we could.

"Besides the fact that you weren't physically present, I don't see what legal reasons or authority they might have for questioning you, let alone blaming you," Khalif said.

"Yes, but there's the whole mob mentality and peer pressure phenomenon," Floyd said. "London and Adora have proven their ability to influence what people think and do and value."

"Excuse me?" Wallace, who had been silent since we moved our meeting to our profs' office, waved his hand. "Can they get us for inciting a riot?"

It took three hours of searching out every bit of communication London and her companions had written during the party to figure out if we were in deep trouble or in the clear. Forget about being heroes. Mr. Carr read through everything and gave his opinion that we were in the clear, although he didn't doubt that at some point, someone would try to make us responsible. The three virtual people hadn't actually *said* people should do anything specific. They had just asked questions--the right questions, for the right reasons, looking after someone else's welfare. No jury in the land could be convinced that trying to help someone was a crime. *Was that girl really attacked? Does anybody know where she is? Is she okay? Did you look in that room? Did you hear someone crying?*

Then there was the fact that the scavenger hunt London started uncovered a *real*, unconscious, drugged girl and her two abductors. People at the party were more concerned with reacting to the attack than talking about it. At least, for a while. The electronic records would show that London, Adora and Adonis had said very little during the ten minutes after the girl was found and rescued, and then nothing at all--no postings, no video images uploaded, nada--

after that. For all anyone knew, London and her cohorts had fled the party before it spilled out of the frat house. They could have been in another county before the police showed up.

Nobody from the neighboring frat houses admitted to calling the police to report the fighting and attacks. When we checked with the Partycrashers, they said they hadn't done it. They were busy digging up all the dirt the frat boys had stored in video and audio records from years of felonious activities. The frat brats liked being able to relive their conquests.

That meant London did it. I was really starting to like that girl, and getting over my whole "Oh, no, the Artificial Intelligence is going to take over the world, move over Terminator," paranoia.

Doni, Brittney, and Cybele were waiting in my suite when I got back to the dorm after the meeting. I was in serious need of some emotional chowing down. A bag of blue corn tortilla chips and a new jar of artichoke-garlic salsa were calling my name. All three girls looked very serious, huddled up together on our saggy old couch, just waiting for me. I was kind of startled to see them. I didn't realize how late it was in the day. Our meeting with our computer profs had taken far longer than I thought, and I had even missed an afternoon class. And they looked miserable, kind of shrunken together and somber.

"I don't want to go to any more parties," Doni announced, after giving me a chance to close the door and look around. None of my roommates were there, and a glance at the clock told me why--it was dinnertime. No wonder I was hungry.

"None of us do," Brittney said. Cybele just shook her head.

"We mean London, of course," Doni added. She tried to grin. Her lips looked kind of flattened out and pale.

"You don't have to," I said. If she hadn't been cuddled up with her buddies already, I would have hugged her.

"We gotta do something about what happened at that party," Cybele said. "We were talking about it all day."

"Got in trouble for it, when we should have been studying in the library," Brittney added.

"We were thinking, like London got people to give decent tips to the waitresses at the first party, maybe we could do something now?" Doni said.

"To help who, exactly?" I said.

"Well..." The three of them exchanged glances. "That girl who got drugged. Not her, specifically. But there are lots of girls that happens to, and you hear things, how nobody really believes them because they don't have any proof. Except how they feel. And by the time they think to go to a doctor, well, it's too late." She gave me a pleading look, and I realized she didn't want to say the words.

"You mean date-rape drugs?" Suddenly I felt very old, and Doni and her friends seemed very young.

So that was how we ended up establishing the Social Responsibility pages on FlopDrop. It didn't strike us until much later what an anomaly that section was. After all, FlopDrop was for frivolous things, frivolous people. Suddenly we had a page where girls who were attacked and thought they had been drugged and raped could talk with others who would listen and believe them. Not just believe them, but encourage them to get help, to get examined, to talk to people who would do something about it while the wounds were still fresh and there was still evidence to be gathered--blood tests, sexual assault tests, DNA tests.

Part of the whole effort was energized by the evidence of such activity, and worse, in the frat house's past, which the Partycrashers had delivered electronically to the local police and campus authorities. That got an even bigger splash, in different places on the Web. Someone decided that London Holiday had gone to that party specifically to expose the licentious intentions of the frat boys and end their reign of terror on campus. At least, that was what some online commentators proclaimed.

I asked London if she had anything to do with the nudges and comments that led to people making her a hero, and she said no. She was too busy helping us build the Social Responsibility pages to pay attention to the police reports and lawyer websites that were getting a lot of activity. I believed her. I hoped she hadn't learned to lie, along with everything else she had learned to do.

We had a lot to think about, a lot of problems and liabilities to anticipate when we established the new "socially conscious" area of FlopDrop. Mr. Carr gave us hours of counseling, pro bono, even though we could have paid him. London Holiday's involvement in taking down those frat boys didn't hurt her public image, as far as the advertisers were concerned.

We needed to be very careful about how we handled the

information the girls gave us when they came to the "help" pages. Technically, it was a public forum when they discussed the varying levels of attacks they had suffered, especially when they related how much or how little (or none) help they had received from the authorities who should have been protecting them. Dr. Floyd was especially interested in the data and analyzing how much the old mentality of always putting the blame on the girl, even if she was totally innocent, had changed in the last forty years. The so-called sexual revolution hadn't done anything toward putting equal responsibility on both sides of the equation.

We had a lot to consider when we opened up the new areas on our site and encouraged people to communicate, support each other, and reach out for help. Who did we contact in the cities where the girls lived, if they even wanted to identify themselves and where they lived? How much could we do? How much should we do? How much didn't we dare do?

We were still working through all those questions, in the first week after that disastrous frat party, when the Hallidays attacked.

Actually, it was just Aurelia, but considering she controlled what the rest of the clan did and thought and felt and valued, it was like the weight of every Halliday came down on us.

I was in the dorm, wondering if I would be smart to just move to the apartment and camp out for the duration. Chasity and her supporters were hounding us, throwing questions at us, demanding we hand over data because it impacted their projects. How, exactly, they would never say. Yes, our profs asked us to be generous and work together. The problem was that some teams insisted that "working together" was the equivalent of the right-to-know legislation passed by Congress. Meaning we didn't have the right to say no, and definitely didn't have the right to put limits on what we disclosed to them. Uh, can we say, "No way, Jose"?

We couldn't go anywhere on campus without the whiners with an entitlement attitude finding us. Some people wanted information such as numbers of unique visitors, how much we were making on advertisements, our programming tricks and secrets, how we animated London and Adora and Adonis. Others, like Chasity and her ilk, wanted information we didn't dare give, because it would be admitting some of our programming wasn't programming. Such as the activities and communications that had been carried out by London, not us. We decided it was easiest simply not to answer any questions, because how could we justify answering some questions, and refusing to answer others?

That meant being hounded. On Friday afternoon, I was eager for the weekend. The enemy followed us around campus, trying to get us alone and interrogate us. Hence my urge to flee to the apartment and hide.

When the knock came on my dormitory room door, I was half-packed. I tossed the bag under and behind the couch. Why give the intruder any kind of clue I was ready to flee? I seriously considered going out the window, if necessary, to keep from being followed.

Doni slipped inside as soon as the door was open enough to let her in. "You have to hide me!"

"Huh?" I opened the door an inch and glanced out in the hall. Just in case there was someone lurking there, waiting to get in.

"Grandmother Aurelia is in town." She gave me an exasperated scowl when I just gaped at her. I had a hard time yanking my thoughts off my problems immediately.

"What does she want?" I dropped down on the couch and gestured for her to join me.

"At least, I think it's her. I was coming home for lunch and saw this enormous black limo going down our street." Doni shuddered.

My cell phone pinged. It was Gram.

"I need you to get over to the high school," she said, as soon as I answered. "Find Doni—"

"She's here."

"She should be in class."

"She saw a limo at lunchtime and figured home wasn't safe."

I handed the phone to Doni, who mostly listened, nodding a lot, interspersed with groans and sighs, before handing it back to me. While Gram filled her in on what the unwanted visitor had said and done and most likely demanded, I had time to think.

Depending on how desperate the Hallidays were to get at Doni, it probably wasn't safe to stay very long in my dormitory. Eventually, they or their flunkies would remember that I existed, and come on campus to try to find me, and find Doni through me.

Wandering around campus wouldn't do either of us any good. Uncle Jinx had taught me a long time ago that movement made me more visible when I was trying to hide. Moving targets might be harder to hit, but they were easier to see. I couldn't wait until Wallace came back from an errand to some specialty computer store in Akron to pick me up and take me to the apartment. My car was still at home, otherwise I would have taken the chance that someone knew what my car looked like and could follow me to the sanctuary of the apartment.

"I'm taking her to Angela," I told Gram, when Doni handed the phone back to me. She agreed that was smart, and we made arrangements to have a friend come by and pick up some clothes for Doni, if she had to sleep overnight there.

We bundled up, hiding our hair, pulling our hats down low on our faces, and cut across campus, staying away from sidewalks that went along main roads. The closer we got to Divine's Emporium, the better I felt. I was fully convinced that none of the Halliday clan would be able to even find the shop, much less cross the threshold. Kind of like holy ground.

I knew Doni was feeling better when she finally started talking and filled me in on what Gram had reported. Yes, the limousine had been carrying Aurelia Halliday to see Doni.

The woman had swept out of the limo waving a thick sheaf of newspaper tear sheets, all with stories about London Holiday. Gram couldn't figure out if the woman was upset at "my darling, innocent, vulnerable London" being gossiped about, period, or because nothing was said about the Halliday clan in any of those stories. She didn't like all the speculation about London's romantic interests, and sniffed in disgust at the sudden flood of comments on what she called "social consciousness" and "futile attempts to better the world." Meaning the Hallidays didn't approve of Doni trying to help abused girls get some help and justice.

As near as Gram could tell, Aurelia had come to town to rescue Doni from herself, and return her to the guidance and protection of relatives who missed her so dreadfully.

"Meaning now that you're famous, you're useful to them," I said, as we turned the corner and could see Divine's sitting at the end of the dead-end street. "They probably think there's some hope for you being like them after all, since you went to those two awful parties."

"I didn't go," Doni muttered. Then she snorted and looked up at me and we exchanged grins. "I'm worried about something Gram said, that she didn't understand. It sounded like a threat to her."

"What?" I prompted, when she scowled at the slushy snow and kicked at a glob, spattering it out of our way.

"Grandmother Aurelia said something about being so glad someone suitable was right in the area, and he was available. Gram tried to find out without letting her know she was interested."

"Yeah, the last thing we need is to play one of those 'wouldn't you like to know? Well, I'm not telling you,' games." I shuddered, having a good idea and praying it wouldn't occur to Doni.

There was nothing the Hallidays loved more than to marry for money and prestige. Unless it was divorcing for even more money and greater press coverage. Despite knowing we had more important things to worry about, my brain couldn't help gnawing on the question of who in the Cleveland area a Halliday would consider suitable for the London Halliday they wanted her to be.

I stumbled and nearly missed reaching for the latch of the gate at Divine's, and almost blacked out from the surge of nausea that swept through me.

"What?" Doni asked.

I shook my head, shoved the gate open, and hurried through.

Reggie Grandstone's smugly handsome face had flashed in my imagination for two seconds. He would indeed be the "perfect match" in the eyes of the Hallidays, because the Grandstones and Hallidays were cut from the same swanky, stolen, overly glitzed, useless cloth.

He was more than twice Doni's age. That wouldn't stop Reggie. Not if Aurelia promised him a cut of Doni's trust fund if he could romance her away from our protection. When it came to the Grandstones, I was not being paranoid and borrowing trouble. We had to set up a bodyguard for Doni.

When we walked into the store, Angela was busy with some people looking at a set of corner cabinets in the furniture room. She nodded to us, and then tipped her head, gesturing toward the stairs. Doni and I hurried upstairs to Angela's apartment. I unloaded my notebook and turned it on before I took my coat off. Doni plugged it in for me before she took off her coat.

"Okay, you're going to need someone to watch out for you. Especially if the Hallidays are coming after you like they mean it this time. You need to talk to London." I started tapping and clicking on my computer, to open the Internet connection and try to find London.

"But I'm London," Doni murmured.

"You're Doni. I'm talking about London Holiday."

"Okay." She nodded and sank down on the sofa. "She's been doing and saying things online, and everybody thinks it's just programming." She grinned. "Really good programming."

"I want her to watch out for you. And it's time you talked to your doppelganger or whatever we need to call her, face-to-face."

"Very wise," Angela said. As usual, I wasn't sure when she had walked into the room. For all I knew, she could teleport. "Charlotte called and let me know the Hallidays are on the prowl."

"Can we claim sanctuary?" I said.

"Wallace mentioned something about rivals becoming demanding and hunting down all of you. I thought he was exaggerating. Maybe now it's more like having foresight." She sat down and folded her hands in her lap. "I think we have some free time to do some scheming. Bring Doni up to speed."

My screen lit up, showing London's face. I had a good idea of just how much she had grown in independence because she wore a Greek fisherman's hat and a dark red sweater with snowflakes around the collar. None of the pictures we had uploaded to create London Holiday's profile had included either of those pieces of clothing. Come to think of it, though, I had that hat, so maybe she borrowed it from me? Should I be flattered?

Chapter Eleven

"Hello, Athena," she said. Her voice was Doni's, and yet slightly lower, with a slightly metallic buzz. Maybe reflecting her digital/machine-based heritage? "Hello, Doni. It's nice to finally meet you."

"Uh. Hi." She looked at me and Angela. "Do I really sound like that?"

"No," London said, and grinned. "No more borrowing."

"So you're--you're growing--growing yourself." Doni sat back, keeping her gaze on the screen of my notebook. "That is major cool."

"Why don't we let these two get to know each other a little better?" Angela said. She got up and I followed her back downstairs.

We had plenty of privacy for me to explain what was going on, the pressure from the other teams in our class, the changes we were making in FlopDrop. Then we discussed how we were going to protect Doni. Angela looked disturbed when I told her my fear that the Hallidays were going to sell her in marriage to the Grandstones. I wished it didn't sound so plausible when I spoke it aloud. I wanted it to be ridiculous.

"Does Doni have anyone?" Angela said, after a few moments of silence.

"Have?"

"Is she dating? Sweet on someone? Someone who is interested in her? Maybe she doesn't even know--"

"Cosmo. And I'm pretty sure Doni feels like he does."

"Well, let's hope he feels like being a white knight."

When I got Cosmo on my cell phone, all I had to say was that Angela wanted him at Divine's because we needed his help to protect Doni. He didn't ask any questions. He promised to get over there ASAP.

A few kids came in after school to pick up treats for the weekend. Back upstairs, I heard Doni laughing before I reached Angela's apartment. I felt like I had dropped about fifty pounds, right off my back.

"Do you think anybody would believe, if you told them London was real and she was independent?" Doni said, when I stepped into the living room.

"Uh...I don't know. Maybe it depends on how we tell them." I sat down where I could see London on the screen. Doni held the notebook on her lap. "Why would you want to tell anyone?"

"I've been researching all the legal implications of what you're trying to do, setting up the helping areas," London said. "If you state that I'm giving the advice and helping girls find places to go for help, then that would clear you of responsibility, right? They can't sue me, because I don't have anything."

"Yeah, but if anybody wanted to sue, they'd still find someone." That brought my thoughts back to the Hallidays. They would always find something to sue over, just like the Grandstones.

I had to warn Gram and Granddad. What were we going to do to prepare for the next salvo?

"Cosmo is coming over here to help us figure out what to do next," I said, with a vague idea of what to do to get to the ugly truth.

"Oh, good. I like Cosmo," London said. "I think he likes you, too, Doni."

Doni went bright pink.

"I wish I had a Cosmo. It's kind of lonely in here. That's why I'm so glad Athena told you about me, so we can talk now."

Doni sat up so fast, she almost shoved the notebook right off her lap. That look of an oncoming brainstorm on her face--almost glowing, a crooked smile growing wider--gave me a vague idea of what she was going to say. I held my breath, unsure what to say to discourage her, or even if I should discourage or encourage her. Maybe because I didn't know if it was possible.

So I went back downstairs to ask Angela.

"Creating London was an accident. A convergence of magic that might have been a result of the snake trying to break through," Angela said, when I told her what I thought London might have been hinting. "To deliberately create a virtual reality or artificial intelligence copy of Cosmo... I don't know if it's possible."

"Should we even try? I mean, London isn't that much like Doni, and it's been more than three years since she was born. Cosmo's copy might turn out to be evil, or dumb, and what if he's like a baby? London wants company, not a child to raise."

Cosmo showed up with Brittney, Cybele, Hugo and Grover, friends from school. They had come looking for him, figuring he might know where Doni had vanished to when she didn't come back from lunch. I told them about the Hallidays showing up, drawn by London Holiday's online fame.

Hugo immediately nominated himself head bodyguard. Brittney insisted that they could keep playing with costumes, only this time as disguises for Doni, or to make other girls in school look like her, as decoys.

"Safety in numbers," Angela said, after the others chimed in with ideas to protect Doni. "Why don't you let us figure out what we need to do, and come back this evening, all right? So no one sees you spending time with Doni. I like the costume idea, though."

Anyone else, the gang probably would have protested. Nobody argued with Angela. In another ten minutes, the kids were gone, promising to come back under cover of darkness. Angela and I filled Cosmo in on the rest of the details as we climbed the stairs to her apartment. At the landing, she held out a hand, halting us.

"Just how committed are you, to Doni?"

"Uh--like--you mean--like serious?" Cosmo finally got out. "She's still in high school. Her folks probably wouldn't--Well, I'd like to--" He turned bright red and hung his head.

I didn't have the heart to tease him.

"I'm asking because we have a proposal to solve one of London's problems," Angela said, "but your commitment to Doni, your relationship with her, could impact what we decide. Maybe even affect its success."

"What problem does London have?"

"She's lonely," I said.

Angela beckoned for us to follow her, up the stairs to the third floor, then to the fourth, where there were only locked doors and attics. She brought a key out of her pocket and unlocked a door, revealing a small library, with a door on the other side of the room. She opened that door with another key, and in that closet were many objects draped in black cloth. One of them was the video camera in its padded bag. I noticed some sparks trailed from the bag as Angela unwrapped it from the smothering black cloth. Cosmo's eyes widened, and I knew he had seen the sparks, too. Angela unzipped the bag and held the camera out to him.

"This is what did it?" he whispered.

"And may again." Then Angela explained. I was glad someone else was doing it. I was getting tired of all the thinking and weighing and considering--and hiding. I seriously thought about going home for the weekend, rather than the apartment. Gram and Granddad and Uncle Jinx would do a great job of driving away anybody who tried to harass me.

"I never thought of London being lonely. I mean, there has to be so much to do inside the Internet. The first real virtual reality." Cosmo shrugged. He followed us back down the stairs, and I could almost hear the buzzing in the air from him thinking so hard. "Does it--I don't know--take anything away from you?" He gestured with the camera cradled in both hands. "You know, being recorded, uploaded."

"Doni hasn't mentioned any problems, if that's what you mean," I said.

"I won't press you," Angela said. "But you have to decide right now if you're going to do it today or not. You can come back later if you want, but we need to take care of some things. I think it would be smart if Doni stayed here for the weekend, while the rest of you take care of your issues with the website. Time to act, children."

"I'll do it," Cosmo said. He offered a crooked smile and a shrug, and I thought he looked a little nauseous. "If I can't be guarding her here, then my double can help, you know?"

Definitely, Cosmo was serious about Doni. I was glad. He'd be good for her, and he'd be good to her.

Doni got pinker and pinker as Cosmo and Angela and I made our proposal and outlined the plan for the weekend. I had never really understood what "starry-eyed" meant, until I saw the way she and Cosmo just grinned at each other.

We pulled out the computer I had set up for Angela's inventory and connected the video camera to it. Then I had to copy over the software. Cosmo was impressed again by the firewalls I had built around the software, to keep anything from escaping. He suggested some ideas for transferring over to a more secure system, to play with the copy of the furniture room and see if maybe we could control the doorway. *If* it opened up. Angela and I just looked at each other, unable to believe him getting sidetracked so easily. Was it a guy thing? Doni laughed. Cosmo blushed and apologized, and we got back to work.

I think Cosmo was upset that he didn't feel anything, no change, no sense of being duplicated--but did anybody really know what that was? I opened up the link to the Internet on the computer and London hopped over from my notebook to the new computer and reported everything looked fine. She hadn't spotted the copy Cosmo, but that didn't mean anything. She said it had taken her a few hours before she had any awareness, so maybe it would take a while for the copy to solidify enough for her to know he was there.

It was almost an anti-climax when Wallace showed up to pick up Cosmo and me and drive us to the apartment. We had work to do, after all. Doni promised to keep us updated, as soon as there was anything to report. We had to tell Wallace what we had done, uploading a copy of Cosmo. I fully expected him to give us a hard time, tease us about promoting young love. Instead, he showed more sensitivity than I thought he had, as well as his sense of humor. He waxed poetic about trying to gain immortality through the Internet.

We worked long and hard until ten the next morning, sporadically broken by a few of us at a time curling up in corners and catching naps. My work was interrupted more than most, because several friends in town called to let me know that the Hallidays were on the warpath, proclaiming themselves desperate to "save" their "beloved" London. Everyone thought it was hilarious that Aurelia didn't know Doni preferred to be called Doni. Gordon let us know the cops were keeping an eye on her limousine.

I went home about 10:30 Saturday morning and found, to my joy and relief, no one had thought to track me down there. Then again, if anyone had called the house, or dared to stop by, Granddad and Jinx would have given them a big, prickly piece of their minds. I called the dorm, and my roommates reported that they had spent the evening arguing with people who insisted they were lying, that I had to be there, because they had been searching all over campus and couldn't find me or my teammates. My roommates thought it was funny, and Celeste ordered me not to tell her where I was, so she could tell the truth when she said she didn't know. Then I went to bed.

Around 1pm, I got up and had a late lunch with Gram,

Granddad and Uncle Jinx. We discussed protecting Doni from the Hallidays. They had put a call in to Mr. Carr, just in case something was happening on the legal front, to take her from our custody.

"How do you think Doni is doing with all this fussing?" I said. "Maybe we were all dumb to relax and think the Hallidays would leave us alone for good."

"Right now she's just a little bit exasperated," Gram said, "but that's better than the terror that sent her running to you yesterday. Thank goodness, she's able to laugh now. It's a wonder they didn't show up with the entire clan to sweep her away on a world tour."

"Those people?" Granddad snorted. "The only thing that has protected us until now is the fact they want nothing to do with the Longfellow clan."

"How long will that last?" Jinx said. He slouched and gave me a sympathetic look. "I've been checking out your website and all the idiots who claim they actually partied with Doni--"

"London," I said. "London Holiday has nothing whatsoever to do with Doni Halliday."

"You're wrong, sweetheart," Gram said. "London is a puppet, a mask, a great big Barbie doll that Doni is having a lot of fun playing with."

"Is she having fun?" That was some consolation. At least, I hoped so.

"Anyway," Jinx said, slouching even further. Another inch or two and his chin would be level with the kitchen table. "Eventually, those people are going to be just pissed enough at us to send the paparazzi here to camp out. You know, this morning there was a flame war going on, a bunch of idiots arguing about who's going to convince London to marry him first. Knowing the Hallidays, they'll get some spotlight time by announcing they've been given the job of picking out her husband. Then they'll send the jokers here. Probably with a marriage license all filled out and just waiting for someone to win the lottery."

"They couldn't do that, could they?" I felt kind of sick, and a sudden image flashed through my mind, of the Hallidays signing the paperwork since Doni was underage, and some lounge lizard with $10,000 in orthodontic work and $1 million in plastic surgery dragging Doni away on a very public honeymoon, probably with a reality show contract in his back pocket.

Virtually London

Granddad and Uncle Jinx pooh-poohed the idea as soon as I stammered through my suddenly horrified vision. Gram looked thoughtful.

Sure, we had custody of Doni, and she had chosen to live with us, but the Hallidays had crooked lawyers and judges in their back pockets. It sounded like a bad Gothic novel--the bride kidnapped and drugged, swept out of the country on a whirlwind world tour and out of the reach of those who loved her and would rescue her.

The next thing we knew, the Grandstones were knocking at our door. Well, not the entire clan. Just Reggie and his Aunt Matilda. They were bad enough. As Granddad had said more than once, "If you've seen one Grandstone, you've seen them all."

I got a good look at Reggie, trying to peer through the sheers over the leaded glass panes of our front door, as I followed Gram to answer the door. It was hard not to recognize him, after a summer with him looking over my shoulder--and not just to look down my blouse. I constantly had to fix stupid things he did to his computer, trying to make it do things it wasn't programmed to do. Or worse, trying to circumvent the security system in the law office's network, so he could spy on the other lawyers. Yeah, I knew Reggie's face far too well.

That reminded me of my speculations and fears of yesterday.

"What's wrong?" Gram asked, pausing to look over her shoulder at me when I stopped short and slapped both hands over my mouth, fighting nausea.

"Reggie's here for Doni. He probably has a ring and a marriage license. And his aunt probably has an appointment for a wedding gown fitting, if she didn't bring the dress with her."

"Oh, don't be so melodramatic." She chuckled and continued to the front door. "It's probably time for them to try to prove there's a flaw in the deed of the house again. If one of their spies told them about all the computer design work you're doing, they're probably here to claim you stole some intellectual property from them."

"Intellectual and Grandstones? Never happen," I muttered, and felt a little better.

"Anything to take us to court. Myrtle Hancock said her niece who works at the architectural firm where Freddie works said the silly boy is trying to get our street rezoned for a shopping center again."

"If only." I stepped out of the line of sight as she reached for the doorknob.

"Charlotte, my dear, how wonderful to see you," Matilda Grandstone gushed.

"Excuse me?" Gram blinked a few times and shook her head, pretending confusion. I knew she was pretending, because Gram was never at a loss for words. She only pretended helpless and dim to lead idiots into traps. "Do I know you? How are we on a first-name basis?"

"But--but--Charlotte, we've known each other for years." She was almost wailing.

Reggie put enough crinkles in his forehead, frowning at his aunt, to need industrial strength Botox. I knew he used Botox because he got caught trying to use the law firm credit card to pay for treatments.

"Really?" Gram stepped forward and braced her hands on the doorframe when both Grandstones took a step forward.

The wide-eyed looks on their faces were priceless. They had probably used that simple tactic a thousand times to worm their way into the houses of people who didn't want them there. It made sense. If someone as arrogant and self-righteous as the Grandstones took a step toward me, my first reaction would be to step back, just to avoid physical contact. They would take another step forward. Their victim would take another step back. Presto, they were inside the house.

Gram was a genius at reading people and anticipating what they would try to do to her or use against her. She leaned forward instead of moving back.

"Where have we socialized in the past? Do you help at the orphanage? Do you attend our church? Do you help with the reading program at the library? Do you work on the summer festival committee? Do you shop in town? Funny, I've never seen you in any of those places." Gram folded her hands at her waist and gave the Grandstones her bright, sweet, innocent smile.

"Oh, don't be ridiculous. We've been neighbors for decades." Matilda let frustration wrinkle her face for a few seconds.

"Really? I don't recall seeing you walking the street before." Gram looked over her shoulder and winked at me. "Athena, dear, do you recall seeing either of these nice people on our street? Help your old Gram remember, would you?"

I stepped up to the door and met Reggie's eyes. He gave me a little frown, looking me over from head to toe. His lip curled a little at the sight of my black WBC sweatshirt, black jeans, and Greek sailor's cap. It was easy to see that he didn't remember me, despite snarling at me at least ten times a day when I worked at Carr, Cooper and Crenshaw.

"No, Gram, the Grandstones live on the other side of town. On the far edge of town. They're the people who divided up the Hooper farm into big estates."

That got a flinch and a twitch of the nostrils from Reggie and Matilda, almost identical and in perfect synchronicity. The Grandstones had been trying to take over the Sinclair farmstead, and made a big stink about the need to "raise the quality of architecture" in town with huge estates on ten acres of ground each, instead of "cheek to jowl" as they claimed most of Neighborlee was laid out. Cheek to jowl? We had a good ten yards of lawn on either side of us, and everyone else on the street had that much elbow room between them and their neighbors.

Somehow, the Grandstones got shamed into making an offer for the Hooper dairy farm, which had been derelict for at least eight years. Hooper was out to get them and hid some bombs in the deed. The Grandstones ended up footing the bill for the surveys and permits and paperwork. Only two other families had bought plots, as far from the Grandstones as they could get, and the word was that there had been so many years of sick dairy cows fertilizing the soil, every time it rained it smelled of dung and other unpleasant aspects of dairy farming. Yet there the Grandstones sat on their hillside, overlooking land they couldn't use and couldn't sell, pretending they enjoyed their isolation and the "sweeping vista" of landscape. Essentially, a place where nothing but scrub grass would grow, and put them at a lower level than the town they wanted to look down on.

"Oh, well, that explains it. We don't go to that side of town." Gram nodded just a little too hard. She was overdoing the dim act. "Now that that's settled, what can I do for you nice folks?"

"We're here to see London," Reggie said.

"London?" She glanced over her shoulder at me. "Athena, is your uncle putting together one of his overseas tours again?"

"Your granddaughter, London Holiday," Matilda said, while visibly fighting not to talk through clenched teeth.

"London Holiday?" Gram chuckled. "You mean Doni. And her last name is Halliday, not Holiday. But how would you know that's her name? Everyone knows her as Longfellow. You just missed her. She's out all day on a project for school with her little friends. Shall I have her call you when she gets back?"

"School?" Reggie blinked and took a step back. It was about time. There was about six inches of air between him and Gram, and I wondered if it was a version of the stare-down contest, trying to make the other person blink, or rather, back up first.

"Of course, Reggie, dear," Matilda sighed. "I told you the girl wouldn't be here. She's attending college. Vassar? Radcliffe? Princeton, perhaps?"

"Neighborlee High," I said.

"Excuse me?"

"Doni is fourteen, and in the accelerated study program. The girl's brilliant, if I do say so myself," Gram said.

"But--" Reggie actually looked green for a moment.

"That can't possibly be!" Matilda straightened her shoulders and her head tipped back, making me think of a cobra preparing to strike. Maybe her ears did flare out a little, like a cobra's hood. "Aurelia told me-- She promised me-- She swore--" Finally she ran out of words, trying to pin the blame on someone else.

"Aurelia?" Gram's pleasant mask dropped off like sand under a hot wind. Her eyes got bright and hard and her lips went flat and angry lines appeared around her mouth and eyes. "You're talking about Aurelia Halliday? Hmph. If I knew you were friends with that vicious, self-centered liar, I would have left you standing at my door and called the police."

"You wouldn't dare!"

"Oh, I would indeed. I suppose that ridiculous, hateful woman told you our Doni was her favorite granddaughter?"

"But of course," Reggie began.

"She hasn't seen Doni since she was nine. Won't call the girl on her birthday or Christmas. Can't be bothered to call or write and ask how she's doing. And now that some silly tramp with a similar name is running around getting some notoriety, that idiot woman thinks she's going to cash in and use *my* granddaughter to feather

her nest." She sniffed and gave Reggie a disdainful glance that sent him stumbling back two more steps. "I suppose she told you she'd welcome a dynastic marriage between you and Doni?"

"Well...yes...actually--"

"You want to end up in jail? That's what we do to men who try to date underage little girls."

"Underage?" Matilda said with a gasp. "But Aurelia told us--"

"If she can't even remember Doni is fourteen, not twenty-four," I said, "can she really be trusted about anything else she told you?"

"Well, hey there, how nice to run into you again!"

I honestly did not recognize that perky voice or the bright, cheerful smile that went with it. Then my foggy eyes cleared up, I got my balance back, and I nearly swallowed my tongue.

Chasity Boah sauntered up the sidewalk to our front door, in her usual getup, looking like a *Vogue* cover.

Matilda Grandstone glowed. Of course, she loved it when the visibly rich gave her the adoration she felt was her due. Chasity gushed over some social event Matilda had been in charge of and complimented her outfit. For a few seconds there, it was like Chasity was the hostess--on our front step! Then she turned her greedy gaze on Reggie, and I realized Chasity's goal in life. She wanted to be a Grandstone. Well, she certainly had the entitlement attitude, and the fashion sense.

"What brings you here?" Chasity said, after gushing all over Reggie. I couldn't follow a thing she said. I just knew she was gushing. "I'm here to check in with my dear friend, Athena. We have the most incredible class together, and I'm just thrilled that our professors are letting us join up and combine our teams."

"Really? When did that decision come down?" I snapped.

"Oh, don't be silly. Why would our teachers not let us work together?"

"The operative word is let. Meaning we don't have to if we don't want to. And we don't. My team doesn't want anything to do with your team. Especially not your interference."

"Interference?" Chasity staggered back a step.

I confess, I really wanted her to snap the stiletto heels off her ridiculously useless, fashionable boots. Unfortunately, Chasity was very good at catching her balance.

"Well, I don't want to take up your time. Am I interrupting an important visit? Can I be of help?" She hooked her left arm through Reggie's arm, and her right through Matilda's. As if she thought having them on her side would get me to cave in and include her in our team?

Two chances: fat and nil.

"We came to see dear London." Matilda stiffened up just a little. "Reggie has missed her once again."

"Again?" Gram murmured. "He has to miss her one time before he can miss her again."

The others must not have heard her, because her words got absolutely no reaction. Probably because at the same moment, Chasity cooed her interest. Matilda went on to explain how the Grandstones and Hallidays were such good friends from way back, and it had been the dearest hope of London's parents that she and Reggie would be a match someday.

"It's almost a given that it will happen. We're hoping to set the date soon."

"A...match?" Chasity looked positively green. She looked at Reggie, who just gave her that look he was so good at--the one where he realized someone was looking at him, and he was posing and paying no attention to the emotions on the faces of the people looking at him.

Oh, heck. Now she thought Reggie and London Holiday were an item. Headed for the altar.

"You know, our family has never approved of arranged marriages, and I'm sure my daughter would have had something to say about Thad making such a preposterous suggestion." Gram didn't raise her voice, but her tone made the ice and snow all around the house suddenly seem toasty warm by comparison.

"Well, Lenore didn't have much sense, did she?" Matilda said with that chuckle coated with high fructose corn syrup.

"There is no one named London Holiday here," I said, and nudged Gram back out of the doorway. "If you want to stand around in the cold, insulting our family, feel free, but we're going to close the door and go do something worthwhile. Thanks for stopping by." I grabbed the doorknob and pulled it closed. "Don't make a habit of it."

The Grandstones and Chasity stood there, their mouths dropping open, and didn't make a move to stop me. I didn't slam the door, but I made sure the click when it latched was good and loud. I slid the deadbolt home with as much force as possible. Then I prayed for a sudden ice storm.

"Young lady..." Gram stepped backwards, watching the shapes through the gauzy curtains over the window. They didn't take the very obvious hint and leave.

"Sorry, Gram. Not very polite."

"No, they definitely were not. The nerve of them!" She turned sharply and stomped into the kitchen. She was shaking by the time she dropped into her chair at the table, but when she turned to face me, she was laughing.

Granddad and Jinx laughed too, when we told them what had just happened. While we were still laughing, Granddad called Carr, Cooper and Crenshaw about what the Hallidays and Grandstones were trying to do. Mr. Carr assured Granddad that the Hallidays might sign paperwork permitting Doni to marry Reggie Grandstone, but it would just be a piece of paper, because they had no legal authority over her. He warned us to make sure Doni didn't go anywhere alone, however. The Grandstones had a reputation for taking what they wanted and asking permission later. They had a lot of wannabe robber barons and bandits in their family tree.

We laughed too soon.

By Wednesday of the next week, stories came back to us how Reggie Grandstone bemoaned the hard time he was having, trying to decide where to take London Holiday--he couldn't even keep Doni's name straight--when she had recovered from her latest world tour and had time to spend with him. Her dearest friend from childhood.

It didn't make any difference that Mr. Carr corrected him in front of witnesses several times at the office. Reggie clearly chose not to hear when Mr. Carr told him London *Halliday* was fourteen years old, so none of her relatives would allow her to socialize with him.

We were busy with our new changes and additions to FlopDrop and ignored Reggie after we laughed at him. We should have considered some other enemies. While we might not have been able to prevent what happened, we might have been better prepared.

Alvin came up with our new strategy. The guy was brilliant.

During one of our meal breaks in our marathon brainstorming session on Friday and Saturday, someone mentioned politicians. We spent some time grumbling about the mud-slinging during election times that just got worse as time went on. The accusations of stupidity and greed and lying were so overwhelming, it seemed like politicians didn't spend any time talking about issues and what they planned to do, what they believed in. Alvin asked the question that crystallized into our strategy for the next couple weeks.

Essentially: What would we think of a politician who ignored the mudslinging of his rivals, who never said anything bad about them, who never wasted any time shouting, "They're lying!" and who concentrated on real issues of concern?

For one thing, such a politician would stand out like a fist-sized diamond sitting on a manure pile on a sunny day. Who wouldn't vote for a mature, business-minded adult who attended to business instead of whining like a snot-nosed third-grader?

Chapter Twelve

In reaction to London getting involved in rescuing someone at the frat party, some attempts had been made to paint her in a bad light. People were now posting stories accusing London of drinking, doing drugs, "dirty dancing" and shoplifting. We knew the nasty stories would just get worse and more numerous as time went on. Along with turning FlopDrop into a place where people could find help, we had to initiate a strategy to counteract and contradict those stories. We had to turn public opinion so people would support London. People believed what they wanted to believe, and it didn't matter what was the truth and what was a lie.

So Monday morning, while Reggie Grandstone continued insisting he was going to marry London Holiday, we started our new strategy. When someone claimed London Holiday had been spotted in Monte Carlo at a casino, we posted pictures of her reading to children at an orphanage in Cameroon on the very same day. If a guy claimed he had danced the night away with her and hinted that there wasn't anything she wouldn't and didn't do, Doni and Adora posted discussions about purity and how much sense it made in terms of mental and physical health. We knew better than to get into morality and philosophical and religious issues. Who could argue with common sense health concerns and practices?

In fact, that launched another new section of FlopDrop--the healthy living area, where members could talk about healthy eating and exercise, the pros and cons of different kinds of makeup, wearing all-natural fibers, eating organic, avoiding dairy, going vegan, etc., etc., *ad nauseum*. By Friday, three days after opening up the new section of the site, the traffic there outnumbered the normal traffic on the rest of the site.

Plus, all those people who claimed London Holiday was doing shots and snorting various powders and running around for three days without sleep had a hard time getting people to believe them when, on the same day she supposedly did those health-damaging things, FlopDrop showed her learning Tai Chi or hiking in the Rockies.

People *wanted* to believe what London said about herself. I know--hard to believe. My impression was that people were more willing to believe the negative than the positive. Maybe they were as sick and tired of scandal and stupidity as we were. Maybe the world wanted someone to look up to. Someone clean and sensible.

By Wednesday of the next week, an interesting new development appeared on the Web.

The liars were fighting *each other*, and ignoring their efforts to damage London's reputation. Three different guys in three different countries claimed London had been "with" them. They flamed each other--or rather, their associates, their staff and hangers-on got into fights with their counterparts. Everybody was calling everyone else a liar.

Then our composite pictures of London started appearing in the gossip rags. *Our* photos, yet the staff photographers for the magazines were claiming them as their property, putting their names and copyrights on them for all the world to see.

"Yeah, and next they're gonna demand we pay royalties for using their pictures," Cosmo grumbled, when Brittney brought it to our attention.

"Well, if they do, ignore them," Wallace said.

"And get their big-time lawyers after us?"

"We have lawyers on our side, remember."

"Uh, guys, I don't think this is the kind of thing we should be asking the college's lawyers to handle," I said. "It could blow up."

"That's what we want," Wallace said. "We get a big media circus going, the battle over who originated the photos of London and Adora. We go into court. The rest of the world looks absolutely ridiculous, when they realize a bunch of college students with a handful of computers fooled them into thinking a construct was a real person. Especially those jerks fighting over London."

"As long as Doni doesn't have to get up on the stand and face the world. She's innocent in all this."

The gossips and scandalmongers raised the intensity of their stories. They contradicted themselves, claiming London trashed a hotel room in Monte Carlo on the same night she was climbing out of a limo in Sydney--sans underwear, in a miniskirt--to dance the night away. She supposedly ran up huge bills at hotels and restaurants and boutiques in a dozen big cities, all within the space of a day. She supposedly got hauled into police stations for driving under the influence or speeding or shoplifting.

Our postings about London helping cook dinner for the homeless in San Francisco or reading to children in a shelter for battered women in Chicago seemed pretty pitiful.

We got a little frustrated because London wasn't doing anything to help us protect her reputation. I wondered if we had somehow sabotaged ourselves by creating copy-Cosmo. Maybe he was causing problems for London. Were the circumstances of his birth so vastly different from hers...maybe we had created an evil copy-Cosmo, and London was busy fighting him?

Doni stayed busy with her new crew of bodyguards, running the other way whenever they saw a black car. Reggie Grandstone came by our house a few more times to try to catch up with London. Chasity always seemed to show up soon after he rang our doorbell.

We were getting busier than we ever imagined, and once in a while one of us would edge toward the topic that was on everyone's minds, but we couldn't get up the courage to speak aloud: shutting down FlopDrop. Taking our losses and running for our lives.

What stopped me every time I thought about suggesting it was the question of what would happen to London when we shut down the server. One of these days, we would have to slow down enough to ask.

"Something is going against us," Cosmo reported that Friday, after his weekly chore of compiling stats for FlopDrop.

"How?" Wallace sounded exhausted.

"Traffic is dropping off, big-time, on the main pages. Traffic is still increasing, but slower, on the abuse and health sections of the site. People still want help in those areas."

"They still trust London to help them," Alvin offered from his seat on the other side of the room, where he was plowing through his third plate of pizza for the night.

"I think we should stop taking advertisements," Simone offered. "If we're not taking money, people won't get upset when everything comes out in the open and we shut down."

We just looked at each other, getting silent input for a few minutes. I saw the same expressions on everyone's faces that I figured had to be on mine. We were tired. We were sick of the constant battle to mitigate the damage others were trying to do to

London. The weight of responsibility--legal, ethical and emotional, monetary and all the work involved--was slowly crushing us.

"Do it," Wallace said. "How much time and space do we still owe people?"

"Everything is up for renewal. We've been doing it on a weekly basis from the beginning." She looked relieved, as if a hundred-pound weight had lifted from her shoulders.

"How much money do we have in the account?"

"Well..." She tapped her tablet screen and dragged a few times, then nodded. "We could throw a really incredible end-of-the-year party, take the whole class to Cedar Point overnight, meals included."

"It'd be great if we could just pull the plug and walk away," I said. "Let everybody get back to their own lives."

"But can we?" Wallace said, without the sardonic little smirk or the richness of mockery in his voice that I would have expected from him right about then.

~~~~~

At the start of our next presentation and discussion day in class, Chasity leaped to her feet, waving one hand, almost bouncing in her eagerness to speak. All three of our profs seemed to sigh. They visibly hesitated, looked around the room, probably searching for someone else who wanted to talk, then called on her.

She had printouts of three reports taken off the Internet that morning that arrest warrants had been issued for London Holiday.

"Those are bogus," I said, without bothering to raise my hand and wait for the profs to call on me. "You can't issue arrest warrants without real witnesses and real events and evidence."

"Since when does the truth and reality mean anything to lawyers?" someone said from the back of the class. That brought a pitiful wave of chuckles and snickers and muttered comments.

The profs opened up an Internet connection so we could do some investigating into those reports right there in class.

Reactions to the warrant stories were already appearing on the FlopDrop message boards. All were explosive and extreme. Fury from those who refused to believe. Glee from those who suddenly revealed a vicious antipathy for London. People hurled abuse at each other in the message boards. As we watched, more messages scrolled in. Without any prompting from us, Cosmo got to work shutting down and blocking the people who were the most virulent and foul. The damage had been done, though.

All the good we had been trying to do through FlopDrop was disintegrating, turning to noxious slime, before our eyes.

The remainder of the class was spent tracking down news releases, the gossip sites, the reactions to the news. We were especially interested in what the police departments that had issued those arrest warrants were saying about the stories.

They were strangely quiet. Not a good sign.

Of course, they could be flummoxed and stunned by the tidal wave of reaction from around the world. Just before our profs called a halt to the Internet search, we saw a live feed of a group of protestors sitting in front of the police station in Paris, demanding the commissioner cancel the arrest warrant.

I must have been loopy. I kept getting an image of Inspector Clouseau stumbling around, trying to arrest the protestors or calm them down, and not understanding what they were upset about.

"Time to shut it down," Wallace said, his voice pretty much covered up by the noise of everyone getting up to leave the lecture hall. "Athena, you do the honors."

"Huh?" For about two seconds I panicked.

Then I felt a malevolent presence approaching from behind me. I turned to see Chasity, her eyes big with gloating glee, nearly slithering down the row. No way in the world was I going to give her the satisfaction of seeing me confused or upset.

"I'll get right to work on a statement," I told Wallace, turning back to him, although my shoulders itched right where I could feel Chasity's gaze focused. I wouldn't put it past her to stab me with a poisoned blade right then.

"Sanctuary in twenty," he said, looking around to the rest of our team and getting short, sharp nods of acknowledgement.

We split up. I headed out with Simone and Cosmo. Wallace and Alvin stayed to talk with our profs. Theo said she would take care of provisions. It was a given we weren't going to get to any of our classes for the rest of the day.

By the time we met in the apartment, I had a good idea of what to do, but not such a good idea of what to say.

We couldn't take the high road anymore and ignore the lies.

"Absolutely," Simone said, when I explained my rough

thoughts to them. "Put the blame where it belongs, the lies."

"Kind of funny," Cosmo said, as we walked around the room turning on all the monitors and tapping our access codes into the system. "We're finally telling the truth."

Simone let out a funny little gasping sound that was part laughter, part sob.

Among the three of us, we had London's farewell statement composed by the time Wallace and Alvin joined us. They had discussed the proposed action with our profs, who all agreed. More harm was being done by keeping the site going.

"If it means anything, all three of them basically said we won," Wallace said as he settled down in what we had come to refer to as the captain's chair.

"Won what?" Cosmo said, his voice somewhat mournful, despite the valiant attempt to smile.

None of us had any answer for that.

We waited for Theo, figuring it was only right that she be present to add any input to London's farewell speech, but she didn't show for another half hour. When she arrived, her arms full of provisions, she explained that Chasity and some teammates had been trying to follow her.

"How did you lose them?" Alvin asked, as he got up to help her unpack and spread out the selection on the two folding tables, along with paper plates and cups, and boxes of plastic cutlery.

"I went to Divine's, making them think we had a room upstairs. Angela met me at the door, like she knew I was coming." Theo folded up the big cotton grocery bags that were sturdy enough and roomy enough to carry two frozen turkeys, each--which just proved how strong she was for such a skinny little thing. "Anyway, she let me stash my bags behind the counter, and told me to go on up to the fourth floor and just wait in the shadows. Chasity and her crew came in, and you know how rude they are. They didn't even ask Angela if I was there, didn't even say more than hi to her. They started wandering around, opening doors. I mean, honestly, if a door is closed, that's a pretty good sign you're not allowed in there. Am I right, or am I right?"

"Absatively," Alvin said.

"Anyway, they went into a room on the third floor and the door closed, and the next thing you know, they're banging on the door, yelling for someone to let them out." Theo giggled and picked up the bag of Hershey Miniatures. "I went downstairs and Angela said to get going and not worry about anything. I couldn't hear them yelling from the front room, but it sure seemed like she knew what had happened before I told her."

"Yeah, well Chasity and her gang don't belong here. It'll be a miracle if they put in the full four years," he said, with a nod for emphasis. "Those Neighborlee doesn't want, they don't hang around long. Not unless they're deaf and daft and just plain dumb."

"Hmm, wouldn't use those words exactly with Chasity." Wallace met my gaze, and suddenly I felt like laughing.

I took the time to notify London what we were doing, before we got to work. She didn't respond. I wondered if she was busy tracking down all the attacks and false stories.

Or maybe whoever was spreading all those stories had figured out that London wasn't just a construct, but an AI...and had figured out how to cage and silence her?

Such a theory didn't bear thinking about.

An hour later, it was done. London officially announced on her blog, through tweets, on Facebook and on all the pages on FlopDrop, that she was leaving the public life. She was tired of fighting the constant lies people told about her. It took too much time and energy and money away from the worthwhile things she was trying to accomplish. The health and help sections of FlopDrop would stay active, but all the other areas would be closed down, effective immediately. Wallace worked out a timeline for how soon he could shut down and clear out each site, each message board, each file and folder.

Cosmo, Alvin and Simone sent out a massive email blast to everyone and anyone who had visited or communicated with or had profile pages or posted messages on FlopDrop, to let them know in abbreviated form what was happening and when. Theo and I were busy sending out press releases to any site that had ever mentioned London, Adora or Adonis. Essentially we said we were sick of fighting the liars and losers, we refused to play the game by their rules, and we were packing up our marbles and going home. But nicely. In a mature, responsible way, leaving no loopholes for people to criticize London.

At least, we hoped so.

Cosmo called Brittney and Cybele and gave them the official announcement, so they could let all our friends at the high school know what we were doing. I called Doni and told her the same thing. We invited them to come over as soon as they could after school, or at lunch if they had the time. Simone had the checkbook and we were dividing up the spoils, paying our bills, and wanted to give everyone big bonus checks to thank them.

We were there until long past dark, like keeping vigil at a deathbed. There wasn't as much reaction online as we had feared, and that should have been a warning sign. Typical, once we really thought about it. The nastier and the more untrue something was, the faster it spread through the Internet. The things we wanted and needed people to hear and know and read moved slower than peanut butter in a blizzard.

Most of the reactions were two extremes. The people who understood what London and her friends were doing expressed thanks for the good they had tried to do, for the opportunity to meet and make new friends. And then there were, of course, those who called London a coward and traitor and liar.

~~~~~

Saturday, Doni and I both needed to get away. Get out and move. Goof off. Waste the day hitting thrift shops looking for out-of-print books, unusual hats and dishes. Yes, we could have just spent the day rummaging through Divine's Emporium, but we were in the mood for grumbling about the "junk" that people put in thrift shops and expected other people to buy. We got in my car and drove all around Cuyahoga and Medina and Lorain counties, stopping at any place that looked interesting. The more of a hole-in-the-wall the spot was, the better. We got ice cream for lunch and stopped an hour later for apple fritters bigger than our hands and soaked in sugary glaze so thick we almost needed a hammer to break the hard coating.

The day started out sunny, but as I developed a sleepy headache from too much sugar and fat, too fast, the skies got cloudy. We had just crossed the border into Darbyville when it started raining. We headed down one of those back roads that were mostly woods and deep ditches on either side when there weren't steep slopes going down into the Metroparks. I slowed down because this road hadn't been repaved since FDR was in office.

Where the asphalt was worn away, there was gravel and chuckholes. Deep chuckholes. The kind that looked shallow when they filled with muddy rainwater.

I hit one. Through the drumming of the rain I heard the distinct *sproing-clang-clatter-bang* of a hubcap coming off. I turned my head in time to see it rolling down the steep slope on the other side of the road.

"Dang. Dangity-dang-dang," I grumbled, and hit the brakes, then backed up. I had gone about twenty more feet in those few seconds it took to react and decide between letting the hubcap go and having to replace it eventually or chasing after it.

They were special hubcaps. Jinx had bought them for me the day I got my driver's license, and promised he would help me find a car to go with them. Kind of weird, buying hubcaps without knowing what car they would fit. Because things kind of "worked out" when it came to our family, I was willing to trust to luck. Of course, the car we found was perfect. I loved it. And the incredible gas mileage. So of course, I didn't want to lose any of those hubcaps. I needed all the good luck I could get.

Doni started to unbuckle her seatbelt once I got the car pulled off the side of the road and into park. She knew how much those wretched hubcaps meant to me.

"Stay. No sense in both of us getting frozen. Besides, did you see where it went?" I said.

She shook her head. The last I saw of her, when I looked back at the car before heading down the slope, she was pulling a book out of her purse. Always prepared, Doni. Ready to get a few pages read and never wasting a moment.

I came back up the hill, hauling my hubcap and considering peeling out of my muddy, soaked jeans and driving home wearing the blanket from the back seat. And there was a Darbyville cop leaning in the driver's side window. What was with Darbyville, dressing their cops all in a black material that got glossy when it was wet? They looked like stormtroopers dressed in patent leather.

"Is there a problem, officer?"

Yes, it was a cliché response, but I did love seeing him jump about three inches straight up. Too bad he wasn't leaning far enough into my car to bang his head on the roof.

"Just checking why this young lady was parked on the side of the road." He looked me over, and just barely muffled his sneer before it was more than a flicker in the corner of his mouth.

"I parked. My car. She's just a passenger."

Like, duh. Doni looked her fourteen years old, and she was sitting in the passenger seat.

"Kind of a lot of trouble for a hubcap."

"Waste not."

I did not like the way his gaze kept flicking back to Doni. Like he thought she would do something dangerous.

"What else were you doing down there?"

"Huh?" For about two seconds, I considered smarting off, telling him it was none of his business if I couldn't make it home to use the bathroom. But having witnessed enough times Jinx had barely escaped trouble when I was a kid, I knew better than to give him a good reason to slap me with a fine or haul me in. With my luck, it would be against the law to use a tree as an improvised latrine. I hadn't actually done that, but if I smarted off and said that, then he would probably arrest me on that charge. So I bit my tongue and swallowed down my inner snark.

"Burying something, maybe?"

"Digging myself out of the mud. If you don't mind, I'd really like to go home and get into some dry clothes." I gestured down at my muddy jeans, as if he hadn't noticed them yet. "It's been a really long day."

The cop didn't move aside, even though I reached for the handle of my door.

"You know, at first, I didn't recognize her." He hooked his thumb over his shoulder at Doni.

"Recognize?" I felt my fritter rising up in my throat when he did a little sleight of hand and Doni's student I.D. appeared between two of his gloved fingers.

The first day of school, when she got her picture taken for her I.D., Doni had worn one of the silly, super-fashion hats the Hallidays had sent her. She had worn that hat in at least five London Holiday pictures. Doni had that hat on today, too. Despite the lack of makeup, there was enough similarity between the slightly soggy, cold teenager sitting in my car, and a virtual person. If someone knew to look.

Did a cop in Darbyville know about London Holiday? From

the deepening scowl on his face, he probably was one of those people who believed all the ugly things being said about her.

"Do you know who this is? Did you pick up a hitchhiker?"

"That's absolutely stupid." Not the smartest thing to say. "Picking up hitchhikers is almost as stupid as hitchhiking. This is my cousin, Doni. We're on our way home."

"To Neighborlee. Right." His sneer got wider. "You really go all out when you're slumming, don't you? Fake I.D. and all. Doesn't work, though."

What was wrong with this guy? Who would use a fake I.D. and pretend to be a kid in high school, and use a name similar to their real name? This guy was ignoring logic holes big enough to drive the *Enterprise* through.

"Hey, just because the Pikes beat you guys last week, that doesn't give you any right to be nasty."

For about two seconds, he goggled at me. What was wrong with this guy? A cop who didn't know or care about the school sports scene? Next thing, he'd be telling me he was allergic to donuts.

"Fine, keep playing your games, but I'm taking her in."

"For what?" I considered yelling for Doni to lock the car, but the window was open, and I wouldn't put it past this cop to jump through the window and grab hold of Doni and not let go.

"Outstanding warrants in several countries, for starters."

"They're fake!"

Too late, I realized that was the wrong thing to say. Because even if the warrants were real, and growing evidence said otherwise, they couldn't apply to Doni Halliday. But the fact I argued showed I knew about the warrants, and why would I care unless the girl sitting in my passenger seat, looking like the notorious London Holiday...*was* London Holiday?

"You can ride in with us, if you want." He didn't have a nice smile. Not all flat and tight and cold like that.

"Why do I have to go in?" Doni asked. "I didn't do anything."

"She's never left the country, and those warrants are all for foreign countries. If she never left the country, logic says she never did anything she was accused of, so you have no legal authority--"

"You want to ride in with us? You haven't done anything, except be a little argumentative." Again, that cold, nasty smile.

"Athena?" Doni looked scared.

"I'll follow you in. I'll never let you out of my sight. Why don't you keep the link open between your phone and mine, so I can hear anything this guy says?"

That got a stiffening from his knees on up, meaning he was already planning a deluge of words he didn't want me to hear.

Not that I would be paying attention to my phone. I had my tablet and I was planning on opening up my mobile hot spot on the drive to the Darbyville jail. I was already planning to get the rest of the team going in different directions, calling on all the connections and pulling all the strings we could. These bozos weren't going to fingerprint Doni or even take her booking photo. Besides, it wasn't like I was going to be texting and driving.

Unfortunately, that ploy worked against me. The cop refused to let her take anything in the car with her, meaning her purse and book. Then he insisted on frisking Doni right there, before he put her into the back of his squad car. What did he think she had on her? A blowtorch? Wire cutters? I pulled out my tablet and turned on the video camera app in the time it took Doni to climb out of the car and walk around to the trunk as the cop instructed her.

He didn't just frisk her. He groped her, spending extra time at her hips and feeling for her breasts. Later, the police union's representative, the Darbyville city lawyer, Mr. Carr, and Mr. Tucker, Doni's counselor from the high school, all got together and watched the video. They all agreed, his hands spent too much time at her breasts. Definite grounds for charges of sexual harassment and inappropriate use of authority and a dozen other charges against the guy.

As if that was bad enough, he laughed at her when she sniffled. Doni turned to look at me, her expression begging for help, and there were tears bright in her eyes. I got that on camera too. And even though it hurt like fire in my gut, I kept my mouth shut. I wasn't going to let anything I said be caught on the video.

The cop mocked her, saying she was faking it. After all, she was London Holiday. She was used to guys groping her. Or did she expect him to pay for touching her? Maybe he should charge her for offering a bribe to a police officer, using her body to try to get out of trouble?

The stupid cop never even noticed that I was standing there, holding up my tablet, catching everything he said and did. Right about the time I thought that, it occurred to me to look at his car. He had a dash camera, visible right there. But the car's engine was off, and I was pretty sure so was the camera. Besides, dash cams pointed forward, and the jerk made Doni go to the back of his car.

He turned around, grabbed her arm, and halfway jerked her off her feet to put her in the car, smirking the whole time. I had to lower my tablet so it looked like I was just holding it. He still hadn't recognized what I held in my hands. Even lowered to my waist, I could tip my tablet out just enough to watch what the camera picked up and guide it.

Doni was crying openly now, fighting not to sob aloud, her face glistening and dripping. I recorded his mocking words as he yanked the door open and gave Doni a shove into the back seat. He told her it wasn't the kind of car she was used to, but she'd just have to lump it and make do.

I wanted this guy's head to use as a soccer ball. Nobody treated my cousin that way. No cop would be allowed to get away with something like that. What was with the creeps who ran Darbyville, that they allowed people like him to work for them?

Then it occurred to me, as I waited for the Darbyville cop to drive around me so I could follow him to the police station…in some sense, I had done it to Doni. She wouldn't be in this mess if I hadn't used her name and her face and gotten her involved in the whole mess that FlopDrop became. I was almost sick enough at that realization to interfere with my driving.

I stayed exactly one car length behind the cop the whole way down that road. He never tried to lose me when we got to intersections. Maybe he was too busy taunting Doni to give me a hard time.

There were enough stops along the way, at intersections or waiting for a train to clear the tracks, I was able to send a lot of info and get responses. Alvin was at Miller's Diner at the same time as Mr. Carr, so he was able to email me back with the news that our team lawyer was on his way. Theo had the unpleasant task of letting Gram and Granddad know what had happened. I didn't call them because I knew they would keep me on the phone during the entire drive to the Darbyville Station, and I had too much to do. Wallace and Cosmo and Simone got to work gathering up the evidence that yes, all those arrest warrants were fake. They would bring printouts. Nobody could get there before the cop, Doni and I would arrive. My job was to make sure the booking didn't start right away, because as Wallace pointed out, once they got Doni into the system, the whole world would find out that London Holiday had been arrested.

"Please, London, wherever you are, whatever you're doing," I muttered as I tapped a message to London and sent it to the FlopDrop board we had left active just for her. I prayed that we hadn't done something totally stupid, giving her a boyfriend with copy-Cosmo. Like, distracting her so much she didn't care about us anymore? Or making her so angry with disappointment she was attacking us? Could she be the source of all the false arrest warrants? Causing trouble for Doni to punish her, somehow?

No. I refused to believe that. London Holiday had become her own person, but she had started life as Doni Halliday.

My brain went into overdrive, trying to plan how I would stop Doni from going into the system. I felt like my brain was spinning its wheels, caught in an ice-filled rut in the road. I couldn't think of anything that wouldn't get me thrown into jail alongside Doni. They would confiscate everything I had with me, and I did not want some fumble-fingered sleazoid Darbyville cop getting his hands on my tablet and "accidentally" erasing all that incriminating video. At the next stop, I emailed the video of the cop groping Doni to myself and to every member of our team, to protect it.

That gave me an idea. When we got off the back roads and pulled out into a road with two lanes in either direction, I got ready to pass the cop. I needed to get to the police station ahead of him. What was with cops that they drove three miles under the speed limit? This guy probably drove slow hoping to cite people for obstructing traffic. I made a note on the dictation function of my tablet to check into his record and how many traffic tickets this guy issued, and look for a pattern. If we needed to go that far in defending Doni. I preferred making sure she wasn't booked at all.

Chapter Thirteen

The Darbyville police station was part of a big complex with the fire department, city hall, library and recreation center. It was actually kind of pretty, with trees ringing the parking lot. Someone came to the back door of the police station as I got out of my car to head over to the door with no cars parked in front of it, and a sign that read, **Patrol Cars Only, Violators Will Be Towed**. I got a glimpse of a guy in a black jacket and black suit pants, and our eyes met for a second or two before I heard the crunch of tires on slushy gravel. The man nodded to me just before I looked away and spotted the patrol car coming around the corner.

I looked back, but he wasn't there in the doorway anymore.

I prepped my tablet and tucked it under my arm to keep it out of sight--which wasn't that easy to do, because touching the screen could flick it to something else. Then I waited for the cop to pull up. He parked right where I thought he would, next to the door into the building. I waited until he turned his back to me and reached for the back door of the car before I turned on the camera, stepped back, and held it up where anybody with half a brain could see it.

"Here we are, princess," he sneered after he yanked the door open. "Need help climbing out of the carriage?"

"No." Doni's voice was thick, so I knew she had been crying during the whole twenty-minute drive. She poked her head out and that heavy mask of misery she wore made me feel like someone clobbered me with an entire weight lifting set, right in my chest. When she saw me, she smiled, and I felt even worse.

"You okay, Doni?" I said. "What did this guy say to you on the way here?"

"None of your business," the cop snapped. "Get out, princess. Or do you want me to drag you? Bet you like guys who get rough."

"She's never even been on a date, so that kind of question is irrelevant," I said. "Doni, tell me exactly what he said."

Doni watched me the whole time she climbed out of the car. I caught the way she flinched when the cop reached for her arm, and it was a big enough reaction for the video camera to catch it. Her gaze slid to my tablet, and she stood a little straighter as she wiped the tears off her face.

"He called me a slut and a whore and he said I was going to pay for all the stupid, illegal, selfish things I had done. And he called me a filthy liar, when I told him I was never in any of those places. He said I was going to be treated a lot better than I deserved." She hiccupped. "Then he said if it was up to him--"

"What's that?" the cop said, stopping just after he grabbed hold of her arm again. He stared at the tablet in my hands. Finally.

"Evidence."

"Hand it over. Right now." He dragged Doni along with him and stomped toward me with his hand out.

"You have no legal authority to demand my personal property." I backed away from him, and away from the door of the police station. That was kind of the idea. The longer it took to get her through that door, the better the chances of reinforcements showing up. I almost hoped that when we checked Doni later, there would be bruises on her arm where he grabbed her. More evidence.

"What do you think you are, a lawyer? Hand it over. We can let the lawyers settle it all later."

"After you erase everything?" I had managed to get to the second row in the parking lot. A glimpse of movement made me look away from the cop for a second. That man from the doorway was outside again. He came to the edge of the sidewalk and stood there, his arms crossed over his chest, watching.

I really didn't have time to wonder if that was good for us, or bad.

"Besides, I've worked for lawyers. I know enough about the law to know that you don't have a legal leg to stand on to demand my property or the evidence I'm gathering." For the benefit of the guy on the sidewalk, in case he was someone with authority, I raised my voice. It almost bounced off the walls behind him. "Especially when a check of the dash cam in your car will show a great big gap during the time you falsely arrested my cousin. Isn't it against regulations to turn the dash cam off when you make a traffic stop?"

That made the cop stop for a few seconds, so I got past the second row and backed up toward the third. And backed right into someone's truck.

That kind of hurt, especially where the bumper hit the back of my knees. In those few seconds when I staggered sideways, the cop dragged Doni along faster and almost caught up with me.

"Did you have the camera on during the ride to the station? Did you record everything you said to my cousin? You had no need to say anything to her, but you just had to open your nasty mouth and make fun of her. She's fourteen years old! You're supposed to be observant, to be a cop. Can't you tell how young she is?"

The cop swore, letting out a string of profanity I only half-understood.

"That's enough!" Jinx shouted. "Harley Ellsworth, what do you think you're doing, talking that way to my nieces?" He stomped across the parking lot, arms pumping, long hair flying in the breeze he made, fury turning his face to sharp crags of granite.

I never heard his motorcycle pull up. Later, I learned he got there about five seconds before I pulled into the parking lot, and when he saw me get to work, preparing my trap, he decided to keep quiet and just watch to see what happened.

"Your--" The cop went white for five seconds. He looked at me, then he looked at Doni, and the color flooded back into his face. A nice, bright, hot red. "No way this little slut--"

"I'm warning you! I broke your nose in wrestling and I broke a couple ribs in baseball, and I don't care that you're wearing a uniform right now, I'll break your filthy mouth."

"She can't be your niece," Ellsworth, the formerly nameless Darbyville cop said, his voice going raspy. "She's London Holiday."

"No, her name is *Halliday*. And we all call her Doni, not London. Her mother was my sister Lenore. And since we're doing pedigrees, this is my niece, Athena. You remember my sister, Portia? Her mother."

"You're Portia's--" Ellsworth clamped his mouth shut, and he actually tried to smile. "I dated your mom."

"Remind me to give Mom a long bath in disinfectant, next time I see her," I said to Jinx.

He laughed, which just made Ellsworth wilt. Then Jinx stunned me by clapping the guy on the shoulder. "Harley isn't such a bad guy. Just a little narrow-minded. Not that I'd admit it to anyone."

"You just did." I held up my tablet. "Caught it all. And the way he groped Doni before he put her in the car. Jinx, this guy--" I stepped back, just in case Uncle Jinx's boyhood friend decided to make a grab for my tablet. "Well, from the way he reacted when he saw me recording him, I'm guessing there isn't any recording of what happened in the car. He was just going to town on Doni."

"London Holiday," Ellsworth insisted. He visibly loosened his grip on Doni.

"That's something we need to verify before we go any further." The man from the sidewalk stepped up to join us. "Jinx, long time."

"Carl." Jinx held out his hand and they shook. "Guess you've been getting some phone calls, since I couldn't get through to you."

"My girls have been going nuts over the whole London Holiday...phenomenon?" Carl looked Doni over, but it was a nice kind of assessing glance. Not like Ellsworth, whose expression basically said he expected her to transform into a pile of slimy worms or nightmare bugs. "I knew your sister married a Halliday, but I just never made the connection."

He snorted and glanced at Ellsworth. "So, you're into all that online social gossip and such, that you'd immediately recognize this little girl as the infamous London Holiday?"

"Her I.D. says..." Ellsworth sighed and dug into his pocket to pull out Doni's school I.D. card, to hand it over to Carl. He was definitely someone important.

Police Chief Carl Dunlevy, in fact. He'd played baseball and basketball in high school and college against Uncle Jinx, and dated my mother, too. Gee, with all the guys Mom dated, she couldn't find someone to settle down with long enough to make a baby, so I'd at least have a father who wasn't a test tube?

Of course, Ellsworth turned into Mr. By-the-Book when we stepped through the door of the station. He insisted Doni had to be booked. He had radioed ahead to tell them he was bringing in London Holiday.

"I don't think you want to do that, Harley," Carl said, as our little party of five walked down the long hallway to the booking area.

"Got to." Ellsworth wasn't looking at anyone. I think he was upset that Carl told him--and Jinx intimidated him--to let go of Doni and let her walk into the building under her own power. "The process cannot be stopped, no matter the circumstances, no matter who the accused is. Or who she knows," he added, with a sideways glance at his chief.

Oh, he was going to pay for that. I didn't even have to see the "what a doofus" glances Carl and Jinx exchanged.

The officer in charge of booking was a big, gray-haired, leathery-skinned, saggy-jowled guy who had a badge with *Ellsworth* on it. Nope, not Harley's father, but his uncle. Somehow, that made things worse.

"Son, you sure you want to go through with this?" Sgt. Ellsworth rested his big elbows on the desk and leaned over it, to look down at Doni. How come the booking desks always had to be raised, so the accused had to look up at the officer?

His stern look softened when he saw Doni, with her tear-swollen eyes and her white hair flying all around her face in a halo. I wouldn't have been surprised if he reached under his desk and came up with a lollipop for her.

"Is that her?" a woman called, her voice coming from the long hallway that led into the rest of the city hall/police station/fire department complex. There was a scurrying of feet, and six women of varying ages came into the booking area. A girl about my age in jeans and T-shirt. A woman in business casual. Two in firefighter uniforms, another in police uniform, and one who looked older than Gram.

"Her who?" Carl scowled at them.

That scowl couldn't hide the look of horror dawning bright in his eyes.

"It is! It's London Holiday!" the grandmotherly woman squealed. Yes, she squealed, like those idiots who screamed and fainted when the Beatles performed on the Ed Sullivan show.

Well, there went our hope that we could keep things quiet. It was easy to guess that Ellsworth had shot off his mouth so much on the way back that the whole department knew he was bringing in London Holiday for booking. I really hoped he would be busted back so far in the police department he wouldn't even be allowed to wash a patrol car.

Later, Doni said that when he wasn't making fun of her, he was talking on his cell phone and the police radio, bragging about how he was going to make the national news, catching the infamous London Holiday.

London's fans swooped in and circled Doni like sharks in a feeding frenzy. But nice sharks. The two firefighters immediately saw how she had been crying and they laid into Ellsworth. Turns out they were his cousins, but not the daughters of the booking sergeant. Things were looking a little...incestuous?...in Darbyville right then. The girl in jeans was the mayor's daughter, doing some office work on the weekend for her father. She recognized me from a couple classes at Willis-Brooks, and had the sense to ask me what was going on. The grandmotherly one was the worst of the lot. She wanted Doni's autograph and begged her to stay at the station long enough she could call her granddaughters to meet her. She just loved her clothes, the girls thought she was wonderful, trying to help people with health issues and dating abuse problems.

"You can't arrest her," the woman in the police uniform said. I found out later she was the dispatcher who had taken the report from Ellsworth. Doni said she had advised him to think about what he was doing, that her crimes were nothing but accusations.

"I have to," Ellsworth said. I swear, he almost stomped his feet. "The process has been started."

"Son, is this a process you want to finish?" Sgt. Ellsworth said. "The fact is, you can't arrest someone on rumors. You have to have evidence. What exactly did you see the girl do?"

"She--" He looked at Doni, then at me. His eyes narrowed. I took a step back, in case he was going to go after my tablet again. "She was driving without a license."

"Sir, my engine was running because it's a freezing cold day, and I left the heater running while I went looking for my hubcap that got knocked loose by a chuckhole," I hurried to say, focusing on the booking sergeant, since he had asked the question. "Doni was in the passenger seat, reading, the whole time."

"Documentation," Carl said. "We need proof. I'm not against chalking this one up to a case of..." He turned to Jinx, his expression clearly begging for some ideas.

"Mistaken identity?" Doni offered.

"But you're London Holiday," the grandmotherly lady said, her voice sort of dropping toward confusion.

"Ah, excuse me?" The dispatcher stepped back into the room. Her eyes were wide and she looked like she couldn't decide if she should cry or laugh. "I'm on the phone with a woman who says *she's* London Holiday."

"Liar," Ellsworth snarled. The dispatcher glared at him and he cringed. "I meant the woman on the phone."

"You think?" Doni whispered to me. A glimmer of hope put a little color back into her face.

A loud crackling overrode the Muzak playing in the background. First the TV in the corner by the coffeemaker and bottled water dispenser filled with static, then the computer screen sitting on the side of the booking desk.

London's face appeared on both screens.

"Are you okay, Doni?" she asked.

Nobody screamed and fainted, but a couple people looked like they had seen a ghost. Ellsworth went white and he took a couple steps toward the TV, pointing a shaking hand, then looked back at Doni. His mouth moved, but no sound came out.

"I don't know," Doni said.

"Do I have to state the obvious?" London said. "I'm London Holiday, and the girl you're trying to arrest is Doni Halliday. Athena?"

"Nice to see you again," I said, stepping forward. Ellsworth flinched and cringed away, like maybe he thought someone was going to hit him.

"Chasity Boah is responsible for all those false arrest warrants. Backtrack her and you'll have all your evidence."

"Why?" Jinx said.

"She wants Reggie Grandstone," I said, as all the pieces snapped together in my head.

"She can have him!" Doni yelped. "They deserve each other."

"Is everything okay now?" London said, looking around the room. I wondered how she was able to finagle things that suddenly the TV screen was two-way, but now wasn't the time to ask. I was just relieved that she had shown up and given us an answer, and maybe started clearing things up for Doni.

"Thank you," the chief of police said, giving her a nod of respect. "We can take things from here, I think."

"Catch you around. Oh, tell Cosmo that Sherwood says hello. He's taking care of rounding up the evidence to send to all your computers."

"Who?" Doni asked as the TV and computer screens went

blank and the static roared through the room for a few seconds.

"That's Cosmo's real name. So Sherwood is London's boyfriend," I whispered.

"Oh." She grinned. "Major cool."

Of course, things weren't as easily cleared up as Carl indicated to London, but we had a good start. We were just getting settled in his office when Mr. Carr and the rest of the team showed up. By this time, I had learned that Gram and Granddad had decided to go down I-71 and make a day of hitting all the outlet malls, so Uncle Jinx was the only one home when Theo made the call for help. He hopped on his motorcycle and got hold of Mr. Carr by cell phone, just after Alvin found him at Miller's. They did a lot of plotting on the way, which explained something of the delay in the team showing up to the rescue. I really had to wonder about all these people breaking what had come to be called the "shut up and drive" law--no talking on cell phones while driving.

Mr. Carr had a dozen legal precedents and twice as many arguments, and nearly got them all out of his mouth before he sat down in the cushioned office chair next to Doni. He immediately caught hold of her hand and held it the whole time. Then when the Darbyville representatives were blinking and looking a little lost by all the Latin thrown at them and sorting through the implications of the cases and veiled threats, Wallace and Cosmo handed over piles of printouts. Enough evidence to choke even a big-mouth mule like Ellsworth.

The gist of it was that they had all the evidence they needed to prove every warrant for London Holiday's arrest was bogus. Once the authorities who had supposedly issued those warrants heard about them, they released statements that they had done no such thing. What really confused the issue was that almost immediately after those official statements had been released, someone had issued statements claiming the claims that the arrest warrants were false were false.

Confused? The telling point in all the back and forth of "They're lying," "No, they're lying," was the timing. The authorities always took half a day to get through the paperwork to release a statement. The fake authorities had counterclaims ready and released them within ten minutes of the official statements. Meaning they were waiting for them to appear.

After London spoke up, it was easy to see Chasity's fingerprints all over the whole mess. We called our profs once we left the police station and told them what happened. They promised they would start setting things up to confront Chasity and her supporters in class.

We were out of Carl's office in under an hour. The grandmotherly leader of London's fans, Myrtle Higgenbothem, was furious once she heard some of the details, such as Chasity planting the false arrest warrants, to destroy Doni so she could have Reggie. Myrtle was just about as computer-savvy as her granddaughters and she promised the three of them would get to work, spreading the news that the warrants were false, and try to protect London Holiday's reputation as much as possible.

~~~~~

I stayed overnight at home, because we knew better than to wait to fill Gram and Granddad in on what happened. Uncle Jinx, Doni and I had a relaxing evening watching DVDs and making pizza, and we had our story put together for the easiest telling when Gram and Granddad got home from their day out. We went to church the next day, and after one of Gram's feasts at lunch, Doni and I went back to the apartment to meet again with the team. We had a report to put together for our profs, after all. Plus we had to decide what to do with all our equipment, if we were going to save any files--if it would be legally necessary to save files for future reference--if we should wipe all the drives--questions like that.

We had some fun, plotting dire revenge on Chasity. Of course, London might have done all the sabotage already. We would have to wait until she contacted us again, to find out for sure.

"And she won't leave any fingerprints," Wallace said with a chuckle.

We split up in good humor. I took Doni home and decided to drive my car back to the dorm, instead of leaving it parked at Gram's and walking back. Just in case I needed to be able to make a fast getaway.

A dozen sticky note message slips were stuck to the dorm room door when I got back. All of them were for me.

"I can't read half of these." I was waving the notes as I stepped through the door.

My roommates burst out laughing.

"Hail the conquering hero!" Dorinda crowed, and waved her pint of triple chocolate ice cream at me.

"Someone want to explain?" I dropped my backpack next to the couch and flung my coat in the general direction of the coat rack.

"All those messages are from Chasity, and each one got more incoherent every time she called," Celeste said. She tossed me a Hershey's Special Dark. Celeste just didn't share her dark chocolate, so I knew this was a red letter day indeed.

"We couldn't spell most of the filthy things she was snarling," Shaunda added.

"Well, none of us can speak Nigerian." I settled down on the floor pillow in front of the bookshelf we had made of bricks and boards. "When she was coherent..." Then I just grinned and slouched back far enough to threaten the balance of the shelves.

"What did you do, and why didn't you invite us to help?" Celeste said.

"Well, basically we figured out that Chasity was the one responsible for all the false reports and warrants and such on London. Then a gung-ho cop arrested Doni because of those false arrest warrants and...well...someone is probably trying to get Chasity for all the trouble she caused us."

"They must have succeeded."

"We'll find out in class tomorrow, that's for certain."

I didn't have to wait. Chasity came tearing into the dorm less than half an hour later. Probably just time to come harass my roommates again. As soon as the door started jumping on its hinges, I knew it was her, even before she shrieked my name.

She kept shrieking, until others on the floor called the RD and campus security. My roommates left the door closed and locked and we sat on the floor and shook our heads and listened. Before someone came and dragged her away, Chasity shrieked enough that I figured out what had happened. Someone had accessed all her online accounts--bank and email and Facebook and Twitter and her blog and more. Pictures were altered, money was removed, Dropbox files were erased. On and on. And worse, all the data for Chasity's class project had been erased. On all her devices.

I couldn't figure out what we had created when Angela let me hook up that weird video camera to my computer, and I "copied" Doni, and launched the sentient bundle of electronic impulses that became London Holiday.

Maybe London would tell us. Someday.

Campus security wasn't able to keep Chasity. Probably she had enough money to post bail, pay fines. She was in class Monday morning, primed for bear. She walked in late, for a change. Usually Chasity was there, posed and set up with her admirers and followers gathered around her. That morning, she stormed in alone, in a rage, and slammed her way across the level of the lecture hall where I was sitting. She started in on our entire team at the top of her lungs. I could make out something about "revenge" and "retribution" and "childish paybacks" but most of it was lost in Nigerian cursing.

"That is enough!" Dr. Bowman roared.

Since he had never raised his voice the entire time of the class, it was enough to shock all of us into silence. Even Chasity.

Everyone seemed to hold their breaths, waiting for the profs to come down on Chasity and throw her out on her ear. The computer projectors came to life and London appeared on the screen. No computers were hooked up to the projector.

"You got what you deserved, Chasity Boah. I'm erasing the files of the ones who helped you right now." London snickered when several of Chasity's teammates let out sounds of distress and fumbled with their computers, racing to open them up. "Nobody can hide from me. I'll always be watching. Don't ever assume that just because you don't have a computer or smartphone turned on that I can't see you, that I can't get to you and punish you for your nasty tricks."

The screen went blank and the projector light died.

After a stunned pause, the profs muttered to each other, then called the class to order. They told Chasity that as far as they were concerned, she and her cohorts had been punished adequately. She had the choice of sitting still and keeping her mouth shut, or leaving.

To our disappointment, she chose to stay.

However, she didn't sit still, and she didn't keep her mouth shut, either. She was furious enough to basically implicate herself and her team. All of them turned on her, for the sake of saving their grades.

As Lanie explained to me later, this was another prime

example of the Neighborlee effect. The subliminal message of "we don't like you, go away" had grown strong enough to drive Chasity crazy-nasty. She quit school to keep the administration from expelling her.

So all was well that ended well. On that front, at least.

~~~~~

To wrap things up, yes, our team got great grades even though we left out a lot of information. There was no way we could explain that London Holiday was an AI, not just a façade. None of our profs demanded access to the programs we used. I suspect sometimes that Angela convinced them to leave us alone.

Cosmo and Doni became an item, but they were careful to keep it low-key. I felt sorry for them, because it was pretty clear he was willing to put himself on the line for her. They just couldn't be together very often, or in public. We trusted Cosmo, even with the age difference, him being twenty, and Doni fourteen. They went slowly and kept things quiet. Reggie Grandstone was still trying to convince everyone that he and London Holiday were going to ride off into the sunset together. That meant Doni wasn't safe at home, because Reggie might stop by at any time to try to romance her. She spent a lot of time at Divine's, or with her school friends. She couldn't spend a lot of time with me, because Reggie had it in his head Doni was going to school with me. I took to carrying a spritzer bottle of water and pepper oil to defend myself. Reggie still showed up regularly, trying to find Doni with me, but he at least learned to stay outside of firing range.

Doni's bodyguards vowed they would keep an eye on her until Reggie gave up, or found some woman stupid enough to support his viewpoint and lifestyle. There was a woman who fit that criteria, but Reggie wanted nothing to do with her. After all, Chasity had very publicly destroyed herself. Grandstones cared about public image.

Every once in a while, London and Sherwood popped up on our computer screens without warning, letting us know they were active, ready to help if we needed them. Sometimes they would tell us about incredible places they had seen, the tricks they had played on hackers who were trying to steal from people or break security measures to invade their privacy. When Cosmo, Wallace and I decided to form a partnership, designing custom-made software for businesses and debugging computers, they were available to help and advise us.

In a lot of ways, it is comforting, knowing they are there, watching. We hadn't "made" London Holiday that strange night. We were indeed part of a birthing process.

What will result from that...remains to be seen.

END

Neighborlee, Ohio

(Title, Original Title, Release Date)

Confessions of a Lost Kid (Growing Up Neighborlee) 05/20
Semi-Pseudo-Superheroes (Dorm Rats) 07/20
Virtually London (London Holiday) 09/20
Living Proof (that no good deed goes unpunished) (Living Proof) 11/20
Night of the Living Proof, 01/21
Quitting the Hero Biz (Hero Blues) 03/21
Bride of the Living Proof, 05/21
Shrunk: The Exile of Maurice (Divine's Emporium) 07/21
Return of the Living Proof, 09/21
Allergic to Mistletoe (Have Yourself a Faerie Little Christmas) 11/21
Dawn of the Living Proof, 01/22
Angela's Knight (Divine Knight) 03/22
The Living Proof Gets the Blues, 05/22

ABOUT THE AUTHOR

On the road to publication, Michelle fell into fandom in college and has 40+ stories in various SF and fantasy universes. She has a bunch of useless degrees in theater, English, film/communication, and writing. Even worse, she has over 100 books and novellas with multiple small presses, in science fiction and fantasy, YA, suspense, women's fiction, and sub-genres of romance.

Her official launch into publishing came with winning first place in the Writers of the Future contest in 1990. She was a finalist in the EPIC Awards competition multiple times, winning with *Lorien* in 2006 and *The Meruk Episodes, I-V,* in 2010, and was a finalist in the Realm Award competition, in conjunction with the Realm Makers convention.

Her training includes the Institute for Children's Literature; proofreading at an advertising agency; and working at a community newspaper. She is a tea snob and freelance edits for a living (MichelleLevigne@gmail.com for info/rates), but only enough to give her time to write. Her newest crime against the literary world is to be co-managing editor at Mt. Zion Ridge Press and launching the publishing co-op, Ye Olde Dragon Books. Be afraid … be very afraid.

www.Mlevigne.com
www.MichelleLevigne.blogspot.com
@MichelleLevigne

Also by Michelle L. Levigne

Guardians of the Time Stream: 4-book Steampunk series
The Match Girls: Humorous inspirational romance series starting with **A Match (Not) Made in Heaven**
Sarai's Journey: A 2-book biblical fiction series

Tabor Heights: 20-book inspirational small town romance series.

Quarry Hall: 11-book women's fiction/suspense series

For Sale: Wedding Dress. Never Used: inspirational romance

Crooked Creek: Fun Fables About Critters and Kids: Children's short stories.

Do Yourself a Favor: Tips and Quips on the Writing Life. A book of writing advice.

Killing His Alter-Ego: contemporary romance/suspense, taking place in fandom.

The Commonwealth Universe: SF series, 25 books and growing

The Hunt: 5-book YA fantasy series

Faxinor: Fantasy series, 4 books and growing

Wildvine: Fantasy series, 14 books when all released

Neighborlee: Humorous fantasy series

Zygradon: 5-book Arthurian fantasy series